RIPPLE

To Linda -
Thank you & Enjoy The Read!
Ron

MARCH 2018

RIPPLE

Rachel Odell Howe

Copyright © 2018 Rachel Odell Howe

ISBN: 1978163657
ISBN 13: 9781978163652
Library of Congress Control Number: 2017916004
CreateSpace Independent Publishing Platform
North Charleston, South Carolina

For David, Ethan, Ava & Trey

ACKNOWLEDGEMENTS

A huge thank-you to Annie, Jake and David Odell, to my husband David, and to all my friends and family, whose support, feedback, and love made this all possible. Thank you to the brave heroes on the Life Star team in CT, especially Sonny, Stephanie, and Craig. Your knowledge, compassion, and professionalism are second to none. Thank you to Scott R. McFarland, Commander, U.S. Coast Guard (ret.) for sharing your experience and expertise. To my editor Jon VanZile, thank you for helping me make the book even better, and to Pam, thank you for always making me look my best. Any way you look at it, I'm one lucky girl.

It is not in the stars to hold our destiny but in ourselves.

— **William Shakespeare**

1

"Jill, you need to come watch this! The weatherman's predicting that big storm is going to hit much sooner than expected," Jillian's mother called from the living room. "He's saying it's bringing in freezing rain and high winds. You might want to think about changing your return flight to today instead of tomorrow, honey. I'd hate for you to get stuck here."

Jillian finished drying a large serving bowl and tossed the damp towel into the sink. She placed the bowl next to the other clean dishes stacked up on the kitchen table before grabbing her mug of green tea from the counter. Blowing the steam off, she strolled over and sat beside her mother. Her body sank comfortably into the worn, familiar leather couch.

"You're kidding, right?" she asked. "Why didn't we hear about this sooner? I thought the storm wasn't gonna hit this area for a couple more days. I can't leave until I know you're going to be okay." She took a sip of her tea and set the mug down on the ring-stained coffee table. A chip was still missing from the left corner, a reminder of the time she fell and cut her eye open just above her brow when she was four. She brushed her fingers across her forehead to feel the scar, now barely visible unless someone knew exactly where to look. Only she could still feel the slight indentation.

Feeling a chill, she pulled her legs up under her and wrapped herself in the hand-crocheted blanket that had been folded over the arm of the couch. The colorful zigzag-patterned blanket had been around as long as she could remember. She caught the slightest whiff of her father's cologne and pulled it a little tighter.

"I'm glad we finally got Daddy all settled in at Revere House yesterday, but my plan is to finish getting the house back in order for you, too," Jillian said, poking her fingers through the looped holes of the frayed blanket. She pulled at a loose piece of yarn. "I still have some cabinets to go through, and there are tons more dishes to wash. I'd forgotten how many cool pieces you have."

Her mother's attention was laser-focused on the television screen across the room and she didn't answer. After a few moments passed, Jillian gently nudged her mother's leg with her own.

"Yoo hoo. Mom, are you listening to me?" she asked, pulling her fingers out from the blanket.

"Huh? Oh, sorry. What's that you were saying, dear?" her mother said, eyes still glued to the screen.

"I was just saying there's still a ton of cleaning to do. I'm also thinking I should probably call someone," Jillian said. "Ya know, someone who could at least patch the ceiling and maybe put a fresh coat of paint on the kitchen walls. The smoke left way more damage than I expected. And you weren't exaggerating about soot getting everywhere. That stuff is a nightmare." She waited again but got no reply.

"I've already washed the walls down twice in there, but they're gonna need to be done again," Jillian continued. "Maybe I'll do that now. Or maybe just go with a darker shade in there. I bet that would easily cover up the stains...and get me off the hook for washing them again."

"Huh?" her mother finally responded during a commercial. "Oh, don't worry about that," she said with a hint of optimism. "It's going to be fine, dear. Charlie from across the street already offered to take care of that next week. He's been painting as a side job for years, so I'm sure he'll know what to do. He told me he owed your dad a few favors, so he isn't even going to charge me for the labor. Just the paint."

"Oh, nice! That actually makes me feel much better about things," Jillian said. "If you want, I can move all the clean dishes into the dining room. Should I do that now?"

"Oh my goodness, don't be ridiculous. You've already done so much. Honestly, you've been a savior to me these past few days, sweetie," her mother answered. "I know you have a lot going on, but getting your father situated yesterday was my biggest worry, and I couldn't have gotten through it without you."

"Yeah, of course," Jillian nodded. "Oh, and don't forget to check their activities calendar online. It sounded like they'll have lots of things planned every week that you guys can still do together. I'm just glad that place is right across town."

"Yes," her mother nodded, then dropped her head. "That's the only reason I was able to leave him there without falling apart." She turned for a moment and wiped away a lone tear, then looked back at Jillian. "Well, enough of this pity nonsense!" she said, pushing the mute button on the remote and setting it down. She took both of her daughter's hands into hers, gently squeezing her fingers. "We knew this day was coming, didn't we, sweetie? Even though I didn't think it would be so soon, I know it's going to be for the best. Like you said, your father is going to be doing so many different things there. He'll probably even make some new friends, which will be good for him."

She looked at Jillian with a brave face and took a deep breath. "One thing is for sure, it'll be nice having someone else worry about him taking all those medications every day. Honestly, I was beginning to feel like a pharmacist juggling all those pills!"

"I'm sure that's true," Jillian said. "You've been amazing, Mom."

"Hey, now that I'll have some free time, I can get out and see some of my own friends. I'm going to get back in with the book club, and the ladies have been asking me to play bridge again on Wednesdays.

You know how badly I've wanted to come and visit you and David out in Boulder. Now I'll be able to, right? Wouldn't that be fun? We could do some shopping and our ladies-only lunch, just like we used to when you were in college. Maybe I could even help with some of the wedding stuff."

She let go of Jillian's fingers, cupped her daughter's face in her hands, and kissed both cheeks. "I just love you so much, my beautiful girl." Her eyes twinkled with a glimmer of excitement, and Jillian could feel her hopefulness.

"I love you so much, too, Mom," she said, giving her a hug. "I'm glad I was able to come out and help. And of course I want you to visit us any time...I've been begging for years! I'll make more time to come back home, too, especially now that Dad isn't here with you." She held on tightly for few more seconds. "I'm grateful I was able to make the trip."

She slowly released her arms from around her mother. Her stomach tightened with guilt, realizing how selfish she'd been just a few days earlier when she'd found out about the fire and dreaded making the trip home.

The weather report came back on the television and red flashes illuminated the screen. Her mother turned the volume back on. An annoying warning signal wailed throughout the report. The meteorologist was amped-up, pointing to the charts and graphs in the background.

"The most current radar is showing the storm steadily picking up speed and heading directly toward the East Coast. It's bringing extremely high winds and freezing rain along with it, folks! The accumulating ice has already been knocking down trees, and we're seeing significant power outages along its path. The saying about March is true with this storm, New Englanders...it's coming in like a lion! Make sure you have those generators gassed up and ready!"

"Holy crap, this thing really is heading straight toward us," Jillian reluctantly acknowledged. "Well, this totally sucks."

"Jill, you really need to get a flight out today!" her mother urged. "It might be your only chance to get back to Boulder in case Logan Airport shuts down. You can't miss your final race, honey. You're gonna need to stay ahead of this mess. I promise I'll be fine. Just go!"

"Really? Yeah, okay, if you're sure. I was actually thinking the same thing," Jillian said. "I really can't miss my race," she reiterated, jumping from the couch and springing into action. As she ran through the house, grabbing her belongings and shoving them into her bags, she felt badly about leaving things half done.

"Are you absolutely sure about this, Mom?" she yelled from the bathroom. "If you need me to come back after we get home from San Diego, I may be able to. I don't want you to have to worry about cleaning the rest of this stuff up by yourself."

She finished getting her things from the bathroom and ran into the bedroom. "Maybe David and I could come back together, you know, to help you with whatever else needs to be done?" she called out. "I could borrow against some of my vacation time if you want. I'm sure it wouldn't be a problem." She was frenzied as she rushed out with two overflowing bags. Her mother grabbed a jacket from the closet and handed it to her.

"Thanks, I would have forgotten that!" Jillian took a deep breath, smiled, and gave her mother a rather rushed squeeze good-bye.

"Let's not worry about any of that right now, Jill. I'm sure it will all work out," her mom said. "Just get yourself to the airport and get home. Call me when you're back in Boulder safe and sound. And good luck at your race. I know how hard you've trained, and I'm sure you'll get the gold this time! I'm so proud of you, honey."

"Thanks, Mom. You'll be the first to know!" Jillian raced out to the car and tossed her bags onto the back seat. The biting cold air sent a shiver down her back as she quickly plugged her phone into the charger and programmed the GPS for the airport. As she drove, she briefly considered calling the airline from the car, but the dread of being on an endless loop with their automated attendants convinced her otherwise. The last time she had needed to change a flight it took her over an hour waiting on hold and three different customer service reps to get it done.

She wondered if there would be any stand-by seats on such short notice. *Ugh,* she thought, *I don't care how much it might cost me; it'll be worth it to pay whatever I need to. At this point, I just need to get a flight out. I'd better not get stuck here.*

Heading onto the on-ramp, Jillian was confronted with darkened grey skies and ominous clouds looming in the distance. Strong gusts were already rocking her economy-sized rental back and forth, and she was afraid they might blow her off the road.

I should've upgraded to that damn SUV, she thought.

"Fucking New England weather!" she cursed, startled by the sudden driving rain violently beating on the windshield. Turning the wipers to full speed, she frantically tried to clear the freezing mess. It was getting difficult to see through the windshield, and clumps of icy slush started to stick to the wiper blades, rendering them virtually useless. Jillian blasted the defroster on the highest heat and wiped the fogged windows with her coat sleeve from the inside.

"This is ridiculous," she snarled, realizing her efforts were futile. Her vision was still impaired as she cautiously merged onto the highway. The road eventually straightened, and she was able to scan ahead.

Well, at least there isn't much traffic on the highway, she thought. *Probably because all the sane people are staying put, which is what I should've done, too!*

After a few miles steadily creeping along, Jillian took a second to look down at the speedometer. *Thirty-five? This seriously feels like I'm crawling. I can do thirty-five on my bike, for crying out loud! This is ludicrous. I'm definitely not going to get a flight at this rate,* she thought.

She pressed the gas pedal, watching the needle steadily climb. Forty, forty-five, fifty, fifty-five. She hated driving in this type of weather, but tried to keep calm. *Okay, Jill, you've got this. It's a miracle this clown car isn't slipping around, but it actually feels pretty steady. Maybe it has front-wheel drive? I think that's good. Wait, is that right? What did Dad used to say? Is it front-wheel or rear-wheel that's better for snow and ice?*

Just then a strong gust shook the car, pushing her halfway into the next lane.

Oh, shit, she thought. *I knew it was too good to be true. This was a huge mistake. What the hell was I thinking trying to beat this storm? Should I take the next exit and just try to go back? Maybe I should just pull over and wait this out?* She tightened her grip and forced the car back into the correct lane.

No, no, I just need to slow down a bit, stay calm, and get myself on a flight, she thought. She visualized being at her house in Boulder with David and tried to shake off the fear. Not familiar with the control panel on the dashboard, she glanced down to try to find a weather report on the radio. Static was the only thing coming out from the speakers because none of the pre-sets she pushed were set to actual stations, and the buttons seemed to be stuck on only AM channels.

Jillian didn't have the patience to figure out how to fix the radio. She could feel her frustration building, but she needed to keep her eyes on the road.

Looking ahead, she could see that she was approaching a substantial hill. She noticed a couple cars pulled off to the side, their hazard lights blinking in steady rhythm. Others were stuck in place on the highway, with only their rear wheels spinning and their back ends fishtailing side-to-side.

"Oh, you've got to be kidding me!" she blurted out angrily. "I'd better be able to make it up this hill in this piece-of-crap car!" She applied a little more pressure to the accelerator. As she started up the incline, she realized that, in addition to the freezing rain, her vision was significantly compromised by a massive tractor-trailer. The rig was plowing along in front of her, its tires relentlessly spitting sludge and ice onto her windshield.

"This seriously can't be happening right now! Could someone please give me a break?" she yelled again. She hit the dashboard as hard as she could with the heel of her palm. "Just get out of my way, you damn nuisance!" she shouted toward the towering beast.

Jillian was determined to pass the mammoth truck before the crest of the hill. Tightening her grip on the steering wheel, she moved into the far-left lane. With no one in front of her, she pressed down even harder on the gas pedal. The car reacted to her command, and she felt herself rushing full-speed ahead. Coming over the top of the hill, she still trailed the truck by several yards.

"Oh, shit!" she yelled at the crest. An unexpected sea of brake lights stopped her cold. The trailer truck had also slammed on its brakes directly in front of her, its red lights lighting up like an inferno. Only, instead of slowing down like it should've, the truck started to violently stutter and sway.

It took a second for Jillian's eyes to register what they were seeing, but when they did, she felt a rush of adrenaline course through her body. Her stomach clenched, and drumbeats sounded in her ears. Her heart was racing out of control.

The back of the rig slid sharply out to the right, blocking all three lanes of traffic in front of her. The front of the cab jammed to the left, and within seconds, the entire vehicle was jackknifing, sliding out of control directly in her path. She caught a glimpse of the driver's face and saw sheer terror in his eyes. He'd completely lost control, and they both knew it.

Jillian quickly took inventory. With cement barriers on either side of the highway, she was trapped.

There's nowhere for me to go, she thought. *There's nowhere for me to go.*

Instinctively, she slammed both feet hard against the brake pedal and clutched the steering wheel, her muscles taut with the force of trying to stop the speeding car.

It's too late, she realized. *Black ice. I must have hit black ice.*

As her car started to spin in dizzying circles, she felt weightless for a moment, gliding along the slick pavement, faster and faster.

Still frantically trying to get the car to respond, she turned the wheel hard and pumped the brakes.

It was no use. Nothing worked.

Her hands, drenched with sweat, slipped off the wheel, and all air was sucked out of the spinning car. She gasped for one last breath and braced herself for the inevitable. Everything went silent except for a tiny voice in her head.

This can't be happening. I'm not ready to die. What about David? What about our plans? What about my race? I need more time.

Time froze for a split second, and then, as if in super slow-motion, she saw the massive truck closing in, then the cement barrier, then the cars behind her, then the truck again. A flash, more brilliant than anything she'd ever seen, was the last thing she experienced before being catapulted into instant and total darkness.

2

MOMENT OF IMPACT
BOSTON

Jillian Richards had never believed that your whole life flashes in front of you the moment before you die. To her, it seemed there would be too many memories and not nearly enough time to recall them all. She figured it would be only the most significant things she'd remember when her time came. Things like the excitement of her first kiss, the thrill of falling in love, or the time she finally won that big race.

She was wrong.

Lying in the wreckage, suspended in the murky space between consciousness and the beyond, two revelations gradually unveiled themselves, eventually coming into focus. First, there are no coincidences in life, and second, nothing is guaranteed.

Her first thought, accompanied by an excruciating ache in her skull, was that she'd never get the chance to do the things she wanted to do most. Her next thought, which was more of an elaboration of the first, really, was that these were things she'd expected to do, that she'd felt entitled to do. No matter...a wave of crippling pain caused her to forget these injustices and temporarily slip back into the abyss.

Time stood still until another conscious thought emerged. *Is this my final moment?* she wondered, then felt her lungs pull for another labored breath of air. A loud throbbing banged in her head. Several fractured images flashed by, reminding her of the old 8mm films she'd watched with her grandparents as a child.

Jillian fought against the darkness. She tried to open her eyes, to move an arm, to scream. It was no use—her body wouldn't respond to any of her commands. The flickering images, a dizzying blend of scattered memories and obscure premonitions, continued to dance in her head.

What do these images mean? I wish someone could tell me what I am seeing.

Everything that had been, and everything that would be, seemed to reveal itself to her in a way that was intricately woven together. It was difficult to comprehend. Her entire existence was summed up within an instant.

As the seconds ticked by, the thumping in her head began to sound more like a distant drum beat. The ache got a bit duller, the once-blinding images suddenly faint.

Jillian wanted to understand her visions before they slipped away. She knew that everything was connected—and that she was at the center of this three-dimensional web. The tangled strands of her life surrounding her represented the paths that she, along with everyone else she'd encountered, had taken. These complex patterns ultimately led her—and somehow the people whose lives she'd saved—to this precise moment...and now they were her only way out.

She sensed this accident should've been her end. Surely anyone who could see her now would agree that a tremendous amount of luck, and certainly a few miracles, would be needed to come out of this accident alive. But she fiercely held on to a single morsel of hope: it was her destiny to survive.

I don't know if luck, or miracles, or destiny even exist for that matter, she thought, a numbness settling in. *But I certainly hope they do...*

Her final wish lingered, then evaporated, as total blackness closed in.

The drumbeats went silent, the pictures gone.

3

"How are the legs holding up?" David glanced over at Jillian, both of them breathing heavily as they pushed up the final hill of their ten-mile run.

"I'm doing just fine, don't you worry about me, tough guy." She smiled sarcastically and nudged her elbow into his ribs. The relentless burn continued to work against her tired legs. She wasn't going to let him know that for the last mile-and-a-half, she'd been willing herself not to quit as the cramp stabbing her in the side steadily got worse—and she certainly wasn't going to let him beat her back to the house again. This was the last long-distance run of her training regimen before the San Diego Coronado Bay Triathlon. The following week, she planned to taper off her training intensity, and then they were going to fly to California for the big race and a couple days of much-needed rest and relaxation. Jillian could almost feel the hot sun on her pale face and smell the salty ocean breeze coming off the bay.

Her heart fluttered with excitement as she realized this was it: this was the last time she'd be training competitively at this level for a triathlon. The only reason she decided to even do this final race was because she had a real shot at winning a national title. After fourteen years of competing, with several finishes mere seconds behind the winners, she was finally the favorite in her age category. She wanted the win so bad that she could taste it, and boy was it sweet.

Starting the first day of training, she'd told herself there'd be no excuses. She knew she needed to do whatever it took to win, like continue to endure the painful ache she currently felt in her quads and keep pushing.

Block out any doubt and fight the urge to give up when it gets tough, she thought, *cuz this final one's for you.* She wasn't about to let anyone or anything get in her way. She'd learned that lesson the hard way years before.

A wave of nausea hit her square in the stomach just thinking about that fateful day. She tried to shake the image out of her head, but it wouldn't budge. It had been the first time she'd been that close to securing a top spot in a qualifying race, but a win just wasn't meant to be. Fate had other things in store that day, and the disappointment had been crushing. The thought of it still made her want to throw up.

This time will be different, she told herself, and she truly believed it. This time, she planned to go out on top and take home the glory. Nothing else would be acceptable, and nothing short of that would do. After a big win, she could finally be done. Really, truly done.

"This is a winning pace today," David said, as if reading her thoughts. "I wouldn't want to be up against you next week."

"Thanks, I appreciate you saying so. I hope that's true," Jillian huffed, just about out of breath. "You know how much I want this."

She imagined accepting a gold medal on the winner's stage and then officially announcing her retirement from the sport. She knew the timing was right. Plus, she'd been promising David they could move forward with their wedding plans as soon as the race was over, and he hadn't been exactly subtle in bringing up the whole "baby thing" every chance he got.

At thirty-five, Jillian knew her biological clock was ticking so loudly that she might as well wear a sign around her neck assuring people there were no bombs in the area and hand out earplugs.

They hit the top of the hill, where she caught a glimpse of their small cape in the distance. Without warning, she broke into a full sprint, leaving visions of weddings, babies, and her damn aging eggs in the dust. As she reached the mailbox at the edge of their property, feeling quite sure of her imminent victory, David came whizzing up from behind.

"Ouch!" she screamed as he slapped her hard on the butt, easily passing.

"Nice buns!" He looked back and winked. "Gave me something worth chasing."

"Oh, c'mon! Seriously? You're such a brat!" she yelled, crossing the informal finish line at the driveway a few seconds behind. She pulled her ponytail out of its soaked headband and flopped onto the grass to catch her breath. Her heart was pounding as she sucked in the cool air. No matter how fast she ran, he always managed to blow past her right at the end.

"So annoying," she grumbled, pretending not to watch as he strutted back toward her with a proud smirk and his chest puffed out like a silly bird looking for a mate. Even though she found it adorable, she would never give him the satisfaction of knowing so.

"Neither your cheesy compliments nor your attempted charms are going to work that easily, bub. Your prowess has no effect on me. Not after that pathetic little show-off attempt, anyway."

"Pathetic, you say? Is that so?" David teased, flexing his arm muscles and posing like a bodybuilder in the midst of a competition.

"Nice try, Arnold," Jillian answered wryly.

"Well, in that case, I might as well just go grab us a couple waters, my blue-eyed beauty.

You probably need to rest here awhile anyway so you can recover from that major ass-whooping," David said, this time using his best improvised macho voice.

"Oh, is that so?" Jillian asked, rolling her eyes. "I highly doubt it."

"I expect it may take several minutes, and potentially even hours, for the humiliation to subside," he continued playfully, kneeling to kiss her forehead before heading inside. "You stay here, me lovely lady. I shall return in a jiff."

"Oh, how chivalrous!" she mocked, giving him a quick kiss in return. "Are you sure it's not too much trouble for such a stud like you? How did I get to be such a lucky girl, anyway?"

She waved her hand to shoo him away and closed her eyes, letting the bright sunshine warm her face. It was mid-March, and the weather had been getting nicer over the past few weeks, perfectly timed for outdoor training.

She felt the trapped body heat inside her jacket begging to be released. She pulled down the zipper, took her arms out from the sleeves, and rolled it into a tight ball, placing it on the grass behind her. Then she lay back with her head on the makeshift pillow. She visualized David's ridiculous smirk again.

"You really are a brat, you know!" she yelled toward the house without opening her eyes. "But somehow, just somehow, I still love you like crazy."

"I know you do, babe," he called back, just before going inside. "What would you ever do without me, right?"

"Hmm…let me count the ways!" she retorted. As she lay there, amused by their witty banter, she started thinking about the years before they met. She'd been single for some time before dating David. She never minded being alone…she was actually quite used to it. Truthfully, she loved her independence and cherished the amount of time she could dedicate to racing. Of course, she'd dated here and there, but never found anyone she could see sharing a future with, and she certainly wasn't willing to settle.

Most of the men she met either had too much personal baggage, no significant direction in life, or still lived in their parents' basements. That made for an interesting sex life. The few she really liked eventually complained about how much training she did and ultimately moved on, never fully understanding the passion and commitment she had to becoming a champion.

David was different. He was her best friend and true partner in every sense of the word. Jillian knew she was lucky to have this amazing man by her side, supporting her, helping to coach her, encouraging her to follow her dreams, and most important, he wanted her to be his wife and share his life with her.

"Just one more race, then I'll be done," she whispered. She stretched her arms overhead, inhaling a calming breath. Her tired body relaxed into the cool grass while a steady breeze lulled her into a peaceful trance. She felt her thoughts beginning to drift off.

The front door slammed shut as David came back out, causing Jillian to startle.

"For God's sake," she mumbled to herself. "I must've asked him to help me fix that damn door a million times. Somehow, it never makes it to the top of the to-do list. I'm just going to have to do it myself, for crying out loud!"

Her annoyance quickly dissipated as she watched him walk toward her. He held two cold water bottles with one hand and her cell phone up to his ear with the other. He appeared to be deep in conversation.

"It's your mother," he mouthed, and Jillian slowly sat up. She gave him an inquisitive look and brought her hand up to her brow, shading her eyes from the bright sun. She quickly recognized something was off by David's pensive expression and immediately became worried.

"Yeah, I understand, Barb," he interjected, obviously trying to wrap things up with the call. "I'm just glad Joe's going to be okay. That must've given you both quite a scare. Here, let me have you talk to Jill. She's the one who'll know exactly what to do." David thrust the phone into Jillian's eager outstretched hand.

"Hey, Mom, what's going on?" Jillian's voice was urgent as she took the phone and quickly stood. The other end of the line was silent. "Mom? Mom, are you still there?"

After a brief pause, she heard the words she'd been dreading: "It's your father, Jill." Her mother's voice was shaky. "I'm afraid things have gotten worse. He tried to cook an egg last night and ended up setting the kitchen on fire. I really need you to come back home, sweetheart. I just can't do this on my own anymore. I'm so worried, it's making me sick. Will you please make a trip home to help me figure this out?" Her usually strong, capable mother sounded both exhausted and overwhelmed.

"Wait. What? What do you mean he set the kitchen on fire?" Jillian's voice escalated as she envisioned the disaster, and panic slowly set in. Her father had been showing signs of Alzheimer's for the past several years, but it had never gotten to this point. "Are you guys okay? Is Daddy all right?"

"Yes, thank goodness. We're both fine. A bit covered in smoke and tired from being up for hours, but really, we're fine."

"What happened, exactly?" Jillian asked.

"He must've fallen asleep on the couch after leaving a pan on the stove and ended up setting off a significant grease-fire. I was eventually able to put it out with some baking soda, but there's some real damage. You should've seen the smoke. Everything is covered in black soot. It's a real mess." She paused as to collect her thoughts. "Everything's going to be okay; it just scared me. It's time to move him into a facility. You know I've been managing this as long as I could, honey, but I really need some help now. I'm so tired, I can hardly think straight. Can you come home and help me sort this out? Please, Jill, I need you right now, darling."

Jillian's heart sank. She knew this wasn't what her mother wanted for her father. They'd talked about it at length many times in the past.

"He wants to be home, and frankly, I want him here, too," she'd told her daughter whenever the subject came up. Jillian had seen her mother give up many of her own interests over the past few years to stay by his side, to make sure he was taking all of his medications and keep him as engaged and active as possible. Every decision she'd made to this point was to keep him close. For her to be saying it was time, Jillian knew it was time.

"Yes, of course, Mom. Of course I'll come out to help. Let me think about this for a second. I guess I can try to catch a flight out either tonight or first thing tomorrow morning, depending on what's available. I can only stay a couple days, though. My San Diego triathlon is next week, and I need to get back in time. I can't miss the race." Her thoughts were spinning as she waited for a response. She only heard silence.

"Hey, Mom?" she prompted again. "Before I get there, you're going to need to make a few calls and find a suitable short-term option for him. I know there are a couple of nursing homes close by. See which ones handle Alzheimer's patients and take your insurance. Once you find a place you like, I'll help you get him settled, and then we can figure out what to do next, okay? It's going to work out. Everything is going to work out. This is best for him in the long run. You're doing the right thing, Mom." Jillian heard her mother crying. A golf-ball-sized lump swelled up in her throat, making it difficult to speak.

"I know it's hard, but you really are making the best choice," she managed. "We need him to be safe. They know what they're doing there, and they have round-the-clock staff. This is what Dad needs now. I love you both so much, and I'll be there as soon as possible. Just take care of him until I can get there. I'll see you soon."

When Jillian finally hung up, her eyes filled with the tears she'd been fighting to hold back. A flurry of emotions crashed over her in waves. She was physically exhausted from the intense training; she was terrified for her father and the panic and confusion he must have felt; she was devastated for her mother, who was losing her best friend and soul mate. Even worse, she was completely dreading the trip back east and felt extremely guilty for thinking that way.

"Aaaaaaaah!" she screamed, throwing the phone down hard against the ground and shaking her fists like a three-year-old in the middle of a tantrum. "Why does everything always have to hit at once? This frigging sucks!" she yelled, pounding her foot against the curb with each angry word. "Somebody needs to make this insanity stop before I lose my nut!"

She stood for a few seconds before David approached and cautiously wrapped his arms around her waist. Even though she feigned resistance, he pulled her close. She knew that because she was physically drained, this level of stress had the potential to push her over the edge. Selfishly, she also knew what she was most worried about was how this affected her race.

As David stood holding her, she could feel her body start to tremble. She clung to him tightly, sobbing into his shoulder. She was grateful that he waited patiently for several moments, allowing her to process what had just happened. Finally, she began to calm down.

"I know this sucks right now, but everything is going to work out," David said. "Try to focus on one thing at a time here, kiddo. I suggest you go help your father get settled first, then when you come back, we can finish your training. I can get you back in the pool for one last swim the day you come back, and you'll still have plenty of time to get another longer bike ride in. I'll help you in any way possible. We can make it all work. I see how hard you've been hustling. You're already prepared for the race, babe."

David leaned back, put his hands on her shoulders, and looked her straight in the eyes. "You so got this thing in the bag, blue-eyes," he said with a wink. "Plus," he added, "I wouldn't worry too much about that whole 'losing your nut' thing. That ship already sailed a long time ago." She couldn't help but crack a little smile as he wiped her cheeks with his thumbs and kissed her tear-soaked face.

Dragging herself inside the house, Jillian started a shower and grudgingly peeled off her running gear. As she stepped in, she felt a surge of disappointment. This wasn't at all how she'd pictured her last couple of days before the race and their vacation. "This completely sucks," she declared loudly as she stood sobbing, her forehead against the shower wall. Not even the warm water running down her back gave her any comfort.

"Hey, babe, you okay in there?" It was David knocking at the bathroom door. Jillian assumed he'd come to check on things after hearing her pathetic whimpers echoing from behind the door.

"Not so much," she answered. "Not so much at all."

It got silent for several seconds, and Jillian started wondering where he'd gone. Just then, the shower curtain was pulled back and there was David, standing completely naked in front of her.

"Well, maybe I can help cheer you up." He flashed his dimpled smile, and she couldn't help but giggle through her tears.

"Oh yeah? How do you propose to do that?" she teased, feeling her sadness start to dissipate ever so slightly.

He stepped in and pulled her toward his long, lean body. He had the perfect swimmer's physique, and she immediately felt the tension leave her body. He raised his eyebrows mischievously and reached around, squeezing her from behind with both hands. Leaning down to kiss her gently on the neck he whispered in her ear, "Well, for starters, how about this?"

She couldn't help but laugh. "You're such a goofball. You know that, right?" she asked, hugging him tight.

"I know," David answered playfully, running his hands through his wavy brown hair and wiping the water away from his face. "But I knew that would make you laugh, and you really do have the nicest buns, just for the record."

After their shower, Jillian wrapped her wet hair in a towel and walked into the bedroom. She pulled on a pair of cozy sweatpants and a grabbed a clean cotton tee from the top drawer. Flipping the light on in the walk-in closet, she reluctantly took her carry-on bag down from the back shelf to start packing. Rather than adding the few skirts, light tops, and wedge sandals she had planned to take to San Diego, she found herself packing jeans, sweaters, and winter socks.

"This is so depressing," she said with a sigh as David finished dressing and headed into the living room to grab his laptop. He'd offered to search for a reasonable flight that would get her into Boston either later that evening or early the next morning.

"I know. The timing stinks," he agreed from the other room. "I'll do my best to get you out and back as quickly as possible. I know a couple of websites that offer last-minute deals; I'll check those first." She wiped a tear away as she heard him tapping away on the keypad.

"Hey, Jill!" he yelled from his spot on the couch after a couple minutes. "There's a decent flight out of Denver leaving in a few hours. It's direct to Boston. I also see a return flight that'll get you back here early Sunday afternoon. There's only one seat left and this is the best itinerary I can find for the money. I'm just going to call and book it."

"I wish you were coming with me," she said. "I'm not saying that to make you feel bad, I just wanted you to know."

"You know I would if I could," he answered. "My ass is on the line with the swim meet Monday. I promised them a state title and we just squeaked by the first round. If I don't get the team to perform, I may be out of a job next year."

As the high school swim coach, Jillian knew David had training sessions with his team over the next few days that he couldn't miss. He'd barely gotten them to the second round of states, and they were counting on him. Plus, the trip would be quick, and Jill just wanted to get it over with.

"No, I know they need you. I'll be home again in no time anyway," she called out from the bedroom. "You'll hardly even have time to miss me!" she added when she got no response. But he didn't hear her; he was already on the phone talking to a booking agent.

"Are you nervous about seeing your dad tonight?" David asked as he loaded Jillian's two overstuffed bags into the back of their car an hour later.

"Yeah, a little, I guess," she answered. "I feel like he must be so confused…and probably pretty pissed that he's getting moved. I wish Mom had let me know things were getting worse. I would've gone back sooner. I would've called more." She let out a sigh as she got into the passenger seat and pulled the seatbelt across her lap. "I definitely should've called more. Ugh. I just hope she doesn't expect me to come back permanently."

"What? Why would you say that? They aren't going to expect you to move back east," David responded, closing the car door and fishing for the keys in his front pocket. "You've been living out here since you graduated from college. They know this is your home now."

"No, I know. It's just, when you're an only child like I am, you feel this enormous responsibility to take care of your parents. They're getting older now, and I'm the only kid they've got."

"Yup, you're their one and only miracle baby, that's for sure." David smiled and pulled down the driveway onto the street. "Your parents love to tell that story every chance they get, by the way," he added. "You mean the world to them. You know that, right?"

"Yeah, I do. They do to me, too," she acknowledged. "That's why I'm feeling like the world's worst daughter right now." She sighed and gazed out the window. As they drove, she recalled her parents telling their story to David yet again the last time they were all together.

"We were already older than you both are now when we had her," her father had started out. "I was forty when I married her mother, who had just turned thirty-seven. I was an accountant for a firm in Boston and she was an elementary school teacher just outside the city. We met at a Memorial Day picnic being hosted by a mutual friend."

"It truly was love at first sight!" her mother had bragged. "He loved me from the moment he saw me, standing at the punch bowl in my polka-dot dress!" she teased.

"Oh, is that right?" he bantered. "I would argue it was the other way around. You wouldn't leave my side from the moment you saw me. I think what really impressed you was when I threw that double-ringer into the horseshoe pits. No matter what I did after that, I couldn't shake you that day. Not that I wanted to, of course!" He ended the story with a wink and a quick kiss on her hand.

The only thing they could seem to agree on was, from that day on, they became inseparable.

"I knew I'd found the woman of my dreams," her father had exclaimed, his face beaming. "I couldn't take the chance of her getting away! That's why I proposed by Labor Day. Some called it foolish, but I thought I was being romantic."

"It was romantic, Joe," her mother chimed in. "Plus, we had both always wanted a child and didn't know if it would even be possible. We weren't spring chickens, after all. That's why it was a wonderful surprise when Jillian was born just a year later."

"That's my little miracle right there, David. You'd better take good care of her."

Jillian could picture her father, his eyes glistening with pride. She reached over and placed her hand on top of David's.

"Hey you, where'd you go? You doing okay, babe?" David asked.

"Yeah, sorry. Must have zoned out for a minute there," she answered, feeling her stomach drop. "I was just thinking about my dad. Did I make a mistake leaving? I can't remember a time when he missed any of my events growing up. He was my biggest fan all those years and I just left him. I hope I'm not too late. I hope he knows how much I love him."

"Oh, my God. Is that what you're worried about? Yes, of course he knows how much you love him! Why are you questioning all of this now?"

"I was just thinking that it's been way too long since I've been back. I should've never waited until something like this happened. I need to make more time for them. I'm going to start going back at least twice a year, especially now that my dad's going to be in a nursing home."

"Yeah, of course. I think that's a great idea. Whatever you need to do." David reached over and placed his hand on her thigh, giving it a comforting squeeze. "We'll make it work."

Jillian closed her eyes and leaned the seat back. Her legs were tired from the run earlier that morning, and she couldn't help but fixate on all the decisions that led her so far away in the first place.

"They knew it was a hard decision for me to move away from them after college," she blurted out. "I would've never left without their full support." She could tell right away that her tone was defensive, and David waited a moment before responding.

"I'm sure they understood. You knew that Boulder was where you needed to be after graduation. Everyone knows it's the perfect training ground for triathlons, and being out here definitely gave you an edge. They knew you always planned to compete on an elite level, right? You needed to be where all the best athletes and coaches are." She knew he was right, but still felt doubt.

"Gabby was the one who enticed me to move out here in the first place. Did you know that?" Jillian asked, eyes stilled closed. "That was thirteen years ago. Thirteen! I can't believe that much time has already passed. It seems like I just got here."

"Yes, I did know that. You two are like peas in a pod. She can talk you into anything."

"That she can," Jillian easily agreed and grinned. "Best friends have a way of doing that. My God, what was I ever thinking letting her coax me into competing in the first place? What a naïve freshman I was. Silly me, I just thought it would just be a fun way to stay in shape. I had no idea what I was getting myself into!"

"Yeah, I can imagine. And now it's such a huge part of who you are. I'm sure she knew deep down that you couldn't give up racing once you'd gotten into it."

"So, what are your plans after we graduate?" Gabby asked one morning on their way to class. It was their senior year at Boston University. "Do you think you might want to stay in Boston and find a job in the city?"

Jillian had been thinking about that more and more. With only four months until graduation, she had no idea what she wanted to do. "I'm not really sure yet," she answered. "I don't have enough cash saved up for my own place, so I guess I'll have to move back in with my parents until I get a decent job. You know how ridiculous the rents are around here. What about you?" she asked. "Are you moving back to Boulder with your folks?"

After several seconds passed without a response, Gabby finally looked over at her and flashed one of her charming smirks. "Uh, oh!" Jillian laughed. "I know that look of yours, roomie! What scheme are you possibly cooking up now?"

After detailing her master plan, Gabby had made a remarkably convincing case for them both to move back to Boulder after graduation. Being there, they could compete at a much higher level and participate in more triathlons together.

"Look, Jill," she argued, "we're already the best of friends, we know we can live together without wanting to kill each other, and the job market is growing fast out in Colorado. Plus, it would be nice to share living expenses, considering all the student loans we both owe!" Jillian immediately saw the potential and agreed it could be a win/win.

"Just wait until you see it out there with your own two eyes, Jill," Gabby told her. "You won't be able to put it into words, it's so incredible. And I promise you're going to fit right in! It literally has everything we love just waiting for us! You know how much I love it there, and I wouldn't suggest it unless I knew it was perfect for you, too. What do you think?"

Of course Jillian was excited. The thought of a fresh start and a higher caliber of competition became more and more appealing the more she thought about it.

"Okay, Gabs," she declared the next day. "Let's do it!"

A few nights later, Jillian sat down with her parents during a visit home. Her goal was to let them know what she'd been thinking, and she hoped they saw the same potential as she did. After dinner, she outlined her plan in thoughtful detail.

"I know it seems so far away, but my gut is telling me I should give it a shot, especially now that I'm serious about competing at a much higher level. I just hate that I'm going to be so far away from the both of you." Her voice cracked. She looked down at the table, afraid to make eye contact, and held back her tears. "Are you going to be upset with me if I go?"

Her mother didn't hesitate. "Absolutely not, honey! Jill, look into my eyes," she said and gently lifted her daughter's chin. "If this is what you want to do, you have our full support. This is your journey, and if it's something you feel like you need to do, we're behind you all the way. Plus, now is the ideal time to take advantage of this. You aren't committed to a job, or rent, or a serious boyfriend. Life has a funny way of opening doors just when the timing is right. If you don't go now, you'll regret it."

Her father nodded in agreement and added, "We just want you to be happy, sweetheart. You've worked so hard to get where you are. We already know you're a champion…now you can go prove it to everyone else!"

Jillian was overwhelmed. In all honesty, she'd been worried they'd be devastated by her moving so far away from them.

"Thank you both so much!" she remembered saying. "Having your blessing truly means the world to me. Gabby just makes Boulder sound so incredible; I have to at least go see for myself. Plus, I'll get to train where all the elite athletes do. And, of course, I'll come back to visit as often as I can. I promise!"

Gabby knew her friend well. Just as she'd predicted, Jillian acclimated to Boulder from day one. The city's spectacular natural beauty couldn't easily be put into words. Nestled in the foothills of the Rocky Mountains, her new home was breathtaking in every way. The months of packing and preparation for their move had all been worth it. One of Gabby's relatives connected them with a friend who had a two-bedroom apartment they were able to rent affordably. Gabby had already arranged to begin working as a teacher at a nearby preschool, and Jillian planned to pick up a waitressing job as soon as they got settled.

Once they arrived, Gabby couldn't wait to show Jillian around. There was so much to do and see; she spent days getting familiar with her new surroundings. She recalled how excited she was to share it all with her parents.

"Mom, Dad, you wouldn't believe it out here!" she gushed on her first call back home. "Gabby showed me this place called Boulder Canyon today. I guess it's a popular site for hiking, rock-climbing, and mountain-biking, and it's beautiful! There's a seventy-foot-high waterfall there named Boulder Falls that we had fun exploring. I wish you both could see it for yourselves!"

"That's fantastic, Jill!" Her mother's voice beamed. "I've heard how pretty that part of the country is. I bet you're fitting right in out there!"

"I am! You should see it, along the western border of the city there's this ultra-cool mountain range. It's called the Flatirons, and the rock formations kinda look like a row of jagged teeth. Gabby was telling me that people come from all over the world to hike and climb out here. It's nothing like we have back east. They're just so picturesque!" She was sure her enthusiasm was palpable.

"One group we met was saying that some of the peaks have an altitude of almost eight thousand feet! Can you believe that? Dad, that's almost three times higher than the time we hiked Mt. Monadnock in New Hampshire. And remember the view from up there? Well, this blows that away. It's just incredible!"

"Are you making new friends out there?" her mother asked.

"Oh, yeah!" she shared. "One of the things I've noticed right off the bat is that everyone is so active and friendly. Gabby introduced me to a group of friends she's had since she was a kid, and I'm finding there's always somebody willing to swim, bike, or run with me. The roads out here go on forever. There are so many types of training terrain, and the traffic is so much less than Boston. Plus, with the altitude, I'm getting more fit than I ever imagined."

"That's great, Jill. We're happy for you. It sounds like you are exactly where you should be," she remembered her parents saying. She recalled feeling like she'd discovered her own private paradise, and just couldn't get enough.

Thirteen years flew by.

"Boulder was definitely the right choice for me," she finally said, after several minutes had passed in silence. "I'd never be where I am today if I hadn't moved out here. Thank you for seeing that. Thank you for reminding me of that." She opened her eyes and straightened the seat back up, stretching her legs in front of her.

David just chuckled. "Well, from the story you told me about your first race, I don't think you could afford to have taken any chances." Jillian shot him an *oh-no-you-didn't!* look and playfully punched him in the shoulder.

"Oh, my God! I can't believe you remembered that! That was a horror show. I'm still plotting my revenge on Gabs!"

"Remind me again what happened. It kills me every time you tell this story," David said. "Especially the part about the pond scum."

Her memory easily drifted back to freshman year in college, and she laughed as she visualized in vivid detail her very first attempt competing at a local triathlon.

"It was a total disaster, to say the least," she reminded David. "For the swim, I had no idea how hard it was going to be trying to maintain any type of racing stroke with hundreds of other people splashing around at the same time. I ended up getting kicked in the face at least six times by other frantic swimmers, which led to me swallowing what felt like a gallon of dirty lake water."

"That's so gross," David said and crinkled his face. "That's why I stick to swimming pools. You know, the kind with predetermined lanes, clearly marked ropes, and lots of chlorine. You girls are bat-shit crazy to put yourselves through that!"

"Yeah, we must be. In hindsight, I should've quit then, but I didn't want to let Gabs down. So mind you, after being traumatized from the swim and feeling like I was on the verge of puking up said pond scum at any second, it took forever to transition from the swim to the bike leg. I remember how wobbly my legs were the whole time on that stupid bike. I ended up walking most of the final running leg because I was so exhausted and nauseous."

"And yet, from what I remember hearing, you did finish with a decent time," David interjected.

"That's true, I did. Although, after that ordeal, I told Gabby flat-out not to ask me to do another triathlon ever again. I can't believe she'd talked me into that nonsense! I threatened her to be on guard, because I'd be working on her payback effective immediately."

Jillian belly-laughed again, this time with tears rolling down her cheeks.

"If only I could've been a fly on the wall back then," David teased. "Man, I would've paid good money to see that race. That would definitely be one to show our kids!"

"Well, thank goodness there's no recorded proof of that disaster!" Jillian declared and leaned into the back seat to reach into her carry-on bag. She pulled out one of the protein bars she'd packed for a snack. After taking her first bite, she thought back fondly of how convincing Gabby had been at the time.

"You never did tell me how she persuaded you to do another race after that," David said. "I don't think anyone would've been able to change my mind after something like that."

"Oh, she had to work for it, that's for sure," Jillian answered. "She pleaded with me every day, 'You can't quit after just one race!' I remember her telling me that everyone did horribly their first time out, as if that would sway me. She even told me about her first race. 'You should've seen my first race. I came in last place in my division. Last place, Jill! I was even behind some eighty-year-old! It was beyond embarrassing!'"

Jillian remembered not being easily swayed.

"I'm not so sure about that, Gabs. What you just witnessed wasn't just embarrassing; I literally thought I was going to die out there! I still think I might need to get my stomach pumped after that. I can literally feel the parasites I'm sure I swallowed boring holes into my intestines as we speak! What have you gotten me into, for crying out loud?"

Gabby just laughed and put her arm around Jillian's shoulder. "Considering how crowded it was, you actually did pretty well your first time out. I have to admit, I'm pretty impressed!" Gabby gave her an appraising look. "Jill, you have what it takes to be really good at this. I mean it—you're a total natural! Even though you hit a few bumps on your first try, at least you didn't come in last like me. Far from it, actually! Maybe I just didn't prepare you the way I should have. That was my fault, and whatever revenge you dole out, I'll gladly accept. Just promise me you'll try it one more time because I guarantee you'll do so much better!"

Gabby persisted and eventually persuaded Jillian not to give up. They signed up for a few more of the shorter distance sprint triathlons being held near their college. They even followed an actual training plan and joined the Boston Tri Club, where they found a great group of friends who supported each other and had structured sessions year-round. The group shared tips and strategies on everything from how to prepare equipment, to what to eat, to how to cut the most time off transition stations. Eventually, Jillian got good. Exceptionally good. Gabby had been right: Jillian was a natural.

By the time she was a junior, Jillian was easily finishing in the top of her age category. It wasn't uncommon for her to place first overall in many of the local short distance races. She also found she was getting a lot of attention from race coordinators and local sports personalities. When approached by a couple of sponsors, she knew she was making a name for herself. It was an exciting time.

With encouragement from Gabby and their friends in the club, Jillian decided to move up to the longer Olympic-distance triathlons, which were twice the length of the sprint races. It was with these that she found her true passion, and she knew she had the potential to compete on a national level.

"I'm glad I didn't give up back then," Jillian said, turning to David and smiling. "If I'd never done another race, I would've never ended up moving out here. And I certainly wouldn't have met you."

"See? Everything happens for a reason. Isn't that what you're always telling me? You're right where you're supposed to be. You've been a good daughter, and your parents are still so proud of you. It's all good, I promise."

The rest of the ride into Denver was quiet. Jillian fell asleep for a few minutes, and once they got to the airport terminal, David pulled up along the curb and shook her on the shoulder.

"Wake up, babe. We're here." He hopped out to grab her bags and placed them on the sidewalk.

"Tell your parents I said hello, and let them know I'm sorry I had to miss them." He hugged her tight. "I love you, blue-eyes, and I'll be here on Sunday to pick you up. Text me when you get to Boston so I know you've landed safely. Don't worry...everything is going to work out with your dad."

"Thanks again, babe. Love you, too," Jillian said, kissing him. "I miss you already, but I'll see you on Sunday. And good luck with your team, I'm sure you'll get them whipped into shape. You're a good coach. Don't forget that."

As he drove away, she hoisted the two heavy bags onto her shoulders and walked through the sliding glass doors. She easily found the ticket counter and checked in, receiving her boarding pass.

Once inside the gate area, she looked for a remote spot to hang out while she waited for the airline attendants to start boarding her flight. The past few hours had been a complete blur, and it still hadn't quite hit her that she was about to fly back home. She walked past her gate and chose a spot on the floor, under a bank of windows and overlooking the busy tarmac. She eagerly dropped her bags and sat down, leaning against the wall.

Casually scanning the crowd, she wondered what purpose her fellow passengers had for going to Boston. Many looked to be professionals returning from harried business trips, laptops opened and fast-food containers littered about. There were also a few college-aged kids meandering around. Jillian assumed they were most likely going home for spring break. It suddenly occurred to her that she hadn't been back to see her parents in almost two years.

She could almost visualize a little devil sitting on her left shoulder saying, "She should've never waited this long," and pointing his finger at her.

"Yeah, but she had good intentions of returning home to visit more often," the imaginary angel on her right shoulder retorted. "It's just that things got so busy in her life, it became easier and easier to put it off."

"That's no excuse," the little devil continued, her mind entertaining the back-and-forth charade. "Her two trips home per year slowly turned into just once during the holidays, then to just once every other year. Not acceptable."

"Whatever, guys," Jillian spoke out loud and quickly realized she might look like a crazy person talking to no one in particular. Thankfully there was no one near.

She shook the silly image out of her head and propped up one of her bags to create a comfortable position to lie back in. She popped her ear buds in, selected a favorite playlist, and rested her heavy head. It took all of three minutes to fall asleep.

"Final call for Flight 714 with nonstop service to Boston, leaving out of gate number forty-two. All passengers please report immediately for boarding. This is your third and final call." The stern voice boomed over the intercom.

"Oh, crap!" Jillian startled and jumped up. Frantically grabbing her bags, she sprinted over to the now-vacant boarding gate. "I'm so sorry! I must have fallen asleep while I was waiting!" She thrust her ticket into the gate attendant's hand. The woman scanned it and quickly handed it back.

"The doors will be closing in a minute, dear. You'd better hurry," she warned. Jillian raced down the ramp and onto the plane as quickly as she could, the hatch being shut and locked directly behind her.

After finding a spot to cram her carry-on and settling into her seat, she hastily fastened her seatbelt and grabbed the flight prep card from the pouch in front of her. The flight attendants were already preparing the other passengers for take-off, and she felt flush from the embarrassment of having everyone stare at her when she boarded seconds earlier. Her heart continued to race, realizing how close she'd come to missing the flight.

"Looks like you just made it. Must be your lucky day." The comment came from an older gentleman sitting in the center seat next to her.

"Yeah, that sure was a close one," she acknowledged and offered a kind smile in return. Taking in a deep sigh of relief, she closed her eyes and rested her head back. The thought of creating small talk for the next several hours was exhausting.

"I'm going to need all the luck I can get over the next few days," she mumbled, just as she felt the wheels starting to pick up speed beneath her. She clutched her hands tightly around the arm rests and braced herself for takeoff.

Within moments, Jillian was in the air, heading back to Boston and her childhood home.

4

TWENTY-THREE YEARS BEFORE IMPACT
BOSTON, LATE JULY

D arkness surrounded Jillian as she lay in the cool green grass in her backyard. She rested motionless, looking up into a clear summer night sky littered with bright constellations. Her sixth-grade class was learning about these ancient patterns in science, and she'd challenged herself to see how many she could identify.

Let's see, I know that's the Big Dipper, she thought as she extended her arm and used her finger to trace the giant-sized ladle above. She kept one eye closed and connected the stars as if the sky was a giant dot-to-dot book. *Okay, I know Cassiopeia looks like a giant W, so that one's easy, and somewhere is the Little Dipper. Oh, there it is!* She had counted seven when the sharp ringing of the phone inside the house broke her concentration.

"Jillian? Jillian, are you still back there?" Her mother stuck her head out from the kitchen window and yelled. "It's time to come inside!" Jillian sat up reluctantly, brushed the loose grass off her overall shorts, and ran to the open window.

"Hey, Mom, I'm right here. You should see how clear the sky is tonight. I found almost every constellation we learned about. Do you want me to show you?" she asked in an attempt to prolong her time outside.

"I'd love for you to show me another time, but right now Amanda wants you to go back over to her house. Her parents asked if the two of you could babysit her cousin tonight. It's okay with me; just make sure you're both watching him closely, and call me if anything comes up. I'll be home all night."

"Oh, cool! Thanks, Mom! I promise we will. See ya later!" Jillian gave her mother a quick wave and rushed across the street to help her best friend. Amanda's younger cousin, Ethan, and his parents had been visiting Amanda and her family from California for the past week. Ethan was easily the cutest kid she'd ever seen. He had big blue eyes just like hers, an infectious smile, and a shock of blond hair. He was only six, but smart as a whip, and he loved spending time with Amanda and Jillian.

Since it was Friday night, all the grown-ups were going out for a fancy dinner. They'd agreed that Amanda and Jillian could babysit as long as they did it together. Amanda had just turned thirteen and Jillian was still only twelve, but both had taken the babysitting course at their school the previous year. The adults knew how eager the girls were to be in charge. Plus, Jillian's mother told her that Amanda's parents and the Carters offered to pay them each five dollars when they got home. The girls couldn't have been more eager, and the adults knew they'd be good with him.

Earlier that day, Amanda and Jillian had played with Ethan in their in-ground swimming pool. Amanda's job was to put him in his arm floaties and carefully lead him up the ladder steps.

"Here he comes!" she would shout down to Jillian, who was treading water at the bottom of the slide.

"Geronimo!" he would screech every time, then come racing down the slippery slide, kicking with excitement. Jillian's job was to catch him after he made his big splash, then make sure he made it over to the edge, so he could pull himself back up and do it all over again. Taking swimming lessons for the last couple of years had made her a strong swimmer, but after several hours of him sliding down and her catching him, she was exhausted.

Little Ethan Carter seemed to have an endless supply of energy. As Jillian headed back over to her friend's house, she was hoping he'd worked most of it out earlier during the day. Luckily, Ethan's parents had already given him a bath and put him into his *Rugrats* pajamas by the time she got there.

"All you girls have to do is make sure he brushes his teeth and put him to bed by ten o'clock. After that, you're home free," Amanda's mother told them.

"After we put him to bed, we can just hang out and watch a movie or something. Plus, I know where my mother hides the junk food!" Amanda whispered to Jillian. They giggled to each other, bonded by their secret plan.

"Here are the numbers you can reach us at if you need to," Amanda's mother said, handing over a piece of notebook paper with two phone numbers scribbled down. "We're going for a drink at the Buffalo Water Tavern first, then dinner at The Harbor Grille. We should be home no later than eleven-thirty. Make sure you lock the door behind us and call if anything comes up."

She leaned down to give Amanda a kiss and Jillian heard her whisper into her ear, "That cheese sauce you love is in the back of the pantry, if you girls are looking for a snack." She winked at Amanda and smiled at Jillian, then grabbed her purse and headed out the door with the rest of the grown-ups. "Be good!"

"Finally!" Amanda looked at Jillian with a spark in her eye as the door closed. "We're in charge!"

"Come play hide-n-seek with me!" Ethan immediately begged, grabbing their hands and leading them both into the living room. "Manda, you can be it first and Jilly and I will go hide!" Ethan was jumping up and down with excitement. The girls took turns being it, and he had a blast finding new places to squeeze in to, giggling like crazy when they got close to his hiding spot. When they finally tired of that, Ethan persuaded both girls to build a giant blanket fort with him.

"We can use all of the pillows and blankets from the couches," he squealed and pulled everything down and onto the floor. Running through the house, he grabbed any extras he could find from the bedrooms.

When their masterpiece was completed, the three of them crawled inside. Lying down in the dark, cavernous space, Amanda had an idea. She ran out and grabbed a flashlight from her hallway closet. When she brought it back, she and Jillian made funny hand-puppet shadows on the blanket roof. Ethan stared up in awe, laughing at their silly creatures, feeling proud of his creation, and loving the undivided attention.

After a few minutes, Ethan scooted out, ran into the bedroom he'd been sleeping in, grabbed a pile of books from his suitcase, and raced back into the safety of the fort. He had both girls snuggle up next to him and read stories, taking turns doing different voices for each character in the book. He followed their lead, adding silly voices of his own and reading right along with the characters they'd brought to life.

After wiggling around for a while, Ethan finally started to settle down and eventually nodded off. The excitement and activity of the day had finally caught up. Amanda and Jillian snuck out of the fort and quietly pulled down the blankets around him. Once he was fully asleep, Amanda carefully lifted him piggy-back style and carried him into his room to put him to bed.

Jillian looked around and saw the heap of pillows and blankets and decided to pitch in. She put all the cushions and blankets back on the couches, then gathered the pile of books and stacked them neatly on the floor.

"Do you need any help?" she called when she heard Amanda rustling around in the kitchen a few moments later.

"Sure! Can you grab the two glasses I left on the counter near the fridge?" she asked when she came back into the living room. She plopped down onto the couch with a huge plate of nachos and melted cheese.

"Yeah, of course! Whoa, those look awesome!" Jillian said as she made her way into the kitchen to grab their drinks. "What do you feel like doing now that he's asleep?"

"I don't care. I'm feeling kinda beat, so maybe we could just put a movie in?" Amanda suggested.

"Sounds good to me," Jillian answered when she came back into the room. She set down the two giant glasses of soda she was carrying, being careful not to spill.

"I feel like such a rebel!" Amanda said with a laugh and grabbed her drink. "My parents never let me bring food in here. Especially not soda!" They clinked their glasses together, pretending to be adults celebrating a special occasion. Amanda took a few chugs from her glass and got up.

Browsing through the rows of neatly arranged movies lining the built-in entertainment center, she started reading off their potential choices. Most were old Disney movies they'd long since outgrown. There were a few boring war documentaries that belonged to her father, and they definitely weren't interested in her mother's old Jane Fonda workout tapes.

"There's not much new here since last time. How about we watch *Home Alone*?" Amanda offered, even though they'd both seen it about a hundred times already.

"Yeah, of course. You already know that's my favorite!" Jillian said. Amanda popped the cassette into the VCR player and fast-forwarded past the previews to the beginning of the movie. They got cozy on the couch and started to devour the heaping pile of nachos, ready to laugh at what lay ahead. They loved the way the would-be burglars got caught up in the many elaborate traps set by the boy home alone, and although they already knew what was coming, they chuckled at the characters' blatant stupidity.

About twenty minutes in, Amanda hit the pause button, yelled, "Pee break!" and scurried out to use the bathroom. Jillian decided they needed refills, so she grabbed the empty glasses and headed toward the kitchen for more soda. On her way, she figured she would peak in on Ethan, who hadn't made a sound since Amanda put him to bed nearly thirty minutes earlier.

Looking into the dimly lit room, she could see that the covers had been kicked off his bed, and Ethan wasn't there. She set the glasses down and went in to see if maybe he'd fallen off the other side and was lying on the floor. She looked around the room and under the bed—no Ethan.

"Amanda!" she yelled. "Ethan isn't in his bed! You'd better come here!" Amanda joined her, and they both started calling his name.

"Ethan! Ethan, where are you?"

No response.

"Ethan, it's not time to play hide-n-seek anymore. Come out right now, buddy! You're not in trouble...we just want to know where you are," Amanda called.

Still nothing.

Frantically, they started to scour every bathroom, every linen closet, and every bedroom in the house. They checked under beds, behind doors, inside cabinets, and in spots he'd hidden in earlier. They didn't find him anywhere.

"I'll check the pantry," Jillian said, thinking maybe he just got hungry and wanted a snack. As she turned the corner leading back toward the kitchen, a warm breeze wafted in and the smell of something familiar hit her nose.

Chlorine. Oh no! Not the pool!

Her mind was racing as she noticed the glass slider was open just enough for a person of Ethan's size to fit through.

Barefoot, she ran out onto the cool cement pool deck and quickly scanned the area. "Ethan! Ethan, are you out here?" she called. It took a few seconds for her eyes to adjust to the dimly lit space, but when they did, she saw a dark figure floating lifelessly in the deep end of the pool.

"Oh my God, Amanda!" she yelled, her heart leaping into her throat. She jumped into the cool, still water and raced to grab Ethan. When she reached him, she immediately flipped his body over to get his face out of the water. He wasn't breathing or moving, and he felt like a heavy sack of potatoes in her arms. She struggled to keep his head above the water while she swam to the edge of the pool, where Amanda was now screaming hysterically.

"Pull him up! Grab him!" she demanded, gasping as water filled her mouth. She could feel herself being pushed under by his weight.

Amanda grabbed Ethan's pajama shirt and heaved him up and out of the water. Even though Jillian's arms were shaking uncontrollably, she managed to pull herself up onto the pool's edge. Her body was trembling as she turned Ethan over and sat on top of his waist. Without thinking twice, she started doing chest compressions.

"One, two, three, four," she called out. "Five, six, seven, eight, nine, ten."

Nothing. She did ten more compressions. Still nothing.

She leaned down, tipped his head back, pinched his nose, and blew two quick breaths into Ethan's mouth. "One, two, three, four. C'mon, Ethan. C'mon, buddy! Five, six, seven, eight, nine, ten," she said as she compressed and counted again. Amanda stood frozen next to them, too paralyzed to move.

Ethan's body suddenly bucked, and before they knew it, he was coughing and spitting up what seemed like a bucketful of pool water. Jillian immediately jumped up and turned him onto his side, allowing him to cough out the rest of the water from his lungs.

When Ethan realized what was happening, he looked at Amanda with terror in his eyes and started shrieking. "I couldn't find Mr. Monkey!" he screamed. "Mr. Monkey was under the slide! Mr. Monkey was scared!" Ethan pointed to his beloved stuffed animal, which had been casually tossed under the pool slide earlier during the day.

"Okay, buddy. Don't worry, just calm down. I'll get it for you." Amanda ran over to grab the stuffed toy. She brought it back and eagerly handed it to Ethan.

"Thanks," he said, sitting up and grabbing it away from her. He wrapped his arms tightly around Mr. Monkey, and Amanda pulled him into her lap. She rocked back and forth. The three of them sat shivering in a stunned silence for several minutes. Finally, Jillian got up and grabbed two nearby towels that were hanging over the pool fence. She wrapped one around Amanda and Ethan, then wrapped one around herself. After she dried off, she held out a hand to help them both up.

When they finally managed to get back inside and warm Ethan up, Amanda called the number to The Harbor Grille, where her parents said they'd be. Making an effort to stay calm, she tried to carefully explain to her now extremely concerned father what had just happened.

"We'll be right home, honey. Are you sure everyone is okay?" Jillian heard him ask again, his voice tense with worry. "Should we call an ambulance?"

"He's breathing fine now, Dad. He's on the couch watching cartoons. Really, we're all okay," Amanda answered. Jillian could see she was still shaking from the ordeal. "Just come home as soon as you can."

In what seemed like no time at all, headlights flashed through the living room window, and the girls heard car doors slamming. Amanda's parents rushed through the front door, with her aunt and uncle following. They were obviously upset and asked both girls to repeat the story over and over until they could make sense of what had happened.

Piecing it all together, they realized that Ethan must've woken up and got frightened because he didn't have his beloved Mr. Monkey. He remembered he'd left Mr. Monkey outside, and when he saw the pool slide again, he wanted to go down "one more time, all by myself" is what he told everyone.

"I won't go into the pool by myself again," he promised his parents, who were clutching him tightly. "Next time I'll get Manda first, okay?" He looked at them with wide eyes, hoping he wouldn't get in trouble.

"That's right, honey," his mother answered with tears streaming down her face. "You need to have a big kid or a grown-up with you every time. You're lucky that Jillian found you when she did. You gave us all quite a scare."

Mrs. Carter was still crying when she stood and hugged Jillian. As soon as she let go, she hugged her again, even tighter than before. "Thank you, Jillian," she said. "Thank you for what you've done. I'm so grateful to you, and we're all so lucky that you got to him in time."

Later, when Jillian's mother came to pick her up, Mrs. Carter pulled her aside.

"Mrs. Richards," she whispered, "Jillian is a true hero, and I don't even want to imagine what could've happened if she hadn't acted so quickly. I'll never be able to repay your daughter for what she's done for Ethan and our family tonight. She is a remarkable young lady and we're just so fortunate."

Jillian could see her mother beaming with pride. She felt her face get a bit warm, flushed from the attention, but she was also proud. "It was a good thing that I had that first aid and CPR course in my swim class, Mom, otherwise I might not have known what to do!" she said. The adults all agreed and repeated over and over that all kids should be made to take that class.

"You should've seen her out there, Mrs. Richards!" Amanda said. "She didn't even think about it, she just reacted. It was amazing. I was so scared, but Jill knew exactly what to do. Thanks to her, Ethan is going to be alright."

When it was time to leave, Jillian waved Ethan over to say good-bye. "Good luck, Ethan. I'm glad you're going to be okay. Thanks for being so brave tonight, buddy. I'm really going to miss you when you go back home." He wrapped his arms around her neck and gave her a big hug.

"You were brave, too, Jilly!" he whispered before letting go, then ran back to the safety of his parents' laps.

As Jillian and her mother walked across the front lawn, back toward their house, she turned briefly and looked through Amanda's large bay window. Inside, she saw Ethan already eating an ice cream cone and laughing with his father. "He's going to be just fine," her mother commented, as if reading her mind, then reached down and squeezed her hand. "He's one lucky little boy."

When Sunday morning came, Jillian decided to go outside in the driveway and test out her new ten-speed bike. It was bright blue with green and yellow swirls, and the chrome was so shiny she could see her reflection in it. Her parents had bought it for her the day before as a reward for her heroics. She'd told them she didn't need a present, but they knew she'd been saving up for one on her own, and they must've thought this was a good reason to get it sooner.

As her garage door opened, she could see Amanda and her family helping Ethan and his parents load suitcases into the trunk of their car across the street.

"Have a safe flight. I miss you already, Sis," she heard Amanda's mother say before giving Mrs. Carter a hug good-bye. She wiped a tear away, then leaned in to help buckle Ethan into the back seat.

"Thank you for everything," Mr. Carter said, shaking hands with Amanda's father. Jillian paused for a moment to watch the scene. For a second, she wondered what it would be like to have a younger brother. She had genuinely liked helping take care of Ethan, reading books, building forts, and making him laugh during the past week. The thought faded as she saw the reverse lights come on and their car backing out of the driveway.

As the car slowly drove past, the Carters rolled down their windows and shouted to her, "Good-bye, Jillian! Have a great summer!" She waved, sad to be seeing them drive away. Ethan pressed his face against the car window and looked right at her with his big blue eyes. He had Mr. Monkey clutched under his arm and a big smile on his face. She watched until their car was out of sight.

"Amanda, come see my new bike!" she shouted, proudly beckoning Amanda to come across the road. Amanda slowly walked over, shoulders slumped and looking rather glum. "What's wrong? Are you upset that your cousin had to leave today?" Jillian asked.

"No, that's not it," Amanda answered, then looked up with sad eyes. She'd been crying. "We found out yesterday that my father's job is moving him to Seattle. We have to leave in just a couple weeks."

The girls became inseparable for the next two weeks. They took turns sleeping over each other's houses every night, and Jillian even helped Amanda pack her stuff into large cardboard boxes. When the moving trucks arrived, they hugged each other tightly and exchanged homemade friendship bracelets. Jillian loved the bright colors chosen for hers, and she eagerly tied the woven gift securely around her wrist.

They promised to write and send letters every week, but after just a few letters, the frequency trickled off. Once school started again, they stopped completely. Jillian was in middle-school now, and cross-country had started. She'd made friends with a few of the girls on the team and had started spending more and more time with them. Eventually, the memories of her summer started to fade, just like the colors on her now-tattered bracelet. When it was just about to fall off, she snipped the final frayed strands and threw it in the back of her junk drawer, the final keepsake from her childhood friend.

5

TWO MINUTES BEFORE IMPACT
BOSTON

I'm *too old to be out here driving in this nonsense,* Mae Roberts thought as she cautiously crept along Interstate 93 north, heading toward Logan Airport. Having her thirteen-year-old granddaughter, Lucy, out from Colorado during her school break had seemed like such a good idea when they planned it a few months earlier. They'd talked about spending their days at the Boston Museum of Science, grabbing lunch at Faneuil Hall, and visiting the Make Way for Ducklings ducks in the Boston Public garden.

Lucy had never been on a plane by herself, and Mae was upset realizing how delayed she would be picking her up. The sound of her ringtone momentarily distracted her from her worry.

"Hello, this is Mae," she answered. "Oh, hi, Miss Jeanne. Yes, I know. The weather is ridiculous for this time of year! The rain is coming down in buckets, and the winds are whipping out here. It's creating quite a mess on the highway. I certainly wasn't expecting it would be this bad so soon."

She waited a beat to hear what her friend had to say. "Yes, of course, you can reschedule. I completely understand. Actually, I've already closed the shop down for the day and planned to reach out to everyone who had an appointment scheduled for this afternoon. I figured my clients would be cancelling once they heard the weather advisory reports this morning," she added with a chuckle. "Now, don't you come out in this storm unless there's an emergency. If I wasn't on my way to pick up Lucy at the airport right now, I'd turn back myself! Looks like I'm stuck in the thick of things, though."

Mae checked her rearview mirror and realized there were several cars behind her, apparently trying to pass. She turned on her directional and slowly eased into the middle lane. Three cars speed past in tandem. Although Mae could handle a lot, being on the phone while trying to navigate in this mess was causing her some elevated stress.

"Listen, Jeanne, I hate to cut you short, but I need to get off the phone and focus on the road. If you call me back tomorrow morning, I promise to get you rescheduled just as soon as possible. I think I can squeeze you in first thing Monday morning." Mae hung up and tossed the phone into the open Louis Vuitton handbag on the passenger seat. She checked the rearview again.

At a youthful sixty-one, with jet black hair, striking dark eyes, a beautiful brown complexion, and a slender build, Mae carried herself with dignity and class. She didn't like to be unprepared for any situation.

Being the owner of an upscale salon and day spa for the past twenty-five years, Mae was also a proud woman. As a single mother in her late-twenties, she had started out catering to her close friends and other black and Hispanic working women in her neighborhood in Boston. She offered haircuts, coloring, and a whole lot of harmless gossiping opportunities from the spare room in her apartment.

After years of hard work, she established her own location and brought along a fiercely loyal following. Mae had gotten popular enough that her clients were willing to wait months just to have her do their hair. She'd even promised Lucy a fancy new hairdo when she came out to visit.

Mae always dressed to the nines, and now found herself regretting not having brought any boots or raingear with her.

The voicemail ringtone on her cell phone beckoned for her attention again. *Oh! I bet this is Lucy now,* she thought, digging for her phone at the bottom of her purse to see who'd left the message. *Please let this be a confirmation that the plane has landed safely at Logan. I sure hope Lucy is just letting me know which gate to retrieve her from.*

Just as she found the phone and held it up to read the first couple words, "Hi Grandma," Mae's attention immediately got diverted. The horrific sound of a crash and the unmistakable screech of metal crunching ahead filled the air.

Coming over the crest of a hill, she was shocked by what she saw and immediately jacked on her brakes. Her new Lexus pulsated and jerked violently, then began to slide out of control after hitting a patch of black ice. Luckily, she was able to find some traction and kept it safely on the road. The car came to a full stop before hitting anything or being hit by someone else.

"Thank the Lord!" she cried out. She took a deep breath. Waves of gratitude washed over her.

Just as she got her bearings, her wipers made another pass, sweeping away the slushy fog clouding her windshield. Coming into focus was a horrific scene. She quickly made the connection between what she heard just moments before and what she was seeing now.

Oh my God! This is bad. This is really bad.

Straight ahead she saw a small silver sedan, or what was left of it, wedged under a massive, jackknifed tractor-trailer. She scanned the gruesome wreckage and realized she was the first person on the scene.

"Please be alive, please be alive, oh Lord, please let them be alive," she pleaded as she instinctively fumbled for the handle. She caught the latch and thrust her car door open.

Making her way into the freezing rain and winds, Mae rushed toward the crushed vehicle as quickly as she could. All was a blur. The driving wind and rain muffled her surroundings, but she thought she heard people on the opposite side of the trailer shouting. "Call 911! Someone please call 911!" a voice screamed.

On this side of the trailer, though, Mae was completely alone. She had to do something, and fast. After several attempts using all of her

RACHEL ODELL HOWE

strength, she was finally able to pry the buckled door of the smashed car open. There she found a young woman, blood trickling down the side of her head, slumped over and unconscious in the front seat. She immediately checked for a pulse and was relieved that the woman was still breathing, though it seemed labored and shallow. A waft of gasoline fumes abruptly hit Mae in the face, and she noticed smoke starting to leak from underneath the hood of the crushed car.

Unbuckling the woman's seatbelt, she attempted to pull her out of the car, away from the danger.

"Oh, no. This isn't working," she said out loud. "You aren't budging. Something must be stuck," she spoke calmly to the unconscious woman. She stopped for a moment to think. "I don't want to injure you further, but I need to get you out of here. What are we going to do?" Mae was still speaking when she knelt beside the open door and peeked under the steering column.

The woman's leg appeared to be trapped under the crinkled dashboard. Mae stood back up and brushed the wet hair away from her eyes. The pelting rain continued to beat harshly against her face. Within seconds, a small fire ignited underneath the trailer. Heavy black smoke began to billow from the car's engine, the cabin quickly filling up. The toxic stench of burning plastic was almost too much to bear.

Mae looked around for help, but no one else had come out from their vehicles yet. A clock started ticking in her head. It was a subconscious alarm, but it became deafening.

Fire, smoke, gasoline. Not much time, and she is really stuck. C'mon, Mae, stay focused here. You can do this! Just think. What can you use to pry her free? There has to be something!

"I'm going to see if there's anything useful in my car," she said out loud. "I'll be right back. I promise I'm not leaving you." As she turned toward her car she called back, "I'm going to help you out of this!" Purely functioning on adrenaline, she set her fears aside.

Leaning into the driving wind, Mae made her way back through the freezing rain to her car. She scanned the back seat and saw only her beauty supply bag. As if by divine intervention, an idea came to her. She snatched the entire bag and rushed back to the woman, who was now hanging limply out of the open car door. There were still no signs of consciousness.

Grabbing a tube of hair gel from the case, Mae forcefully squeezed an entire handful into her palm. She smeared it down the woman's pinned leg, reaching through the smoke to get as far under the dashboard as possible. She tugged again and felt a little movement, but was still unable to pry her free. Mae was slipping on the wet, frozen ground and knew she needed more leverage.

The clock's *tick, tick, tick* was getting louder and louder in her head.

Breathe, Mae, she told herself. *Think. Think. The seatbelt! I can use the seatbelt!*

She knew exactly what she needed to do.

Grabbing the razor-sharp scissors from her bag, she cut a long stretch of seatbelt off at two ends. Quickly, she wrapped it around and through the woman's legs, then around her own waist. She threw off her heels and braced both feet against the open doorframe of the crushed car. Using all her might, she grabbed both ends of the belt, wrapped her arms tightly around the woman's torso, and pushed off. A loud crack startled Mae as the pinned leg came free, and both she and the woman landed with a jarring thump against the hard, unforgiving pavement.

Mae winced as a sharp pain radiated from her tailbone. "It's okay, pretty lady, you're going to be okay," she said with a huff, then stood and grabbed the woman from underneath both arms. "I've got you now. You're going to be okay," she repeated again. Using small, calculated steps, she labored to drag the woman several yards back, away from the accident. Her feet were raw and numb. Within seconds, the crushed car was engulfed in flames. Choking clouds of noxious smoke quickly filled the air.

By this time, the driver of the tractor-trailer had stumbled away from the truck. He was on the phone with emergency services, shouting for help. Mae heard the blare of sirens approaching in the distance. She knelt and cradled the injured woman's head in her lap, covering them both as much as possible with her rain-soaked blazer.

"Hold on, sweet lady, help is coming. Just hang in there. You're going to be just fine," she said to the still unconscious woman. By the looks of things, Mae wasn't totally convinced this was true.

The vibration of her phone in the jacket's pocket diverted Mae's attention. A sudden wave of panic shot through her body. "Oh, no!" she shouted and fumbled to reach for it while still attempting to shield the woman's face. "Lucy!" Mae already couldn't stop shaking from the bone-chilling winds and rain. Now panic set in as she envisioned Lucy, all alone, waiting for her at the airport.

Her attempts to call Lucy back were unsuccessful. After several tries, she sent a text, only to get an "Out of Service Area" reply. "My poor Lucy," Mae whimpered. "My poor baby. I need to get to her. She'll be sick with worry if I'm not there for her."

6

"Lucy!" Mae whispered loudly, squeezing her granddaughter's hand and settling back into the cushioned recliner in the darkened theater. "Sorry it took me so long to come back. Have you girls been worried?" Mae looked toward Lucy and her friend, who were intently watching the colorfully animated movie playing on the gigantic screen in front of them.

"Huh? Oh, no Grandma, we're okay," Lucy answered and looked over, smiling with wide, bright eyes. "Where were you? Did you go to get us some more candy?" The girls hadn't even seemed to notice that Mae had been gone for so long.

"No, dear, maybe on the way out. Let's just finish the movie for now, okay?" Mae leaned back as the cool theater air sent a shiver down her sweat-drenched back.

Mae had been looking forward to this visit with her daughter Grace and her family out in Boulder for some time. It had been two years since she'd last made the trip from Boston. It was hard to be so far away, and Mae missed them all terribly, especially the grandchildren. Taking time away was always a challenge because the salon was busy, and her clients rarely trusted their hair to anyone else. But since her granddaughter Lucy's eleventh birthday was coming up, Mae had promised to come out so they could spend some quality girl-time. She always made good on her promises.

"What have you got planned for your big day out with the girls?" Grace had asked her mother earlier that morning. "It's all Lucy's been talking about for weeks!"

Mae smiled.

"Oh, is that so? I've been looking forward to it as well, I have to confess! It's not every day that I get to spoil her the way I like to. What do you think she would love to do most?"

Grace suggested to her mother that she take Lucy and one of her friends shopping to buy an outfit she'd been asking for. "You know that girl of mine…any excuse to go to the mall and she's happy as a clam! I think I know where she gets that gene from!" Grace winked at her mother. "You are like two peas in a pod, I must admit!"

"Well, how could I say no to that? You know that itinerary is right up my alley!" Mae was ecstatic. Grace knew her mother loved to shop and had a great eye for fashion and trends. Taking her granddaughter to the mall would be just as much fun for her as it would be for Lucy.

Once they got there, the girls spent hours going through the racks at Nordstrom and Macy's, trying designer clothes on, playing dress-up with the fancy gowns, and pretending they were runway models in their high heels. They even convinced Mae to let them sit at the beauty counter to get a complimentary make-up session. She allowed them both to pick out a flavored lip gloss, even though they had begged for bright red lipstick. "Lucy, you know your mother would kill me if I let you take that stuff home!" she had warned. The girls just rolled their eyes, most likely knowing she was right but trying to get away with it anyway.

Mae helped the girls choose skirts and matching tops, and encouraged Lucy to find a pair of wedges to match her new outfit. She wanted the girls to feel like movie stars, leaving the store with fancy packages and overflowing bags.

"Thank you, Grandma," Lucy said, grinning from ear to ear and skipping along. She reached over and grabbed Mae's hand as they walked toward the elevators leading to the parking garage. "That was the best birthday present ever!"

When they finished loading the car with their bags and were all buckled in, Lucy had an idea. "Grandma, would you bring us to go see a movie before we have to go back home? The theater is right across the street." Mae was happy to oblige her granddaughter and spend more special time together.

"Well, I was going to take you ladies for an early dinner, but I guess we can grab a few snacks at the theater if that's what you'd rather do." The girls bounced up and down, obviously filled with excitement.

"Yes, please, that sounds perfect!" Lucy's face lit up and she gave her friend a high-five. Mae called to let Grace know they wouldn't be home for a couple more hours, but that everything was going well.

Once they arrived at the theater, Mae decided to let the girls have a treat as their dinner. After all, it was Lucy's birthday, and if this made her happy, Mae couldn't be more accommodating. She bought a big bucket of popcorn with extra butter and let them both pick out their choice of candy and a frozen slushy drink. She knew she would be hearing about this later from Grace, but she didn't care—she would do anything to see that smile on her granddaughter's face. The girls raced into the theater with their snacks and started up the steps.

"Up here, Grandma. We like to sit up here. Is that okay?" Lucy said and pointed toward a row of seats in the back of the theater.

"Yes, that's fine, baby girl," Mae agreed. "They never had these Pixar movies or these stadium seats when I was a girl. We had to watch movies with our necks cranked back and hope no one tall sat in front of us! You two sure are lucky you get to watch such fancy movies, and in such fancy seats!" The girls just looked at each other and giggled.

About halfway through the movie, Mae started to pick at the remnants of the popcorn left in the bottom of the bucket from the two girls. She ate a couple small handfuls, thoroughly enjoying the salty, buttery treat. Feeling a persistent tickle in her throat, she snuck a sip of Lucy's melted raspberry slushy to try to clear it away, but got no relief.

It didn't take long for Mae to realize that a half-popped popcorn kernel with a jagged edge must have lodged itself at the back of her esophagus. Her subtle attempts to quietly cough it out were not successful, and she certainly didn't want to cause a scene. It was becoming more and more uncomfortable by the second. She motioned to the girls that she would be right back and headed down the steps toward the exit. She located the brightly lit restroom sign and quickly entered the nearby ladies room.

Mae was grateful to have some privacy as she walked into the empty bathroom. She was already embarrassed enough and just wanted this fiasco to be over. Tipping her head to the side, she took a few sips of water from the sink's faucet to see if that would work to clear the kernel from her throat. It did not, and even worse, it became more irritated. When her attempts to forcefully cough the kernel out also didn't work, Mae began to panic.

With her heart nervously racing, and while trying to cough it out again, she inadvertently inhaled the popcorn piece even deeper into her windpipe, making it nearly impossible to breathe. After several moments struggling for air, Mae fell to her knees.

No one knows I'm in here, she thought, the realization that she might choke to death washing over her. Sweat pooled on her back, palms, and forehead.

You need to get back to Lucy, she urged herself, before becoming so light-headed and dizzy that she was sure she would pass out. Mae tried to stay alert, but her vision slowly began to fade, and her remaining strength was slowly leaving her body. It was as if she was traveling through a dim tunnel, and she knew that the light at the end was just about to burn out.

"Ugh!"

A hard squeeze to her abdomen shook her from behind. When the second, more forceful squeeze came, her mouth involuntarily shot open. The popcorn kernel flew across the open room, landing near a toilet in an empty stall several feet away. A large gasp of air brought her back into the moment, and she slumped onto the cold bathroom floor.

Mae's hands began to shake as adrenaline pumped through her body. The shock and embarrassment hit her at once. She was overwhelmingly relieved, realizing that the kind young woman standing over her had just saved her life, and although she knew she should have been happy, she simultaneously felt completely mortified by the whole experience.

"Here, let me help you up," the woman offered as she reached down and carefully took Mae's arm. She gently helped Mae back up onto her feet and led her over to the sink, where she grabbed a few paper towels, wet them down with cool water, and handed them to her.

"Are you alright?" the woman asked with a deeply concerned look. "That was a close one! Here, use these to cool yourself down. I think you might be in shock. Are you breathing okay now? Did we get everything out?" The woman waited for Mae to respond.

"Oh, yes, dear, thank you," Mae finally answered, patting the damp towels against her forehead. "I'm so sorry about that. I guess I hadn't realized how large that popcorn kernel was. I'm quite embarrassed!" Mae kept her eyes diverted and spoke sheepishly as the blood rushed back into her face.

"Oh, please don't apologize. There's nothing to be embarrassed about. I'm just glad I came in when I did!" the young woman said with a smile, then turned to pick up the spilled contents of the purse she had dropped behind her.

Mae panicked and made a mad dash for the door. She hurried out of the bathroom as quickly as her feet would take her. Without looking back, she eagerly scurried into the next theater where the girls were waiting.

Now sitting there in the dark, Mae took another deep breath to calm herself further and glanced toward Lucy and her friend again. She saw the delicate outline of her granddaughter's face as she gazed in wonderment toward the brightly lit screen in front of her.

I couldn't bear the thought of missing out on seeing her grow up or putting her in harm's way like this ever again, she lectured herself. *I need to be more careful when she's in my care. I feel such a fool.*

Still feeling ashamed and embarrassed, Mae decided she was better off not telling the girls or her daughter Grace what had happened. She didn't want to put a damper on such a perfect day or risk losing her daughter's trust.

"Everything was perfect," Lucy told her mother when they got home. "The best birthday ever, thanks to Grandma!"

"That it was, Lucy," Mae agreed. "That it was."

7

EIGHTEEN MONTHS BEFORE
IMPACT (JILLIAN)
BOULDER, COLORADO

"Why am I so nervous, Ashley?" Jillian asked over speaker-phone while she sat at her vanity, putting on the finishing touches of her makeup. She was excited to finally use the new liquid eye liner pencil she had bought the previous week and was trying to hold her hand steady as she added the final details.

"I'm not sure, Jill. It's not like you haven't already been spending almost every day together at your swim lessons. I think it's because you really, really like him," Ashley answered.

"Yeah, I guess that's been pretty obvious," Jillian agreed, putting a second coat of mascara on to bring her pale blue eyes into sharp focus. Her naturally highlighted auburn hair, usually pulled back into a ponytail, fell softly to her shoulders. She looked into the mirror and smiled. It had been too long since she'd gone out on a date, and she was looking forward to the night ahead. Butterflies floated about in her stomach, and she felt like a schoolgirl with a silly crush.

"I just want everything to go perfectly. You know I've had the major hots for him since we started training a couple months ago. By the way, if I haven't thanked you enough for introducing us, thank you, thank you, thank you!"

"It was my pleasure, you goof. David's a good guy, and I genuinely think you two make a cute couple. I hope it works out. Good luck tonight, and I want all the juicy details in the morning! Don't do anything I wouldn't do and I'll see you at the pool at six-thirty," Ashley said. "Let's see if you can keep up with me this time."

The last time they got together to train, Ashley's lap times had gotten so much faster, Jillian could hardly believe it. She remembered being blown away when they came out of the pool.

"I just have to ask," Jillian said, "what have you been eating lately and how do I get some? You were like Nemo on steroids out there! Seriously, what have you been doing differently with your training? That was amazing!"

Ashley just smirked.

"Oh, I could tell you, but then I'd have to kill you!" she joked, using her best pretend mafia hit-man voice. "Actually, all the credit really needs to be given to my new coach. He's amazing. He swam for the University of Michigan, and I heard he even tried out for the Olympic team at one point."

"Whoa. That's impressive. So what's his secret?" Jillian asked.

"Honestly, he's just really good at breaking down the mechanics of each stroke. He gave me a ton of tips on how to improve my overall technique. I can't believe how much time we've shaved off. I'll give you his number if you want. I think he is still taking new students right now, too. Oh, and he's pretty cute, by the way. Actually, he's really cute. It sure makes those 6 a.m. training sessions a little easier to get to! Too bad I already have a boyfriend!"

Ashley blushed as she gave Jillian her swim coach David's contact information. "Don't you dare tell him I told you that or I really will have to kill you!" she teased. Jillian called his cell number on the way home that morning, setting up a session for herself the very next day.

David proved to be an excellent coach. He was able to identify Jillian's strengths and weaknesses in the pool right from their first lesson. With his expert eye and encouraging coaching style, he was able to teach her ways to shave seconds from her lap times almost immediately. Plus, Ashley was correct: Jillian thought David was ridiculously good-looking from the first moment she set eyes on him. He was not only boyishly handsome with wavy brown hair, a squared jaw, and an adorable dimple, but also well-built, with a tall, lean frame. He was without a doubt the most experienced swim coach she'd ever worked with. Plus, she found him easy to talk to, and he had an excellent sense of humor.

Jillian was confident the attraction was mutual. She'd been enjoying the subtle flirtations throughout their training sessions, and when she found out he had asked someone about her dating availability, she knew there could be something more there. After practice one afternoon, and in a moment of complete bravery, she asked David if he would like to go see a movie with her that next weekend.

"Well, on one condition," David answered her in a surprisingly serious tone. "I'll only go if you allow me to take you out for dinner beforehand. This is non-negotiable and a complete deal-breaker if you don't agree to these terms."

Jillian, of course, followed his lead. "Well, if you could have the proper papers drawn up in advance I'll have my lawyer take a look. If acceptable, I'll get the contract notarized and stamped with an official raised seal, and we should be able to proceed accordingly. Let's reconvene at six o'clock next Saturday night at my place."

"Okay, I accept that deal," he said, extending his hand to meet hers.

As they shook hands, she was laughing. "Well, I guess that makes this a legally binding transaction now."

"Well, I guess it does. I look forward to seeing you then, Miss Richards." David held on to her hand a few seconds longer than necessary before letting go. Her heart was pounding, and she definitely felt her stomach do a flip. She couldn't wait.

Glancing at the clock on her dresser, she noticed it was just before six o'clock. He would be there any minute. She took one final look in the mirror to make sure she hadn't forgotten anything.

At six o'clock on the nose, the doorbell rang. Jillian grabbed her jacket off the bed and hurried out of her room to answer the door. David greeted her with, "Well, Miss Richards, I assume you have the signed papers before we proceed with the evening?"

He waited a beat and she just rolled her eyes. "Just kidding. You look very nice tonight, by the way. Although, you may be a little over-dressed for the Quickie Mart microwave-burrito buffet I was planning, so I guess we'll have to pick another spot. And on such short notice. Hmm. What are you in the mood for? Preferably something a tad more upscale? A place that won't cause quite as much intestinal distress, I would imagine?" David chuckled, amused by his own joke.

Jillian thought for a few seconds, then offered, "As tempting as that does sound, and believe me, I always love a good convenience-store burrito, how about we try that new microbrewery that just opened across from the theaters? It might not have the same ambiance that you were going for, but Ashley raved about it last time we spoke."

"Well, I have to admit that Ashley seems to have exceptionally good taste. The referrals she's sent my way so far have all been winners, so count me in!" David responded, giving her a wink and his signature smile.

That dimple is going to be the death of me, Jillian thought as they walked to his car. He politely opened the door for her and she got in, her butterflies in full flutter-mode.

After a delicious dinner, David looked at his watch, then back into her eyes as the waitress cleared away their empty plates. "Do you think we have time for one more beer? I wanted to try their new IPA, but I don't want to be late for your movie."

"Absolutely! Let's do it!" She smiled and held up her empty glass. She was happy to agree to another round of drinks before they left. "Besides, even if we are a little late, they usually have at least twenty minutes of previews. We should be fine!"

Jillian was having so much fun, she totally forgot to keep tabs on the time. David had been making her laugh hysterically with stories of the pranks the boys on his high school swim team had pulled on each other before their larger meets. She especially loved the story of how a few of the kids switched their team captain's Speedos for a pair two sizes too small, just before he needed to get ready for the diving competition.

David lit up reliving the details. "Because he knew he would be disqualified if he didn't come out of the locker room, he ended up squeezing himself into the suit and strutting out as if that was completely normal. I almost had a heart attack when I saw him, of course. I mean, those things are tight! And in all the wrong places, I might add. So anyway, he proudly climbed up to the platform and performed his dive as the rest of the team gathered around, laughing hysterically and pointing from the sidelines. I was so embarrassed in front of the other coaches; I must've looked like an overly ripe tomato about to explode! There may have been actual steam coming out from my ears, come to think of it. Luckily, he managed to score pretty well; otherwise they would've all been doing extra laps until the next millennium!"

Jillian enjoyed seeing how passionate he was about the talented kids on his team and how proud he was of them. She could tell that he loved what he did for a living, and she found that extremely attractive.

When their drinks arrived, she took the opportunity to share similar escapades from teams she'd been on and teams she'd coached. They found they had more in common than they realized. The conversation flowed smoothly and effortlessly. David learned that she'd been head coach for the girls' cross-country team at the private Boulder Academy for the past several years, and she discovered that in addition to teaching private lessons and being the head swim coach at the local high school, he was also an avid runner.

"I can't believe our paths haven't crossed sooner," David said and waved for the waitress to bring the check. With a wink he added, "I'm just glad they have now!"

By the time they made it to the movie theater, they were running several minutes behind. "I'll get in line for the tickets and grab some seats while you run to the ladies' room," David offered as they entered the lobby. Jillian had gulped down her last beer rather quickly and had jokingly commented that she didn't want to be suffering with a full bladder throughout the movie.

"Yeah, perfect idea, thank you! I'll meet you in the theater in five." She gave him a little wave and headed off in the opposite direction. "Make sure you grab us a good spot!"

Upon entering the ladies' room, she immediately noticed an older woman down on her knees and clearly in some distress. "Are you okay?" she asked and walked around to the front of the woman, trying to see what was happening. "Ma'am?" she asked, leaning down to see her face.

As soon as she realized the woman was struggling to breathe, she threw down her handbag, wrapped her arms around the woman's diaphragm, and gave a firm upward squeeze.

Nothing happened.

Jillian took a deep breath, braced her legs, and squeezed a second time, even harder. This time the woman's mouth flew open, and a small object hurled across the bathroom floor. The woman gasped for air and fell back limply onto the floor. Her hands began to tremble uncontrollably.

Jillian gently helped the woman to her feet. "Are you able to breathe okay now?" she asked. "Is there anyone I should get for you? That certainly was a close one," she added. The woman seemed a bit disoriented and did not respond right away. "Did we get it all out?" she asked again.

After a few moments, the woman finally responded. "Yes, dear, thank you. I'm so sorry about that. I'm quite embarrassed," she replied in a whispered voice, wiping her face with the damp, cool paper towel Jillian had handed her.

"I'm sorry that I caused you to spill all of your things," she said, pointing to the area behind Jillian. When Jillian looked down on the floor where she had dropped her bag, she realized most of its contents had spilled out and were scattered about.

"Oh, it's no worry," Jillian answered, then turned and bent down to start picking her belongings up. "I'll have this cleaned up in a jiff. The important thing is that we got you taken care of, right?" When she turned back toward the woman, she saw the bathroom door closing behind her. Surprised, Jillian quickly grabbed the final few items, shoved them into her bag, and attempted to go after her.

When she opened the door, the woman had already vanished. A walk through the lobby and a scan of the concession stand showed no sign of her. With fourteen theaters, Jillian knew she could have easily slipped inside one undetected. There was no way she would be able to find the mysterious woman now.

She made her way over to the theater where David was waiting. He waved her over toward their seats as soon as he saw her come in. Settling in beside him, she leaned in and quietly relayed the story. "You won't believe what just happened," she started out. By the time she had finished detailing her encounter, David was in disbelief. "Well, if nothing else, this is certainly going to be an interesting first-date story to tell your friends," Jillian offered.

"You aren't kidding!" David agreed. "Plus, I don't think I've ever been on a date with a real-life superhero before."

"Oh, you have no idea," Jillian joked. "But that's a story for another time."

"Well, in any case, I think I'm going to start calling you Popcorn Girl from now on. And I'll be sure to only eat popcorn while in your presence from this day forward." David put his hand over his heart as if making a solemn pledge.

"Okay then, I guess that means we'll be seeing a lot more movies together!" Jillian teased. David reached over and took her hand into his, sending a shot of electricity up her arm.

"I guess it does," David answered, then he looked into her eyes and flashed his adorable smile, adding, "Lucky me!"

The previews finally started, and the theater got quiet. Just as Jillian had predicted, there were about ten new movies getting promoted. Most looked horrible, and they took turns letting each other know with either a two-thumbs-up or two-thumbs-down gesture if they would see the movie or not based on the preview. When a trailer for *The Fault in Our Stars* came on, David leaned over to say something to Jillian. His silliness had turned to sadness. She could see in his eyes that something had changed.

"I actually had a cousin who died from leukemia when she was only seven," he whispered. "It was just awful seeing what she had to go through. I bet that movie is going to be really sad." Jillian nodded in agreement, surprised but impressed to see such a sensitive side to him that soon.

The previews finally finished and the theater became completely darkened. Jillian leaned back into her chair as the feature movie began. Rather than paying attention to the film, though, her thoughts drifted back to her senior year in high school.

8

"Why are they calling us down for an assembly now?" Jillian asked her friend Sarah as they met each other in the hallway. "It's strange that we're getting dismissed so early from class. I'm supposed to be taking a calculus test right now."

"I think it has something to do with Jake Morgan. Something about a blood drive I heard," Sarah answered. They shuffled down the corridor, following the bulk of the senior class into the gymnasium. Sarah and Jillian filed in and took their seats on one of the top rows of hard, wooden bleachers that lined the far wall. They were careful not to sit near any of the used chewing gum wads stuck to the wall behind them.

"I'm just glad this is getting me out of my boring history class," Sarah added. "I was literally about to fall asleep in there for the second time this week. I think I was actually drooling onto the desk last time."

The girls started giggling until they noticed a few privacy screens set up in the back corner of the room, blocking what appeared to be medical beds. When they saw a few adults sitting somberly in the center of the room, they knew something important was happening.

For the next several minutes, they sat silently and waited to hear why they'd been assembled.

As soon as everyone was in the auditorium, the principal stood and spoke into the microphone. His tone was serious. "Thank you, ladies and gentlemen. Please find a seat as quickly as possible if you haven't already done so. This will only take a few minutes. I'd like to have your total cooperation and ask that you show respect for our guests, please." He looked around the room and waited for complete silence.

"I want to take this opportunity to introduce Mrs. Pamela Wagner, the director of the Boston Blood Bank. She has a few things she would like to share with you today. Please give her your undivided attention."

A well-dressed woman in her mid-forties rose from her seat next to Jake's parents in the center of the auditorium. She cordially smiled up at the students and walked purposefully toward the microphone sitting atop a podium bearing the school's logo.

Sarah leaned over and whispered into Jillian's ear, "I know Jake has been really sick, because I haven't seen him at school for most of senior year so far. It's so weird to see his parents here without him, though. They're usually so private; I wonder what this is all about." Jillian, along with the rest of her classmates, had no idea what Jake had been going through until the woman spoke out.

"Thank you all for being here today. I'm sorry that it couldn't be under better circumstances. As some of you may have heard, your classmate Jake has been going through intensive chemotherapy over the past several months. He's been bravely battling with an aggressive form of leukemia called AML, which is a type of blood cancer. His doctors have been doing everything they can for him, but unfortunately he's still very sick. They've just recently let him and his parents know that he will need a bone marrow transplant to save his life."

The woman took a moment to let the news sink in. There was a collective gasp from the students, and Jillian saw a few girls start crying in the row in front of her. She felt Sarah grab her arm and squeeze in disbelief.

"His parents, who are here with us today, have contacted our organization in hope that their community, including all of you, will consider donating blood today to see if we can find a suitable match for him," she continued. "We often find that the best donors end up being neighbors, friends, or people who grow up in the same area. You may be surprised to find out that you, or even the person sitting right next to you, might be just the person to save Jake's life." A hushed silence fell over the room.

"You're under no obligation to do this, of course, but if you're at least eighteen and would like to participate, we invite you to come sign a few forms and donate today. It'll only take a couple of minutes, and only a small blood sample is needed for the test. Jake's parents have agreed to cover all expenses, and thank you in advance for your help and continued support for Jake." The woman walked back toward where the Morgans were sitting.

"I'm definitely doing it," Sarah said firmly. Without hesitation, she jumped up and pulled Jillian's arm to follow her. Most of their classmates were slowly making their way down the bleachers. Multiple lines were starting to form near the privacy screens.

Jillian had never known someone with leukemia, and she began to feel sad for Jake. Not only was he missing his senior year, but none of them even knew quite how sick he'd been all that time. She joined Sarah in line, where she couldn't help but think about the nurse drawing a small sample of blood from her arm.

"You know I hate needles," she whispered to Sarah as they stood waiting. "And the sight of blood makes me queasy." She began to feel a little shaky when she realized it was almost her turn. She contemplated making up an excuse to bow out, but after seeing the look of hope in Jake's parents' faces, she reconsidered.

As if Sarah was reading her mind, she leaned toward Jillian. "Look how grateful they are watching all of their son's friends standing in line. We're definitely doing the right thing, Jill. Just try not to worry; it goes fast. And remember to look away before they put the needle in. That's usually the worst part."

Jillian nodded. "I just hope that someone here can be a match for Jake. I can't imagine what his parents are going through right now."

"I know. This must be so scary for them. It must be just awful. Poor Jake."

When her turn came, Jillian quickly scanned the paperwork they handed her and signed at the bottom. She rolled up her sleeve and watched as the nurse wrapped a rubber tube around her bicep, which caused the vein in the middle of her arm to slightly bulge. After being swiped with an alcohol swab, she looked away in anticipation of what was coming. She could feel herself tense up.

"Ouch!" she screamed when the needle poked into her arm.

"That was the worst of it," the nurse empathized and offered a comforting smile. Jillian got embarrassed thinking everyone was now staring at her. She felt her face get red hot when a few of her classmates standing nearby started to giggle and gave her a funny look. She tried to laugh it off, pretending that it didn't bother her.

"When will we know if any of us are a donor match for Jake?" she asked, trying to sound cool and collected again.

"Oh, it usually takes a few weeks to do all the screening with a group this size. Someone from the blood bank will reach out if anyone does come through as a match, though. You just never know," the nurse answered, pulling the needle out and placing a small adhesive bandage on Jillian's arm before moving to the next student in line.

9

"**I** can get this, Coach," Nikki Jamison said as she grabbed the four extra bats leaning on the fence and stuffed them into her already overcrowded equipment bag. She was eager to show how helpful she could be.

"You sure those are all gonna fit in there?" he responded, watching her cram them in with all her might. "Looks like that bag weighs more than you now!"

"Yeah, that's probably true, Coach!" she agreed, laughing.

Joining the travel softball team was one of the best decisions Nikki had made, but she desperately wished they had an equipment manager for these weekend tournaments. She usually got stuck carrying more than her fair share since she was the newbie on the team. This day was no exception. Her awkwardly heavy bag continuously bumped the back of her legs wherever she walked. Normally it wouldn't have mattered that much, but this complex happened to be one of the largest in the state.

Nikki had made numerous round trips from the team bus to the locker rooms, then out to the fields, then back again several times over the course of the two days. By the time she got home, both her thighs and calves were covered with painful bruises.

"We should probably have a doctor take a look at those now," her mother suggested a few days later. She slid her reading glasses down her nose and examined her daughter's legs while she stood making a sandwich at the kitchen counter, but Nikki, a tough, freckle-faced, thirteen-year-old, just scoffed.

"This happens all the time in sports, Ma. It's not a big deal. Just like always, I'm sure these will go away in another few days or so," she answered. "I'm tough, ya know, I can handle a few bruises, for crying out loud! Geez!"

Instead, in the following weeks, purplish-green bruises continued to pop up all over her body, starkly standing out against her pale, sensitive skin. Nikki had gotten bruises before, of course, but never like this. Now they seemed to be appearing for no reason and not going away. It wouldn't have been a problem, except that Nikki had also been feeling abnormally tired and even skipped a few practices. That was completely unlike her. Eventually, just walking up the stairs became exhausting. Her parents finally persuaded her to let them take her to the doctor.

"Nik, these bruises are probably just a sign that you've been working too hard at practice or not eating enough iron or something like that. Maybe you're just not getting enough sleep, or there's even the off chance that you've come down with mono. We're sure your doctor will be able figure all this out."

At her pediatrician's office, most of the common culprits were quickly ruled out. She didn't show a temperature, there were no signs of an infection, and her heart and lungs sounded clear.

"What else can we do then, Dr. Vazquez?" her mother asked, knowing that something was just not right. "She hasn't been herself for weeks now, and we've never seen her quite this tired before."

The doctor nodded.

"I agree…something is definitely a bit off. Nikki has always bounced right back after she's gotten sick in the past. I recommend we run a few higher level tests to see if we can get to the root of the problem here," Dr. Vazquez suggested. Turning her attention to Nikki, she added, "I'm going to send you down to the lab to get some blood drawn right now, and we should know within a day or so what's going on. In the meantime, go home, get some rest, and make sure you're drinking plenty of fluids. I'll be in touch as soon as I hear back."

Early the next morning, the Jamisons received a message from Dr. Vazquez's receptionist asking them to meet with her in person. "The doctor would like to see you in her office this afternoon. Please make whatever arrangements are necessary to be here. We'll see you all at three o'clock."

Sitting in the doctor's office, Nikki had a bad feeling in the pit of her stomach. Her parents had tried to be optimistic to keep her calm, but she could tell they had been on edge all day.

When Dr. Vazquez walked into the room with a dire expression, the three of them held their breath and waited for what they antici- pated could only be bad news.

"Nikki, I'm afraid I have some discouraging news, and I'm so sorry to have to tell all of you this. Based on your lab reports, we've narrowed down the possible cause of your symptoms. We'd like to perform a bone marrow biopsy for final confirmation, but we're fairly confident that you have an aggressive form of cancer called acute myeloid leukemia, or AML."

The Jamisons sat paralyzed by the news, staring blankly at the doctor.

"What this means is that Nikki's bone marrow isn't working prop- erly, and as a result, cancerous blood cells have crowded her blood- stream," Dr. Vazquez continued. "This is leaving her with too few red cells to carry oxygen, which explains the exhaustion. It also means that her white cells are unable to fight off infections, and she may not have enough platelets to clot injuries. That is why you've been notic- ing so many bruises."

Nikki looked to her parents as tears welled in her eyes and spilled down her face. They remained transfixed, motionless and stunned.

"On top of all this," the doctor continued, "it appears that her particular cancer may include a mutation called FLT3, a sign it may be extra resistant to standard treatments. I'm recommending that she go see an oncologist right away. I'm referring her to an excellent team at the Chicago Cancer Center right across town. We've already made an appointment for Nikki to be seen, and they're expecting you at four o'clock today. They're among the best in the country, and I know they'll be able to answer all of your questions and get you the optimal treatment."

She paused, waiting for the news to sink in. "I'm going to give you all some time to digest this, and I'll be back in a few minutes with copies of the labs for you to take with you today." Looking directly at Nikki, she added, "I know you're a tough kid, Nikki, and I have every confidence you will beat this."

With that, Dr. Vazquez got up and gave them some space to process the bombshell she had just dropped on them. Nikki turned to her parents, who were both clearly devastated.

"Cancer?" Nikki could hardly speak the word out loud. "I have cancer?" She looked toward her parents in stunned disbelief. Her mother was trembling, and her father was as white as a sheet. Together, they embraced their daughter, sobbing, clinging onto each other as if for dear life.

When they finally made their way across town to the cancer center, the Jamisons were still in shock. A team of pediatric oncology doctors met with the family to go over the preliminary diagnosis and possible treatment options. Trying to comprehend all of the information was completely overwhelming for both Nikki and her parents. They couldn't fully accept that she was so sick.

Her mother pleaded with the doctors, "How can she be this sick? She rarely even had a cold as a child! She's only ever been a healthy, active, and strong kid. She even keeps up with her two older brothers. She plays on a travel softball team and just won a home-run derby in her last tournament. This just cannot be! There must be a mistake! Is it possible the labs weren't done correctly? We demand a second opinion!" The doctors listened empathetically.

"You have to understand, this is completely out of left field for us," her father added a bit more calmly. He took his wife's hand into his and looked sincerely at the team of doctors. "Most of her childhood has consisted of climbing trees in our back yard, playing touch football with all the neighborhood kids, and always being the best athlete on every team she's been a part of. She's so tough. We just can't understand how this could be happening. Are you absolutely sure the tests are correct?" he asked, still desperate for this all to be a horrible blunder.

"We know this is quite a shock, and you have every right to be angry. We are, of course, going to run a few more tests to confirm the original findings, but with Nikki's symptoms, we're fairly certain this is what we're facing. What we can tell you is that we're going to use every weapon in our arsenal," the head oncologist said. "We know it's a big ask to put your trust into a group of people you have just met, but we do have a calculated plan. Nikki is going to have access to the very best treatment plan available. This is one of the top cancer centers in the country, and we'll do everything in our power to make your daughter well again."

None of them could imagine what actually lay ahead. Everything felt so foreign to Nikki and her parents, as if they were being spoken to in a different language. As she took it all in, Nikki reminded herself that she was a fighter and wasn't going to let this get the better of her. Finally, after hours of explanations and lots of crying, Nikki knew she needed to be brave enough for all of them.

"Mom, Dad, it's all going to be okay. You know I'm going to fight this thing with everything I've got, and I'm willing to do whatever they think it will take to get me out on the fields, playing sports again. Just promise me you'll fight this with me and stand beside me no matter what." Nikki held onto her parents as they nodded in agreement, obviously too choked up to speak.

With her parents by her side, her journey into the unknown began.

The first eighteen months after Nikki's diagnosis were a relentless and brutal battle. Her initial round of chemotherapy landed her in the intensive care unit twice. First for a nasty infection, then again to deal with a 104-degree fever, complicated by fluid that had seeped into her lungs.

The chemo had taken its toll in other ways, too. She had lost all of her hair, felt nauseated most of the time, and her throat and mouth were often lined with painful sores. Nikki's teammates tried to visit as much as they could in the beginning, but eventually they got busy with their own lives. In time, visits with friends became less frequent. Her parents tried to keep any excitement to a minimum, as she needed her strength to focus on her treatments.

After the first round of chemo was complete, Nikki and her family met with the team of doctors to go over results and get the updated prognosis. The news wasn't good.

"We're so sorry, Nikki. Our tests show that your bloodstream is still riddled with leukemia. We feel that it would be in your best interest to do a second round." The Jamisons' spirits were crushed. This wasn't at all what they had hoped for, and watching their daughter go through the process had been excruciating. Nikki once again had to be brave.

"I know this isn't what we were counting on," she said. "But if they think this is the best option, I need to do what they're telling me." Things felt grim and their morale was low, but Nikki insisted on giving it another go. After several conversations, a second, equally grueling round of chemo was administered.

For a brief time, the second wave of treatment seemed to be working. The disease showed a few signs of being beaten back. Nikki started to feel a little better and got some energy back, and she could tell that her parents felt a glimmer of hope. They allowed themselves to be optimistic and started planning for a return to normalcy.

The excitement was premature. After just a couple of weeks, Nikki started to feel sick again. Additional blood work confirmed their worst fears. The oncology team at the Chicago Cancer Center asked to meet with the Jamisons once again.

"After trying to fight Nikki's cancer with the most advanced medicines and treatments we have available here, we've concluded that chemotherapy alone will not be enough to save her life. For Nikki to beat this thing permanently, a bone marrow transplant will be necessary. Because we've already tested the both of you and her two older brothers and discovered that none of you would be a good match for her, we're recommending you allow us to put a request out to the national donor registry."

The Jamisons were devastated and heartbroken, but agreed to consider moving to the next phase, even though they had heard a few discouraging rumors regarding the donor process from other families at the cancer center. Unsure of which direction to take, they asked some tough questions of the medical team before moving forward.

"If we go ahead and put ourselves through all of this, what are the odds that we'll actually be able to find a match for Nikki? We've heard that it's like playing, and expecting to win, the lottery. We don't want to set ourselves or Nikki up for another huge disappointment. She has already been fighting this for close to two years. It's more than anyone should ever have to endure."

"Once we get your go-ahead, we'll be able to submit an urgent plea for a new donor through the national system, which can happen within just a couple of hours," the doctors responded. "Based on your daughter's condition, you should know that even though the odds are poor, they're not impossible. Your concerns are valid, but the important thing is that we pursue every option available to her. We have a specialist on site who is going to be able to lead you through the process. Once you meet with her, you can let us know your final decision."

The liaison who met with Nikki and her parents carefully outlined the possible scenarios involved with a bone marrow transplant. "Many times a suitable donor is found, and things work out as planned. I've dealt with several families who have chosen this option and everything went smoothly and successfully. That's the best-case scenario and certainly what we hope for Nikki. However, you should be aware that there have been times when even if a match was found, complications came up that were out of our control."

"What kinds of complications?" Nikki's parents asked. "We want to hear all the potential scenarios so we can be prepared either way. The fact that nothing is guaranteed is what makes us most nervous. We just don't want to get our hopes up again if this is a complete long shot."

"Well, I can certainly understand where you're coming from. The truth is, we've seen a few unfortunate cases where the donor bank finds a match, but may not be able to physically locate the donor. It could be due to something as trivial as a change in address or a new phone number. It's also possible that the donor may have had a change in their circumstance. He or she may have had a change in health and is no longer able to donate. We want to make sure you are prepared for any of these outcomes, no matter how unlikely they may be."

"What do you think, Nikki?" her father asked. "We want to respect your choice in the matter. You get the final say in this, honey."

Nikki, looking and feeling completely exhausted, took a moment to compose her thoughts.

"Mom, you're the one who taught me that a cup half-full is always better than a cup half-empty, right? I still think it's worth it to try." She spoke quietly, offering a slight smile in an effort to comfort her worried parents. "I'm not ready to give up yet, guys. It may be the bottom of the ninth, down by a run with two outs and two strikes against me, but you know I'm still going to be swinging for the fence!" She mustered a little energy to laugh at her joke, knowing they would appreciate the metaphor.

Her mother pulled her close, held her tight, and whispered, "Of course you would. That's my Nikki. I'm so proud of you my courageous, beautiful girl." They signed the paperwork and prayed for a miracle. Their daughter's fate would now depend on a complete stranger, and the odds were heavily stacked against them.

After nearly two years of fighting her disease with every ounce of energy and every shred of tenacity she could muster, Nikki finally got lucky.

Really, really lucky.

Within just one day, a woman from the national registry called with incredible news. "We've found a match for Nikki," she said, her voice amplified over the speakerphone in Nikki's hospital room.

"The young woman who meets the criteria is from Boston and had been part of a donor drive for a very ill high school classmate just a month or so ago. Although she wasn't a match for him, when your data hit the national data bank, it was discovered that she was potentially a perfect match for Nikki."

Nikki covered the phone with her hand. "Is this too good to be true?" she whispered to her parents. She felt her lip begin to quiver, and tears welled in her eyes as she fought back an uncontrollable wave of elation. "Is this really happening?"

"I know you may still be a bit apprehensive, but here's the best part: the match has already agreed to do the bone marrow donation remotely and anonymously from Boston. The tissue they withdraw there will be flown to Chicago, where Nikki will receive the transplant when she's ready to accept it. Congratulations, Nikki. This is the news we've been hoping for."

Finally feeling hopeful for the first time in months, the Jamisons eagerly met with the oncology and transplant teams to put a plan into place. Their optimism unfortunately turned to discouragement when they found out that the doctors needed to do an additional round of chemo before the transplant.

"We know this is not what you wanted to face again, but we need to prepare her body to accept the new tissue. It's her best shot at a successful take," they explained. Once again, the Jamisons had to break the news to Nikki.

"It's been nothing short of gut-wrenching to see you lying so helpless in the hospital bed, weak, exhausted, and so frail with each treatment you've endured. It doesn't seem fair that you would have to undergo this hell again, Nikki. Are you sure you want to put yourself through this another time right now? What if it's just too much for you to handle again?

"We would never forgive ourselves if we pushed too hard and something awful happens because of it. If you need time to try to build your strength back up first, you have to be honest with us."

Nikki understood that she would have to dig deeper than ever to mentally prepare herself for the grueling transplant prep she was about to face.

"Mom, Dad, I know I can do this. I have to at least try," she decided, knowing it was quite likely her last shot. "I just want the chance, and this may be the only one we get. I can't risk losing this opportunity."

After careful reflection, the decision was made. "If anyone can do this, it's you, Nikki," her parents agreed. "We have to let you try. This is your wish and we, of course, honor that. Whatever happens, we promised we would stick by your side. That will never change."

With that, the operation was scheduled, and the treatments started again. Nikki could not have imagined how difficult things would be.

She was given two more rounds of chemo to force her leukemia into temporary remission. "This will provide the best-case scenario for her new immune system to accept the donor tissue," her doctors explained, as if trying to make it easier to accept. Each round wreaked additional havoc on her already weakened body.

Just three days before the transplant, Nikki was given a final dose of yet another blend of toxic chemicals. These were administered with the sole purpose of completely killing off the contents of her bone marrow. Entirely void of an immune system at this point, Nikki was left utterly vulnerable to illness—even a common cold would have been enough to kill her.

Her doctors administered antibiotics as a precaution and contacted the Boston transplant team, giving them the go-ahead. All Nikki and her family could do now was to wait, staying as optimistic as possible that the healthy tissue being flown across the country would be exactly what was needed to save her life.

10

Daniel Bryant was relieved he'd decided to work from the home office. The weather reports predicting the winter storm would hit the East Coast earlier than originally anticipated were spot on. From the sound of it, things were already in full effect. He stood, pushing his custom Massimo swivel armchair back from the large mahogany desk situated in the middle of the spacious room.

He'd been working steadily since early morning, and he could feel the stiffness in his muscles as he rose. Extending his arms overhead, he stretched side to side, relieving the tension that had built up in his lower back. Grateful for the break, he slowly strolled over to look out onto the backyard of his multi-million-dollar home. He stood mesmerized for a few moments, watching the freezing rain pelting the large windows. This side of the house overlooked the extensive stone patio and Caribbean-themed pool cabana. Tiny frozen droplets danced and pinged off the taut pool cover.

Most of his businesses had already been shut down for the day. Daniel had allowed his weekend employees to go home earlier that morning to beat the impending storm. Safety always came first when it came to his people, and this day was no exception.

I might as well call it a day myself, he thought, catching a quick glimpse of his salt-and-pepper hair in the window reflection. *I doubt much is going to be happening with all of this mess going on. I would much rather spend some quality time with my girls, anyway.*

Just then, his youngest daughter, Annie, ran into the office and wrapped herself around both of his legs. She looked up with her big, brown eyes. "Daddy, Daddy, come play with me. The wind is so loud outside of my room, and I'm scared!" He lifted her into his arms and kissed her rosy cheek.

"You don't need to be scared, sweet pea. I won't let anything bad happen to you! Our house is stronger than those silly winds outside, and I promise it won't fall down! Remember the story of the three little pigs? It can huff, and it can puff, but what can't it do?"

"Blow the house down!" Annie screeched, delighted.

"That's right! Nothing can blow this house down, not even the Big Bad Wolf!" Daniel teased as he tickled her tummy, enjoying her giggles and laughter. "Now, what do you say we go see if Mommy wants to help us bake some yummy chocolate-chip cookies right now? Would you like to be my special helper today?"

Annie's ringlet curls bounced up and down as she writhed in his arms and shrieked, "Yes, yes, yes! I want to do the beaters all by myself this time. Let's go, Daddy! Let's go now!" She wrapped her arms around his neck and hugged him tightly.

As they turned to head toward the kitchen, the phone on Daniel's desk rang, catching him by surprise. That phone only rang when there was an emergency his staff couldn't handle, and that hadn't happened in some time. He set Annie down and walked over to pick up the phone.

"Mr. Bryant?" the caller asked. "Is this Guardian Enterprises? This is the number I was directed to call, as no one could be reached at the main dispatch office. The lines must have been knocked down with these winds. Is it okay to call you on this line, sir?"

Daniel was curious and responded graciously, "Yes, of course. This is Daniel Bryant. You have in fact reached Guardian Enterprises. What can I help you with?"

"Oh, good, I'm glad I reached you in person. This is Officer McHale with the Massachusetts State Police Highway Division. There's been an accident on 93 northbound. We're calling to request that your Medi-Vac rescue helicopter be dispatched to the site immediately. A woman has been seriously injured, and the roads are completely blocked due to multiple accidents. We can't get emergency ground vehicles here quickly enough for her with these conditions. The local hospitals won't dispatch their contracted helicopters due to these winds. We were told you had pilots trained especially for these types of situations. Can you get your helicopter to the site in this weather? The victim will need to be transported to Boston Memorial because there's a head injury involved. The hospital is awaiting word back. Time is of the essence, sir."

"Oh, I see. Yes, of course. We do have pilots specially trained for this. I'll call my guy now, and if he gives me the green light, we'll dispatch a crew within minutes. Stand by for an ETA once I can confirm flight details," Daniel said. He carefully took down the trooper's contact information. He also wrote down the coordinates of the accident scene and called his best pilot Garrett, who was on site at the Medi-Vac hangar. Although the Medi-Vac helicopter hadn't had to fly in conditions this challenging since he started this nonprofit venture two years earlier, Daniel had every confidence his people were uniquely qualified to do the job.

"Garrett, I know these conditions are outside the documented risk levels we normally tolerate," he started the conversation. "But this is the victim's best and maybe only chance…that's why we were called. I trust you to make the decision based on the wind gust, cloud ceiling, visibility, and other pertinent conditions before you commit. Go no-go. What do you think? It's completely your call, along with the rest of crew, of course."

"Thanks, Mr. Bryant. Yeah, we have been closely monitoring the storm all morning from our computers. As you know, they're linked directly to the national weather site. The screen has pretty much been lit up all morning with yellow and red dots, indicating the areas with the worst weather. I can see the larger storm front moving in from the west, but I also see a few local pockets that haven't been hit with the freezing rain yet."

"Okay, so what's your take based on the coordinates for this accident? Be straight with me."

"I know the conditions will be demanding, but I feel confident I can get the aircraft and the crew there safely, especially if it may be the victim's only chance. We're ready for this, boss. The location of the accident is fairly close, and I'm calculating I can get out and back before icing causes me any trouble. It looks like the temp in that area has come up a bit in the last five to ten minutes, but I'm not sure how long that will last. This might be my only window, but we need to go now. Where's dispatch? Why didn't they call me directly on this? Are you going to be the point man for this mission today instead?"

"Yes, our main phone lines must be down, and I still haven't been able to get through to them on their cell phones. I want you to keep me posted directly. Stay safe out there, and notify me when you've landed at Boston Memorial. Call me on my cell if you need anything, or if anything changes," Daniel finished. He scanned the top of his desk and found the piece of paper he had scribbled his notes onto.

He quickly called and relayed the flight information back to the state trooper.

"The crew is being dispatched now and should be there within minutes," Daniel confirmed. "Make sure that all traffic is stopped in both directions on the interstate, and that an adequate landing zone has been set up and clearly marked for my pilot. He needs to be able to make a safe landing or he'll turn around." The police officer gave Daniel his assurance that everything was set up and ready to go.

After he hung up, he glanced toward the large photo hanging on his wall. Medi-Vac's team of seasoned crew members stood beside the Airbus H145 state-of-the-art medical helicopter valiantly displayed in the oversized frame. Daniel could see the smiles and proud faces of his team.

I hope this was the right call, he thought, hearing a howling outside and knowing that the winds were still whipping. *I know Garrett is trained for this exact type of thing. I'm sure the mission will be okay.*

Daniel reached out to pick up the phone again to call it off in a sudden bout of self-doubt, but quickly pulled his hand back. *No,* he decided, *I just have to trust Garrett's judgment and have faith they know what they're doing out there. These are the moments I know we're needed most. This is how I'm making a positive impact.*

"Daddy, Daddy, pick me up again! Up, up, up!" Annie demanded with outstretched arms, pulling his attention back to her. "Can you show me all your trophies again?" she asked with a big grin, pointing to the awards lining a display case at the back of his office. Daniel was distracted, but couldn't resist his little girl.

"Um, sure, honey, let's go see." He lifted her and carried her across the room. Setting her down a few feet away, he carefully opened the two glass doors on the front of the case.

He let her hold each award for a few seconds before having her place it gently back in its position. He was still humbled every time he was reminded of the accolades he had received over the past few years for his charitable giving and contributions to humanity.

"Why did you get all these trophies, Daddy?" Annie asked, just as she did every time she was allowed to hold them. "Are they prizes like I get in my gymnastics class?"

"Well," he answered, "Daddy actually got these as thank-you presents for helping people who need it the most, sweet pea. Sometimes people don't have the money or the resources to do the things that we take for granted, like drinking clean water or going to the doctor when we get sick." Looking into her curious, bright eyes, he added, "Even though I'm the one helping them to be able to do these sorts of things, they're actually helping me, too. It's really me who is the lucky one."

Her eyes stayed fixated on his face, as if trying to understand what he was saying. "Why are you lucky, Daddy? Because you won all these trophies?"

"Well, that's part of it," he chuckled and scooped her back up. "But mostly it's because I know that each day I'm here with you and Mommy and your two big sisters is a gift. Being able to share what we have with others and make a difference in their lives is what makes the difference in mine."

Daniel reflected for a moment as he stood with Annie. It was only a few years prior that he decided his legacy would be to start and fund companies that would help save lives. Over the last thirty-six months, he'd already been involved in building fresh-water wells in several impoverished countries and had sponsored a team of doctors to travel abroad, administering much-needed vaccines.

Most recently, he'd decided to start a life-saving transport company in his own home state. The dire need for rescue aircraft in extremely high-risk situations had been brought to his attention by one of his favorite clients, the CEO at one of the largest Boston hospitals. Because of Medi-Vac, dozens of lives that otherwise wouldn't have made it had already been saved. At fifty years old, Daniel felt extremely grateful for being in a position to make a contribution.

It almost hadn't been possible.

11

D aniel was forty-two years old and living on top of the world. He felt like a big shot, having already reached the pinnacle of success. This sensation, along with the attention he was getting, was all new to him. He'd never been the best-looking, tallest, or most athletic guy growing up. In fact, he'd never been the best at anything. Until now.

Now he was one of "them." One of "those guys." He was the kind of guy that people wanted at their dinner parties, whose kids were always invited first for play dates, and whose lives were the envy of most. Having worked his way up the ladder quickly in the financial world, he was living his dream as a stock fund manager at a firm in Boston, dealing with hundreds of millions of dollars for his clients. He was the wiz kid with a knack for picking the right stocks. He had steady returns year over year and was a shining star. Times were good. He had his health, he'd been sober for over twenty years, and he'd made a name for himself.

Daniel was enjoying the high life and all that went along with it: a million-dollar estate in the suburbs, a fancy penthouse apartment in the city, vacation homes on Martha's Vineyard and in the Caribbean, luxury cars, and designer everything for his gorgeous wife Kate and their two beautiful twin daughters. Things couldn't have been any better.

Overnight, the climate began to change in the markets. In September, a wave of volatility hit the financial community. During their weekly staff meeting, one of the firm's partners pulled all his large fund managers aside. "As you know, there are major concerns over the ability of financial institutions to cover their exposure in the subprime loan market right now. We feel that this is what's causing so much instability. With the future becoming more and more uncertain, we need to find ways to counteract the negative market reactions and find new places to make money. I'm counting on this team to protect our assets and continue to grow. Your jobs depend on it. All of ours do."

October hit and things got even shakier. Every day, Daniel read in the *Wall Street Journal* about additional large financial institutions and banks filing for bankruptcy. Panic was ramping up to all-time highs. News stations were making the floundering markets their lead story night after night. Like a house of cards whose base was slowly getting yanked out from below, the dream life he had built started to crumble, and Daniel felt helpless to make it stop. Darkness began to creep into the cracks of his foundation.

Although he'd been sober for most of his adult life, Daniel began to seek solace in his old comforts. He started going out for drinks a couple nights a week after work with his colleagues. "Misery loves company," they would tease, egging each other on in their "self-medicating" sessions. Eventually, just a few nights a week turned into almost every day. Daniel found that he was often the first one to get to the bar and usually the last to leave.

One night after getting particularly drunk, one of his coworkers insisted that Daniel hand over his car keys. "Danny, I know it's none of my business, but I think you should try to take it easy on the drinking for a while," he said with genuine concern as he loaded a very drunk Daniel into the back seat of his car to drive him home. "I've never seen this side of you, and to be honest, a few of us are getting worried."

"Worried? You guys are getting worried? What the hell are you talking about, man? Aw, take the skirts off, ladies. Really, Ma, I can handle myself just fine," he slurred, trying to be funny. "You're all just jealous that I can hold my liquor better than you. Bunch of wusses." He laughed dismissively and leaned his head against the cool glass of the car window. He closed his eyes until he felt the car stop moving. When he opened them again, he saw that his friend had pulled up in front of his house.

"Okay, okay, I will admit it. I *may* have gone a little overboard tonight," Daniel said, brushing it off as he stumbled out of the car and onto his driveway. "But you have nothing to worry about, really, Officer," he added sarcastically, crossing his heart and coming over to pat his friend on the back through the driver-side window. "Anyway, thanks for the ride, man. See you tomorrow." Daniel saluted as if a cadet in the army, then turned to head inside.

The truth was that Daniel had no intention of either slowing down or stopping his behavior. It was the only way he knew how to numb the anxiety and depression he'd been feeling. It was the same coping mechanism he had used back in high school, and although he knew it was tempting the fates, it gave him a familiar escape. Eventually, he started to drink at home, too, trying to hide it as best he could. He knew he wasn't fooling anyone.

One night after struggling to fall asleep, Daniel snuck down into his office to retrieve a bottle of vodka he had stashed. He thought he had cleverly hidden it behind a stack of books on the top shelf of his built-in bookcase. When he reached behind, he found nothing but an empty pocket of space. Enraged, he whipped the books off the shelf and frantically searched the rest of the case, throwing everything into a big heap onto the floor.

"Damn it!" he yelled in a violent frenzy. He could feel rage bubbling up from his core. Frustrated, he grabbed a weighted bookend and hurled it across the room, where it smashed into the wall, leaving chunks of plaster spilling out on either side. When he looked up, he saw his wife Kate standing in the doorway with her arms crossed. It had missed her head by only a few inches.

"I dumped it down the sink," she said. Her voice was calm, and she kept a cool demeanor. She glared at him in disgust for several moments before mumbling something under her breath and walking away. Daniel felt ashamed and humiliated, his ugliness exposed.

What the hell are you doing, man? he asked himself. *You're going to ruin everything, you fucking asshole.*

He wept into his hands, slumping pathetically to the ground.

When they had gotten married ten years earlier, Kate knew about the trouble he'd had with addiction in his youth. Daniel had grown up poor, going to school and working part-time from a young age to help support his single mother and grandmother in their small run-down apartment in South Boston. He never knew his father, and his grandfather had passed when he was just three.

Living in an area surrounded by projects, Daniel had been exposed to more than most see in a lifetime: people on welfare, drug dealers on every corner, domestic violence, and instability everywhere. This had been his normal. If he hadn't been so talented in school, he probably would've fallen into the same traps as most of his friends and ended up in prison, selling drugs, or dead due to gang violence.

Doing well in school had always come naturally to Daniel. He was smart, but never applied himself more than he had to. Getting by was good enough. His guidance counselor, Mrs. O'Connor, knew he could make something out of his life if he had a little direction. She knew his mother had been diagnosed with mental illness and was most likely addicted to drugs. His grandmother tried the best she could, but she was still working full-time and taking care of Daniel's mother in her spare time. Mrs. O'Connor had kept her eye on Daniel throughout his years at high school, helping where she could. That's why, when he was sent to talk with her after arriving at school drunk for the third time during the first month of his senior year, she finally laid it on the line for him.

"Daniel, it's disappointing on so many levels to see you like this again. There comes a time in every young man's life when he has to make a choice. Guess what, pal? Today is the day when you have to make that choice. The choice is to either become a victim and product of your environment, or—and I strongly recommend this one—to make a conscious decision to forge your own path and become what you're meant to be in this world."

Daniel hung his head.

"I think you have the talent and the ability to do something great with your life," she continued. "But you have to grow up and stop making these bad decisions that keep landing you in hot water. You need to completely stop the drinking and get some help for your addiction. You need to stop hanging around with the kids who are getting into trouble and start making friends with people who actually care about you. With your potential and smarts, I can likely help you get a scholarship to college if that's even something you want. I need to know that you can clean up your act, commit to staying sober, and start focusing on your future. Are you even willing to do that?"

Mrs. O'Connor waited patiently for his response. When he didn't reply, she followed up with a final threat. "I'm not going to waste my time and energy if you aren't willing to do the work here. And frankly, time is running out for you. What's it going to be, Daniel?"

"Yes, ma'am, I think I can do that," Daniel eventually answered, feeling ashamed and embarrassed by his actions. He knew he hadn't been making the best choices, and he hated the feeling of letting someone down who'd been looking out for him. There were so few people who did.

"Are you serious about helping me get into college?" he asked sheepishly, peeking his head back up. He looked surprised this might even be an option for him.

"Well, I can at least try. But you have to do your part, too. I won't put my neck on the line unless I know you can get—and stay—clear of the booze. You need to stop all this nonsense. You have to show me that you're serious about wanting something better out of this life. You have to get your grades up, and no more skipping class. I mean it. You need to smarten up right now. If you can commit to following through on what I'm saying, then I will try to help you. But if you screw up even one more time, I'm out. No more chances. Do we have a deal or not?"

Daniel stood and put his hand out to shake hers.

"Yes, ma'am. We have a deal. I hear what you're saying, and I really do want to try. And I promise I'll stop the drinking starting right now…just please don't tell my grandma on me, okay? Thank you, Mrs. O. Thank you so much. I won't let you down!" For the first time in a long time, Daniel felt hope.

Daniel made good on his pledge to stop drinking and even stopped hanging out with the troubled kids. Each week they picked one day after school where they met in her office, and she helped him fill out college applications and financial aid forms just as she'd promised. He joined some extracurricular clubs and eventually made friends with other kids on the same positive track. He worked with a tutor, and his grades moved up in every class. For the first time, he made the honor roll and his name got printed in the newspaper. By far, his proudest moment came when he earned a perfect score on his SAT in math and it was announced over the loudspeaker one morning before first period.

When the admission decision letters finally came out that spring, Daniel brought his still-sealed envelopes to Mrs. O'Connor's office.

"I'm too nervous to open these," Daniel said as he plopped them down on her desk and sat in the chair across from her. "Can you please open them for me, Mrs. O? Honestly, I haven't been able to sleep since they came in the mail yesterday. I feel sick to my stomach."

"Yes, of course," she answered. "It will be an honor." She pulled a letter opener from her drawer and carefully slit open each envelope. Daniel held his breath as she quickly scanned each one.

"Daniel, you can relax," she said and looked up at him with a wide smile. "I'm so proud of you. You have been accepted to every school you applied to. But this one is perhaps the most exciting." She held one of the letters up and turned it toward him so he could see the writing.

"Congratulations, Mr. Daniel Bryant! You have been accepted on a full academic scholarship to Boston College."

The hair on his arm stood up, and he could hardly believe his luck. For a moment he felt like he might faint.

"What? Are you sure? You aren't playing with me right now, are you, Mrs. O?" he asked. She handed him the letter so he could see for himself.

"I don't even know what to say, Mrs. O! I couldn't have done any of this without you." He sat for a few seconds, shaking his head in disbelief. "Thank you. Thank you so much for believing in me. You were the only one who did, you know. I just can't believe this." Daniel had a tear in his eye as he stood and walked over to give her a hug. "I'm going to work really hard so that you'll know you didn't waste your time on me, I promise."

"I know you will, Daniel. I know you can do great things in this life. Just keep your nose clean and promise to come back and visit once in a while." With that, he rushed home to share the news with his mother and grandmother, both of whom were thrilled.

That fall, Daniel headed off for college. While at school he stayed clean, worked hard, and visited home when time allowed. His mother, inspired by his hard work and success, signed herself into a treatment program and got clean while he was away. His grandmother sent him care packages and some spending money whenever she could spare it. After four years, he graduated Summa Cum Laude with a degree in finance.

When he finished there, he went on to Columbia for his graduate degree. It was there where he met and fell head over heels in love with Miss Katherine Brewster, the girl who just happened to have her seat assigned right next to his in many of their classes. Daniel thought she was the smartest, most beautiful girl he had ever seen. Kate was sophisticated and classy, and Daniel knew she was way out of his league. She inspired him to work harder than anyone else there. He needed to prove that he was worthy of her affections. He convinced her to give him a shot, and eventually his charms won her over.

After graduating, they continued dating and even found an apartment together. Eventually they decided to get married and build a life together.

I can't believe that was fifteen years ago, Daniel thought. He sat slumped in his office, still ashamed and surrounded by the mess he had created. He knew his behavior the past several weeks had been a complete disappointment.

She has a right to be worried, he admitted and sighed, realizing how pitiful he must look. *You're a fucking idiot. You made a promise to her that you would stay clean and sober. You're breaking that promise to her every day. She doesn't deserve this. She doesn't deserve the pain you are putting her through. You're going to ruin everything!*

He was paralyzed by guilt, but unable to stop on his own. The self-sabotage continued, and the drinking became even more frequent.

"Things have gotten way out of control," Kate finally said one night after she put the twins to bed and found him passed out on the kitchen floor for the second time that week. She took him by the arm and led him over to the couch. With tears in her eyes she gave him a stern warning, "You've got to pull yourself together and get some professional help, Dan. I can't live like this, and I won't have the girls grow up with a drunk for a father! You made me a promise, and I trusted you. You need to snap out of this little pity party and be the man I married, or I can assure you that this is going to end." She left him to sleep it off with the ultimatum spinning round and round inside his inebriated head.

Meanwhile at work, and despite every effort, Daniel and the other managers at the firm were unable to find any solid footing in the market. No matter what angle they played, they couldn't stop the catastrophic slide. For five straight trading sessions in early October, things went from bad to worse. During that week, the Dow Jones Industrial Average fell over 18 percent. In that same week, the S&P 500 fell more than 20 percent. Billions were literally lost overnight.

The pressure wasn't letting up. Daniel knew he was on the brink of losing everything that mattered to him. His phone was ringing off the hook with clients calling, demanding that he sell off their holdings. "I understand your concern," he repeated the same message over and over as each client called. "We strongly recommend that you do not liquidate all of your positions, because fear and panic are now controlling the markets. Your best strategy is to stay the course and wait for a correction."

He was unable to convince any of his clients to weather the storm and ended up losing millions of dollars for his firm, his clients, and himself. He'd never felt so defeated and broken, the stench of failure oozing out from every pore.

Like many of his colleagues and peers, Daniel also found himself tragically underwater on his personal properties. Kate had no clue about the second mortgages he'd taken on both vacation homes. His career was basically finished, and his drinking was still spiraling out of control.

"I think we need to separate for a while," Kate eventually said after seeing no change with his behavior. "I can no longer tolerate your drinking, your belligerent moods, and the horrible behavior you're displaying in front of our girls. I just can't believe you are doing this to us. What's worse is that it doesn't even seem to matter how upset I have been. You've broken my heart, Daniel. I want you out of the house as soon as possible. You need to go get some help."

The demands of his family, his debt, and the fact that he was public enemy number one to his clients, many of whom were also once his close friends, was too much for Daniel to handle. He found himself desperate for a reprieve from the disappointment and insurmountable anguish he felt every moment of every day.

I just want a way to make this stop, Daniel thought. *I just need to make it stop.*

The following night, after another intense argument with Kate, Daniel grabbed a half-full bottle of Glenlivet eighteen-year and headed into the living room to drink until he went numb. The couch had been his bed for the past several weeks, and empty liquor bottles, dirty laundry, and trash had started to pile up around it.

"I'm so fucking done with this bullshit," Daniel said with a grunt as he took the final sips from the bottle in his hand, then tossed it onto the ground. "You want me gone? You all want me gone? Fine! Tomorrow is your lucky day, ladies," he mumbled angrily right as he was about to pass out. "Everything's going to change tomorrow..."

The sounds of an early morning garbage truck rumbling by woke Daniel from his drunken slumber. It was a cool, crisp morning in late October. Without a word, Daniel pulled himself up from the couch, his head still groggy from the night before. He crept up the stairs and slid undetected into his bedroom. He moved quietly past Kate, who was sleeping alone in their king-sized bed, took a hot shower, shaved, brushed his hair, and put on his best suit. He chose his finest shoes, polished them into a glassy shine, and picked out his most expensive tie.

Oh yes, this one is perfect, he thought, reaching toward the back of the rack. *Katie gave this to me on my fortieth birthday,* he recalled fondly. *She always remembered my favorite color. She always remembered everything. She deserves so much better.*

He walked down the hall, gave both of his sleeping girls a kiss good-bye on their foreheads, and headed out the door. Instead of getting on the highway and going into work like he had almost every day for the past fifteen years, Daniel made a quick stop, then drove to a remote spot by a lake just outside of the city. He had hiked the trails that circled this lake many times and had always found solace in their serenity and tranquility. A thin layer of fog hovered just above the still waters. It was as beautiful as he'd remembered.

Daniel got out of the car and breathed in the cool, damp autumn air. He casually walked around his car, popped open his trunk, and took out a newly purchased bright green garden hose, a roll of silver duct tape, and an old beat-up rag. Using an old fishing knife, he cut off the plastic tabs and cardboard that held the hose in its packaging. Tearing it out, he mindlessly discarded the trash on the ground near his feet. Walking backward in steady, even steps, he carefully uncoiled the hose and set it on the sandy ground along the driver's side of the car.

Next, Daniel took the sturdy roll of duct tape and pulled off several lengthy strips. He carefully and methodically walked around, taping the windows and doors of his $104,000 Lexus at every possible seam. Finally, he knelt behind the car and placed one end of the hose up into the exhaust pipe, sealing it with the old rag and taping it securely in place.

That should do it, he thought as he opened the door and slid into the driver's seat. Reaching into his front jacket pocket, he carefully pulled out a handwritten letter addressed to his wife. Daniel arranged the letter face-side-up and perfectly centered on the passenger side seat.

There's no way they'll miss this, he decided, then he sat back and took a deep breath in.

After a few moments, he pulled the loose end of the hose into the driver's side window. He closed the door and fastened the hose as best he could to the inside roof with a few more small pieces of tape.

I need to make sure I don't crush it, he reminded himself and closed the window as tightly as possible, pinching the hose between the glass and the window frame.

Just a few more strips right here, he calculated, sealing the last few open cracks with the remaining duct tape.

"It sure is peaceful here," Daniel said out loud. He gently rested his hand on the letter and stared out at the motionless body of water before him. After several minutes sitting in complete stillness, he placed his key into the ignition and turned his wrist to start the engine.

"Good-bye, my love," Daniel whispered out loud. "I hope you can forgive me."

He closed his eyes and reached down to find the button on the side of his seat, reclining it back as far as it would go.

As he lay there, Daniel visualized a tropical Caribbean vacation he had taken with his family two years earlier, when times had been good. He imagined his twin girls running up and down the beach with pigtails and giant toothy smiles, collecting shells and playing tag. He pictured sitting in their custom-made Adirondack chairs, holding Kate's hand as they watched the tropical sunset. He imagined pushing the windswept hair off her face, gently tucking it behind her ear and tenderly kissing her lips.

The life insurance money will get her out of the debt I created and give her and the girls the life we had always dreamed about, Daniel rationalized. He began to feel a little dizzy and detected a dull ache starting to creep around from the back of his head. Wanting to throw up from the nausea, Daniel fought the urge, hoping it would pass quickly.

You're so pathetic. Can't you even get this right? Don't you dare open that door, you weakling.

He felt his legs get heavy and numb. He finally sensed the pain leaving his body and slowly drifted off toward sleep. The world around him became completely calm as the demons he had been fighting against so intensely finally went silent. An eerie stillness set in.

Just as Daniel was about to take one of his final breaths, a large rock smashed through the driver-side window, shattering it into thousands of marble-sized pieces. He sensed a cool rush of air across his face as the car door was pried opened, and he was forcefully pulled out onto the damp, cold ground. Choking and coughing, Daniel was completely disoriented and utterly confused. His vision was impaired and his hearing oddly distorted.

Rubbing his eyes, he turned his head and saw what he made out to be a blurred female figure running up the nearby hill. He could hear her yelling for help, but still couldn't make sense of what was happening.

Where am I? What the hell is happening?

Get up! You need to get up! the voice in his head commanded as he tried to foster enough strength to get onto his knees.

The woman shouted something unintelligible in his direction again, then ran up and over the hill, completely out of sight. Sheer terror set in as the realization of what had happened finally occurred to Daniel.

"Oh my God!" he uttered, pulling for air. "Oh my God! I need to get the hell out of here!" He forced himself to his feet, stumbled backward, and tore the hose from the back exhaust pipe. Once it was free, he jumped into the car and erratically sped away. Dirt and gravel shot back from his spinning tires, leaving nothing behind but a set of wild tracks, some broken glass, and the discarded debris.

With his heart pounding and a loud ringing in his ears, Daniel started to sob uncontrollably. He felt remorse and humiliation, and he immediately regretted allowing himself to succumb to such cowardice.

"What have I done? What have I done?" he cried out, still shaking from the ordeal. When he was finally able to pull over, he found a remote spot to remove the remaining tape from the car. As he was clearing out the remaining broken glass, a pivotal realization sank in.

I can never speak of this day to anyone, he pledged. *I'm so ashamed. This is not who I want to be, and I can't believe I almost lost everything that's important in my life. I'm making a promise right here and now that I'll stop the drinking, do whatever it takes to rebuild my life, to take care of my family, and to be the man they were all once proud of. I just hope it isn't too late.*

Daniel did just as he promised. He started by apologizing to Kate for his inexcusable behavior, begging for her forgiveness and a second chance. She agreed to allow him to stay on the couch as long as he stayed away from the booze and got some help. He proved he was committed to being sober by going to support meetings on a regular basis. He stayed clean, worked the program, and spent more quality time with his wife and girls. Once his family was back on the right track and he was feeling stronger, Daniel then pleaded for his job back.

When he finally got back to work, the markets had started to stabilize. He used his well-tuned charms and successfully persuaded some of his wealthiest clients to give him another shot. Daniel was so focused and talented at what he did that he was able to systematically rebuild many portfolios back to their former levels. Eventually, substantial bonuses and even the offer of partnership were presented to him. He continued to make highly lucrative investment choices and found himself and his firm rising from the rubble. Daniel was back in the game, and he was playing to win.

Five years passed quickly, and a not a day went by when Daniel didn't stop to acknowledge the fact that all he'd accomplished was possible because he was lucky enough to have been given a second chance. Eternally grateful, he decided to take his reversal of fortune and turn it into an opportunity to create a more meaningful life in the long run for himself and his now growing family. He talked about his vision with Kate, and together they decided to set their plan into action.

With plenty of money in the bank, investments that he felt confident would continue to grow over time, and just three years until he was fully vested in his firm, he devised an exit strategy and an early retirement. Together, he and Kate formed Guardian Enterprises, a nonprofit corporation whose mission was to sponsor philanthropic, life-saving causes around the globe. In addition to taking care of their new baby girl, Kate also helped lay the groundwork for their new venture and maintained the day-to-day operations until Daniel could retire from the investment firm at age fifty.

Once he did, he enthusiastically took over the helm and found projects that he could pour his passion and interests into. He was proud of what they had built, but was even more proud that he had done all this as homage to that still unknown young woman who saved his life on that fateful day, years ago.

12

EIGHT YEARS BEFORE IMPACT
BOULDER: LATE OCTOBER

"Hey, Mom, sorry it took me so long to call you back. The cross-country team has been training hard every day after school for the upcoming meet. They need to win to qualify for states. On top of that, my own training has been exhausting. I'm managing to squeeze three to four hours every day, if you can believe that! Of course, I'm usually up by four a.m. but what else is new, right?" Jillian sat perched at her desk in her office at Boulder Academy. The team had gone home for the day, and she was catching up on some paperwork and returning phone calls.

"Jill, you're going to wear yourself out, honey. I just wish you could slow down once in a while! Actually, that's what I had called you about earlier. Do you think there's any chance you could take a few days off and come home for a visit?"

"Why, Mom? What's up? Are you guys doing okay?" She knew her mother wouldn't be asking her to miss days off from work and fly all the way back east unless it was something important.

"I'm not really sure, honey. I think so, but to be honest, your father has been acting a little strange again lately, and I just think some time with you would do him a world of good."

Jillian paused to let this sink in.

"Strange how? Is he still forgetting things and getting confused like he was before? Have you brought him back to see the doctor yet?" she asked. She'd been suggesting to her mother that he be seen by his physician more often. With her being so far away, she wanted to make sure he was getting the supervision and support he needed, rather than all the responsibility falling onto her mother's shoulders.

"Yes, but things seem to be happening a little more frequently lately. His regular doctor has set up an appointment for us Thursday with a neurologist. I'm hoping you will consider flying out and taking him there with me. It would be helpful to have another person help me understand what's happening with him. Plus, I know how much he's missing you. Maybe you could fly in Wednesday night and stay through the weekend? I would just love having some time together. And, Jill, just wait till you see the foliage. It's incredibly beautiful right now. Would you please come? It would mean so much to me."

Jillian was caught a bit off-guard, but happy her mother asked for her help rather than taking on all the responsibility by herself. "Sure, Mom, I think I can do that," she agreed. "Let me reschedule a few things on this end, and I'll call you with my itinerary as soon as possible. Give Daddy a hug for me. Love you both."

Since everyone had already left for the night, Jillian had to wait until the next morning to clear it with her boss. "Chip, I need to book a flight home for a few days. Something's been going on with my father, and I need to help my mother out. Would you be able to run the next couple of practices without me?" she inquired. "I think I can get a flight out tomorrow morning if so."

"Of course, Jill," Chip said. "Take whatever time you need. I'll call if anything important comes up while you are away, otherwise just focus on your dad. I'll make sure the kids are ready for the meet next week. Just leave me a few notes on what you think they still need to work on. Don't worry, we have them looking strong."

Jillian was grateful. She'd never worked for such a supportive boss and didn't want to jeopardize the opportunity she had in front of her. This was the first job she'd had where she could see a real future for herself.

When she first moved to Boulder, she knew she didn't want to be tied down to a forty-hour-a-week job while she trained. Being a serious athlete required lots of flexibility and the ability to train whenever she could. For the first few years living in Boulder, she mainly took jobs waitressing or bartending. She also worked an occasional shift at her local gym, just to help make ends meet. Money was always tight in the beginning, and after a while she knew she needed to find something more substantial. One night while closing up at the gym, she let her manager know that she was on the hunt for a full-time job.

"I desperately need to start making more money," she told him. "My car is on its last legs, and I need to think about buying something newer in the next couple months. If you hear of anything interesting, let me know."

A few days later her manager called on her cell. "Jill, I might have a good lead for you," he started. "I overheard one of our trainers mention that they're looking for an assistant cross-country coach at Boulder Academy. Do you know the place? It's the private high school on the north side of town. Anyway, I thought it would be a good fit with your background. And it might allow you to continue with your training. You should check it out."

Jillian was immediately interested.

The next day she walked into Boulder Academy with her resume in hand. She asked to meet with the athletic director and was lucky enough to catch him during a free period. Although she was only twenty-five at the time, her passion and experience were too good to pass up. He hired her on the spot.

Jillian's new role had her working under Chip Donahue, a cross-country star in his own right. He had built the running program at Boulder Academy up over his tenure to the point where they were winning state and national titles year after year. Chip had planned to retire and needed time to groom a replacement who had his same mentality and vision for the sport. Since he and Jillian had a similar philosophy, they were a terrific fit from day one.

"Thanks so much for everything," she expressed again. "You can always reach me at my parents' home in Boston if anything comes up while I'm gone. I'll leave the number and those notes on your desk before I head out."

Driving back to her apartment to pack, she realized she was actually looking forward to a break and some time with her parents, especially if it included some of her mother's homemade cooking. Being single and constantly busy made it hard for her to eat well most nights. Since she didn't like to cook for just one person, most of her meals consisted of protein shakes with a handful of nuts and a piece of fruit. She could almost taste her mother's famous lasagna as she finished packing her bags.

When she was ready to leave the next morning, she double checked to make sure she had her running gear in her carry-on.

Okay, Jill, she prompted herself, *what else are you going to need? You have your workout stuff, your music, a laptop, and a couple of magazines. I guess that should do it.*

She locked the door behind her and headed straight to Denver International Airport. With a four-hour flight ahead, she planned to catch up on some much-needed sleep. Luckily, the flight wasn't full, and she was able to take two seats and spread out. She nodded off as soon as the plane reached cruising altitude.

As the wheels touched down in Boston, she was jarred awake from her deep sleep. She wiped away the pocket of drool that had gathered in the corner of her mouth and suddenly worried that she may have been snoring the entire flight.

"I hope I didn't disturb you too much," she said politely and smiled to the woman who'd been sitting beside her in the aisle seat. "I've been training hard for an upcoming race. I guess I didn't realize how exhausted I've been!"

The woman just gave her a blank stare, then turned away, rolling her eyes.

Well, alright then. So nice talking with you, too. God, some people can be so rude, she thought. She stood in awkward silence, painfully waiting for everyone in front of her to grab their belongings from the overhead bins and exit the plane.

After what felt like an eternity, she started to move forward. *Hopefully the line at the rental car place won't take this long,* she worried. *I just want to get home.* She checked her watch and made her way into the terminal area.

"Hey, beautiful!" Jillian turned toward the sound as she came out from the jet bridge door. When she did, she saw that her mother was waiting at the gate. She felt her face light up. She immediately dropped her bags, ran over, and gave her mom a giant hug.

"What are you doing here, Mom? Did I forget to tell you I was going to rent a car once I landed?" she asked. "I didn't want to put you out by having to come get me, but the truth is, now that you're here, I'm really happy to see you." She squeezed her again.

"Yes, you did tell me that, but I thought it would be fun to surprise you. I took a taxi in and figured we could drive back together in your rental. That way we can catch up a bit before you see your father. I hope that's okay?"

"Of course it's okay!" Jillian blurted out. "It couldn't have been a better surprise. I'm thrilled to have your company!"

On the way home from the airport, Jillian pressed her mother for details on what had been going on with her father. She wanted to be prepared.

"Oh, Jill, it's something different every day, honey. Yesterday he forgot to turn the water off in the bathroom, today he left the freezer door wide open for hours and everything just about thawed out. He's constantly losing his keys or his wallet, or forgetting where he's going when he's driving. Just before I came to get you today, he asked me five different times where I was going. He's just acting so strangely, and I'm getting worried!"

"I'm sure the doctor will be able to tell us what's going on, Mom," Jillian said. "Maybe his blood pressure medication needs to be adjusted. Or maybe he should be spending more time out on the golf course with his buddies." Her mother didn't look like she was convinced. "Either way, we will find out together tomorrow. Right now, I just want to get home and eat whatever you've cooked up. I'm literally starving!"

Jillian's father greeted them at the door. He had a huge smile and waved her in.

"Hello, my sweetheart! How was your trip in? I'm so happy to see you. You look thin. Have you been eating enough out there in Boulder? Do you need some money for food?" he asked in rapid fire. She just shook her head and laughed.

"Hi, Dad. Yes, I am eating enough in Boulder. No, I don't need any money for food. I am in training mode right now, so I get pretty lean. You know the drill." She hugged him tight.

"You're working too hard out there. Look at you. You need to put some meat on those bones!" he teased, spinning her around. "Now, come and sit down. Your mother has made us a feast."

"I told you having his daughter around always put him in a great mood," her mother said, winking at Jillian. "Isn't that right, Joe? I knew you'd be happy to see her."

He was chattier than usual at dinner, and Jillian noticed he asked her the same questions over and over again. "It's probably just the excitement of having me home," she suggested to her mother while they finished up the dishes. In her gut, she knew something wasn't quite right, but she tried to sugarcoat it for the time being.

"Hopefully that's all it is," her mother replied. After everything was cleaned up and they'd put a kettle on for tea, they all settled down in the living room to watch television. After just a few minutes of watching the news, Jillian sensed her eyelids starting to get heavy. She rested her head against a pillow and closed her eyes. She felt her mother cover her with a blanket and kiss her cheek before turning the television off and heading to bed. "C'mon, Joe," she heard her call to her father. "Let's let her sleep. She must really need it."

"Jillian!" her father whispered loudly, nudging her shoulder to wake her up. "Jillian, wake up!" A beam of sunshine came through the blinds, lighting the whole room with a warm glow. She rubbed her eyes and glanced at the wall clock.

"Is that clock right? I can't believe I just slept ten hours straight!" she said, sitting up and looking groggily at her father. "What's going on, Dad? Is everything okay?"

"Yeah, of course. I thought we could go get coffee and bagels before your mother wakes up. Let's surprise her," he said with a twinkle of mischief in his eye. "A new spot just opened up right down the road about a month ago. They have those asiago cheese-covered ones you used to eat. You'll love it!" He smiled from ear to ear, excited to have his daughter all to himself.

Jillian pulled herself up off the couch, slipped on her sneakers, and grabbed her jacket. As quietly as she could, she closed the front door behind her and followed her father out to the car. It was just six in the morning, and the cool New England air filled her lungs. *Oh, how I miss this,* she thought.

They drove for several minutes before her father broke the peaceful silence. "Hmm, I thought the shop was right up here on the corner, but I don't see it. I must have made a wrong turn a couple blocks back. Then again, maybe it is a bit farther than I remembered," he said with a shrug. After a few more minutes passed and there was still no sign of the coffee shop, his temper and voice started to escalate.

"Did you see the sign with the dancing coffee beans back there? The sign, Jill...did you see the sign?" He waved his hand around angrily.

"No, sorry, Dad. I wasn't paying attention to any signs. Should we just turn around and go back? Do you think we missed it? I'm sure we are just a block or so off." Jillian watched her father's face. She saw the confusion and realized what her mother had been talking about.

"It's okay, Daddy. Really. Let's not get so upset," she suggested. "Why don't I just drive us back home and we can stop at that coffee shop on the way back from your appointment later this morning? I would almost rather wait and get an iced coffee then, wouldn't you? It's going to be okay, Daddy."

Jillian gingerly convinced him to pull over, where she switched into the driver's seat. She drove them back home with a heavy heart. What her mother had been saying was true: something just wasn't quite right.

When they walked back into the house, her mother was already awake. She'd made a pot of coffee and laid out her husband's medications. "Oh, there you two are. We need to leave soon if we're going to get there by seven. Where were you off to so early this morning?"

"Dad thought he would pick up some bagels, but we couldn't find the place he likes. I told him we could pick some up on the way back from his appointment later this morning instead. Right, Dad? They have the cheese ones I like. That'll be a nice treat for tomorrow," Jillian answered, trying not to make a big deal out of things for his sake.

Her mother shot her a quick knowing glance. "In any case," Jillian added, mostly as a way to redirect the situation, "I'm going to whip us all up a veggie omelet. Let's have a quick breakfast before we have to leave for Daddy's thing."

Her mother left it alone for the time being.

"Mr. Richards?" The nurse directed her voice toward Jillian's father in the waiting room of the neurologist's office. "The doctor will see you now." The three of them stood and followed her through another door, down a hallway, and into an unoccupied exam room.

After taking his vital signs, the nurse let them know that the doctor would be in as soon as possible. They were already forty-five minutes behind schedule, and Jillian could see her father was getting antsy. After sitting for a few minutes in complete silence, she decided a distraction might be a good idea.

"Hey, Dad, tell me that story again about the time I put the Lego in my ear when I was little."

He laughed out loud.

"Yes, yes, that's my favorite. Oh, let's see. You were only five, but I remember that day like it was yesterday. You had been playing with your Lego pieces on the living room floor when you came running over to me, real upset. 'Daddy, Daddy, it's stuck inside. Get it out!' you shouted at the top of your lungs. You were adamant that you had shoved a Lego into your ear and that it was still stuck deep inside. I couldn't see anything, of course, but you were convinced that it went in and never came out. Oh, you were something! No matter how much we tried to talk you out of it, you downright insisted that we bring you to the emergency room." He looked over to his wife with wide, bright eyes. "Remember that, Barb? She made us rush her right over!"

Jillian could see her mother was enjoying seeing him so happy. "Yes, I do remember that. What a day that was for all of us. Go ahead, tell her what happened next, Joe."

He jumped right in, full of enthusiasm. "So, there we are, desperately trying to convince the doctor that he needs to take an emergency x-ray of your entire head, you know, to see how far the Lego has traveled down into your ear, when you decide to do a cartwheel right there in the middle of the exam room." Jillian's father stood up excitedly and added some animated gestures.

"Flip-flop, over you went, only to have the bright yellow Lego piece fall right out of your front shirt pocket and onto the floor directly in front of us! You squealed, 'Oh, there it is!' as happy as a clam to have found your missing building block. We were horribly embarrassed, and there you were, without a care in the world, just twirling around the room." He twirled on his tiptoes to imitate the young Jillian, and they found themselves laughing hysterically. It was a cheerful and welcome diversion from the long wait.

Finally the doctor came in, apologizing as he shut the door behind him. "I'm so sorry to keep you folks waiting. I got held up at the hospital with another patient this morning. In any case, I'm here now, and you have my undivided attention. So, what brings you here today, Joe?" He had a kind smile, and Jillian trusted him immediately.

"Well, Doc, it appears that my lovely wife and daughter thought I should probably see someone because, as they will try to convince you, I tend to get a little confused sometimes. Oh, and once in a while I may get a little turned around on how to get somewhere when I'm driving. I personally think it is just old age, but these two beauties insisted." He pointed toward his wife and daughter and playfully winked.

"Fair enough," the doctor said, adding, "I think I know a few things we can do to try to set their minds at ease. I'll tell you what, let's start by reviewing your medical history and any medication you're taking, then we can talk about any other symptoms or recent changes that you can think of. I'd also like to conduct a few quick tests, mostly to rule some things out. How does that sound so far?"

Joe nodded in agreement.

"We should probably do a complete physical evaluation while you're here today as well. That way we can see if you have other health conditions that could be causing or contributing to your symptoms, such as signs of past strokes, Parkinson's disease, or other medical conditions. And if it comes to it, we may decide to check for thyroid problems or vitamin B12 deficiency."

"Oh, is that all?" Joe asked with a grin and a note of sarcasm. "I'm not looking for clearance to go to the moon here, Doc. Just kick the tires and look under the hood. I think you'll see I pass the muster!" They all laughed at his silly visual. Jillian and her mother had been worried, fearing that the signs were pointing to dementia or Alzheimer's, but they could clearly see his sense of humor was still intact. Sitting here with him now, they hoped the doctor would find an easy explanation.

The doctor completed his initial round of tests and called the ladies back into his office while Joe got dressed. "I'll be calling you in the next day or so with the results and any follow-up tests we may want to run," he said to Barbara. "In the meantime, I would suggest that Joe not do any driving on his own, just to stay on the safe side. I'll be in touch soon."

Getting back home, Jillian decided to go for a run. She was feeling a bit overwhelmed. It had been tough being so far away, knowing that her mother needed her support at home. Running always helped clear her head and focus on the larger picture. She knew exactly where she wanted to go.

The trails that looped the nearby lake had always been her favorite place to train when she lived in Boston. She felt excited to go back there. She slipped into a pair of running tights, laced up her sneakers, and grabbed bottled water from the fridge.

"Mom, I'm going for a trail run down by the lake. I'll be back in an hour or so," she called out as she grabbed her keys and headed out the door. She couldn't wait to be surrounded by the beautiful views, the calm water, and the serenity the lake brought her.

There were several loops that circled the lake, but her favorite by far was the five-mile stretch that followed the water's edge. The first mile was entirely in the woods, but then it opened up and ran alongside the shoreline for a good distance. When she started out, there wasn't another soul in sight. It was late October, so she didn't expect to see anyone else on the trails. That was why she was surprised when she came out of the woods, heading toward the lake. Next to the boat ramp, she saw a lone black car parked in the distance.

That's odd. It's unusual for a vehicle to be out here this late in the year, especially since no boating is allowed after Labor Day, she thought. She decided to approach with caution and instinctively reached for the mace in her pocket.

Oh crap! I didn't bring it with me. Normally she carried a small canister of mace when she ran by herself, but knowing she wouldn't have been allowed to bring it on the plane, she left it behind.

She hoped this wasn't going to be a problem.

She momentarily froze when she got close enough to the vehicle to realize she'd stumbled upon something rather horrific. It took a few seconds for her brain to register what she was seeing. There before her was a long green garden hose running from the exhaust pipe into the driver's side window, silver tape covering most of the seams along the doors and windows, and an idling car. The shock hit her like a ton of bricks. Her legs went weak beneath her, and her heart started pumping with a surge of adrenaline.

Once she willed her legs to move again, she ran over, looked into the car, and discovered a man lying in a fully reclined position in the driver's side seat. Screaming at the top of her voice, she demanded, "Can you hear me? Can you hear me?" She pounded on the window with both fists. When she got no reaction, she desperately tried to pull the door handle open, but to no avail. A quick check confirmed all the doors were locked and a dismal thought crept in: *Am I too late? Oh God, I must be too late. Why is this shit always happening to me?*

Frantically, she scoured the area to see if she could find something, anything, to break a window. She quickly spotted a large metal trash barrel near a grove of picnic tables about thirty yards away. Sprinting over to grab it, her heart sank when she saw that it was attached to a metal chain and anchored down by a cement block.

"Shit!" she yelled. "Who the hell is going to want to steal a fucking garbage can, for Christ sake?"

Think, Jill, think. There has to be something you can use. She scanned the area again and saw a few downed branches littered about, but nothing sturdy enough to break a car window.

She could feel time ticking away, so she ran back to the car and pounded on the window again, still hoping to alert the person inside. Just then, she caught a glimmer of some larger rocks about six feet into the lake. Without hesitation, she waded waist-deep into the frigid water and pulled out the largest rock she could lift. Holding the rock against her chest, she trudged out of the water and made her way over to the idling car. Raising the heavy rock as high above her head as possible, she smashed it down into the car window.

A booming echo reverberated across the lake as the glass window exploded into hundreds of small pieces the size of rock salt.

Reaching through the shattered glass, Jillian fumbled to unlock the door from the inside and pulled it open. The man inside was completely unconscious and all color had drained from his face. She wasn't sure if he was still alive.

Using all her might, she yelled, "C'mon! C'mon!" and dragged the man's limp body out of the car and into the cool, damp air. She brushed some of the shattered glass away from his neck and face, trying her best not to make any cuts. Her intention was to give him CPR, but after just a few seconds of lying on the cold, wet ground, he flinched, desperately gasping for air. The coughing and wheezing assured her that he was alive, but she knew she'd need to get help, and fast.

"Wait right here! Don't move!" Jillian demanded. Running up the nearby embankment, she shouted at the top of her lungs, "Help! Help! Can anyone hear me? Call 911! Somebody help us!" She paused for a second to see if anyone responded, but of course nothing came back. She was sure they were too far into the woods for anyone to hear her plea.

"I'm going to run for help. I know there are some houses about a half-mile this way," she yelled toward the man, pointing the opposite direction. "I promise I'll be right back! It's going to be okay! Just wait here!" The man was just starting to move about.

Jillian's legs were heavy, still numb from the extremely cold water. Although she felt like two anchors had been tied to her ankles, she ran as fast as she could until she reached the street where there were a few houses within sight. Luckily, someone was home at the first door she knocked on.

The door was opened just a crack by an apprehensive-looking older gentleman.

"Oh, thank God!" Jillian said with a gasp, still trying to catch her breath.

"Can I help you?" he asked in a cautious tone. Once Jillian explained what was happening without sounding like a complete lunatic, the homeowner allowed her to call 911. She waited outside the house for a cruiser to come meet her. Within minutes the officer arrived, and they drove toward the boat ramp together.

In all, just fifteen minutes had passed since she left the man, but when they got there, both he and the car were gone. A set of erratic tracks led up and away from the boat ramp.

"I swear he was just here a few minutes ago!" Jillian said, her hands on her head in disbelief. She and the police officer walked around the site, gathering the discarded hose, the packaging, and the ripped tape as evidence. They cleaned up the broken glass and placed it into the large metal trash barrel.

"You're really shivering, miss. Would you like me to get you a blanket from the cruiser?" he asked her once they'd finished. "We always keep a spare in the trunk."

"Yes, please, that would be great. I think the chill has gone to my bones," Jillian answered, pulling her legs into her chest and sitting at one of the empty picnic tables. The officer brought her a blanket, wrapped it around her shoulders, and sat beside her.

"I'd like to take down a few notes for my report if you wouldn't mind," he told her. "Can you describe the scene for me again? Please tell me exactly what happened in the order you remember it." She did her best to recall every detail about the sequence of events, the vehicle, and the man.

"All I can remember is that it was a black luxury car, maybe a Mercedes or a Lexus, and the man inside seemed to be about in his early forties. He had dark hair. Oh, and he was wearing an expensive suit and a bright blue tie. I thought it was a little odd that he was so dressed up in light of what was happening."

"Uh huh," the officer replied, marking a few notes down. "Did you happen to catch the license plate? Or any part of it? Even the first few letters would be helpful."

"No, I'm sorry. I was so focused on getting the man out of the car that I wasn't paying attention to much else."

The officer finished writing and closed his notepad. After he did a final scan of the area, he offered to drive Jillian back to the trail entrance where her car was parked.

"Thank you for your help today, ma'am," he said. "Here's my contact info in case you remember anything else. Any little detail might enable us to find him. We'd like to make sure he's okay." He handed her a business card and waited until she was safely back in her car before pulling away.

Getting back to her parents' house, Jillian shared the incredible story with her mother. Neither of them could make sense of what had just happened. "Jillian, you're like a good luck angel!" her mother declared. "That man most likely would have died if you hadn't found him exactly when you did." She wrapped her daughter warmly in another blanket and gave her a hug. "I can't believe you did this again, sweetheart."

"What do you mean again?" she asked.

"Don't you remember back in high school, honey? That blood donor thing you did your senior year?"

13

SEVENTEEN YEARS BEFORE IMPACT
BOSTON: MAY

"Mom, I just got a call from the National Marrow Donor Bank. Remember that blood drive we did for Jake Morgan about a month ago?" Jillian asked, setting the phone down and walking over to her mother, who was busy grading papers at the kitchen table.

"Yes, of course I remember that. I thought they came back saying no one from your school was a match for him. Are they thinking you might be a good match for him now?"

"No, I'm still not a match for Jake, but I guess I'm a perfect match for some fifteen-year-old girl who lives in Chicago. From what they said, she's really sick. Some type of leukemia, I think the lady was saying. They asked me to let them know as soon as possible whether I'm still willing to donate. From the sounds of it, she doesn't have much time."

"How did they even get your information, honey? I thought you were just being tested for Jake. Did you take down the person's name and number who just called? I will call them back if you'd like me to." Her mother sounded concerned.

"The lady told me that the waivers we signed permitted our information to be sent to the national registry, I guess. To be honest, I didn't even read the forms that closely. I was more worried about the needle going into my arm. You know how much I hate needles." Jillian sat for a few minutes thinking about the call. She felt herself begin to get choked up, overwhelmed by the enormous responsibility she'd just been handed.

"It's up to me, Mom. Some other person's fate all depends on me," she said, looking to her mother for comfort as tears started to stream down her face.

"What am I supposed to do here, Mom? I'm kinda freaked out about this." She felt herself start to tremble. "When they told us what we might have to do if we were a match for Jake, it sounded pretty awful. I'm afraid that what they're going to do to me is going to hurt too much. Plus, what if I'm not able to run for a while? What if I miss competing this season?" She knew her voice was escalating. "I don't even know this person, Mom! I mean, if it were for Jake that would be completely different. He's my friend. But I don't even know this girl! I have no idea what I'm supposed to do."

Jillian's mother stopped what she was doing and pulled her daughter in close. She let her cry for several moments, then responded, "Jillian, you need to calm down. You're working yourself into a frenzy. Everything is going to work out, sweetie. You don't have to decide right this second. Just take a deep breath. We're going to figure this out."

Jillian spent that evening talking it over with her parents. They tried to look at the situation from every possible angle. With all the demands of school and sports, Jillian was feeling strapped for time already and didn't want to have to give up the things she loved to do most.

"It's the end of my senior year. I wanted this to be a fun time, and I have a real shot at setting some records in track this year. You know this would slow me down. My coach and my teammates are counting on me. This could ruin everything!" She felt selfish for acting this way, but couldn't help it.

"Look, Jill, we understand why you're so upset, but you don't have to make a rash decision. We have discussed this thing backward and forward, and I think we all agree that there's a lot to think about," her father said. "It's getting late. I think it would be best to talk it out again after a good night's sleep. We'll figure this out tomorrow."

Seeing the dilemma was still agonizing her the next morning, her parents offered some advice. "Bottom line, Jill, this isn't about you, sweetie. It's about this other girl," her father started off. "You could make such a difference in her life, and in the life of her family. If the situation was reversed, wouldn't you want that person to be brave enough to donate and possibly save your life? I couldn't imagine knowing that someone was out there who could make that difference for you and didn't come forward."

Jillian listened intently.

"Plus," her mother added, "the part you have to do is just temporary. You'll be back to full strength in just a few days. I'm sure they'll make the whole process as comfortable as possible for you. Didn't you tell me we can do the procedure right here in Boston, then they just fly the tissue out to her? We'll be able to stick by your side every step of the way, honey." Her mother's voice was calming. She said just what Jillian needed to hear to put things in perspective. "I know it's scary, but I also know you. If you don't do this, I think you may regret it in the future. You don't get a second chance with things like this."

It took Jillian a few moments to let this all sink in.

"Yes. You're absolutely right. I know I would regret it," Jillian finally whispered, taking a deep breath. "Of course I'm going to do this. I don't even know why I was weighing the pros and cons. I guess I'm just scared." She embraced both of her parents tightly before going over to pick up the phone. She dialed back the number for the donor bank and asked for the woman she had spoken with the day before.

"Sign me up!" she let out, surprised at her own excitement. "What do I need to do next?"

After a battery of tests and final confirmation that she was, in fact, a perfect match, the procedure was scheduled. Based on the sick girl's age and type of leukemia, it was decided that the best chance for her survival would be to receive healthy stem cells from Jillian's bone marrow. The registry set up an appointment for her and her parents to meet with an affiliated doctor in Boston.

A few days later, they met with Dr. Patel, the surgeon who would be performing the operation. He carefully went through his list and explained each step of the donation process.

"Plan to arrive at the hospital outpatient facility the morning of the donation. You'll most likely be in the hospital from early morning to late afternoon that day," he began. "Based on the type of donation Jillian will be doing, I'll be doing the procedure in an operating room. She'll be given anesthesia to block the pain during the marrow donation. Since general anesthesia will be used, she'll be unconscious during the donation. The average time of the surgery is less than two hours." Dr. Patel directed his attention toward Jillian.

"During the bone marrow donation, you'll be lying on your stomach. I'll be using special hollow needles to withdraw liquid marrow from both sides of the back of your pelvic bone. This is done through several small incisions. The incisions are less than one-fourth inch long and don't require stitches. Remember, because you'll be under anesthesia, you won't feel any of this." He waited a moment, then asked, "Do any of you have questions so far?"

Jillian's mother, who'd been feverishly writing everything down, looked up from her notes. "How can Jillian expect to feel after this is done? Is she going to be able to walk right away?"

Dr. Patel handed her a list outlining all the possible side effects, then went on to explain further.

"Any discomfort or side effects after the donation vary from person to person, but most marrow donors will experience at least a few of those listed on this form. The most common are back or hip pain, fatigue, muscle pain, and bruising at the collection site. She may feel some soreness in her back for a few days or so, which is completely normal. Most donors are back into their usual routine within about a week. And yes, she'll be able to walk the same day." Dr. Patel winked at Jillian and added, "Seeing that your daughter is a track star, I wouldn't be surprised to see her bounce right back from this. She's going to do just fine."

"Are you still okay with all of this, Jill?" her father asked. "You still have the final say, honey. We want to make sure that you're completely on board before we all sign the paperwork." He looked at her, and she could see the sincerity in his eyes. "I admire how brave you're being right now, but I need to hear it from you."

"I'm sure, Dad. This is something I have to do." Jillian knew she would be sore for a few days after the procedure, but she easily justified any short-term discomfort that would come, especially when she thought about what this might mean for the girl in Chicago.

When the day finally arrived, Jillian drove into Boston with her parents. It was early, and they were on the road before most of the commuter traffic. Although the highway was almost empty, the hospital was buzzing with activity when they arrived. They signed in at the outpatient desk, filled out some additional paperwork, and watched *The Today Show* on the overhead television in the sitting area. While she waited to be called in, Jillian fidgeted with her hospital bracelet, spinning it round and round on her wrist. She had a nervous stomach and just wanted to get started. She hoped the process would go quickly.

When it was finally time to go in for the procedure, she kissed both her parents good-bye. "Thank you both for being by my side," she said. "I love you so much." As the nurse led her into the pre-op area, she was feeling more worried about the needle being put into her arm for the anesthesia than the actual procedure itself.

"Just so you know, I'm not very good with needles," she said apprehensively. "Try to go easy on me," she added with a nervous laugh.

The last thing Jillian remembered after being wheeled into the operating room was Dr. Patel asking her to count backward from one hundred. She got to ninety-seven.

"Hi there," her mother was gently rubbing her forehead when she opened her eyes. Jillian was still a bit groggy coming out from the anesthesia. It took a few moments to adjust to the bright lighting and regain focus.

"Where am I?" she asked, immediately feeling a dry scratchiness at the back of her throat.

"You're in the recovery room, sweetie. It's all done. The doctor said everything went well. You did just fine. The tissue they took out is already on its way to Chicago. Can you believe that? We're so proud of you, Jill."

"When can I get out of here?" Jillian asked slowly and tried to sit up. Her mother placed a cool, damp cloth on her head.

"The nurse said as soon as you're able to eat, drink, and walk on your own, we can go. I can get her when you're ready to try." Jillian was anxious to get up and going, but still feeling quite dizzy. Trying to move had made her nauseous.

"I'm so thirsty, Mom. Can you please get me some water?" she asked, leaning her head back against the pillow. Before her mother could even finish pouring her a cup, she fell back asleep. Another half-hour passed before the nurse came over to wake her again.

"Before we get you up and on your way home, there are a few things to remember," the nurse started out. "First, it may take a couple of days for you to feel like your old self again. You may experience a few symptoms, including headaches, fatigue, muscle pain, back or hip pain, bruising around the incision site, and difficulty walking. These symptoms may last as little as a couple of days or as long as several weeks. Just be patient and get plenty of rest." She smiled and wrapped a cuff around Jillian's arm to take her blood pressure. "Do you have any questions for me?"

"Just one," Jillian asked. "What would I need to do if I decide that I do want to find out what happens to the girl who's getting my donation?"

"Well, there are very strict guidelines in place for everyone's privacy," the nurse answered, taking the cuff off and putting a thermometer under Jillian's tongue. "As you know, we were able to give you the age and gender of the recipient, and of course her condition. If you'd like, we can provide you with up to three updates on how she's doing in the first year. Just keep in mind that if you do get updates, it's important to prepare yourself for the possibility that she may not have survived the procedure, or other complications may have come up in the meantime. In most cases these donations are successful, but I just want to make sure you have all the information before you make that decision."

Jillian thought about what the nurse had said while she waited for a ginger ale and some saltine crackers to be brought over. She knew she could not bear knowing if something didn't go right and the girl didn't make it. She needed to believe that going through this process was the right thing to do and that she had made the difference in the life of the girl and given her a future.

When the nurse came back, Jillian said, "I'd still like to keep my donation anonymous, and I've decided not to find out about the recipient. I'm just going to have faith that whoever is on the other side receiving my bone marrow is lucky enough to be given a second chance because of it."

14

"Let's go, Nik, we just got a call!" Garrett Holden popped his head into the break room at Medi-Vac Rescue Helicopters. It was Nikki's turn to be on call, and she was always happy to be there with Garrett, whom she'd developed a major crush on. She grabbed her phone off the charger and retrieved Liz, the transport nurse, who was resting in one of the private rooms in the back.

"Liz, a call just came in. It's a Code 100," Nikki relayed. "Garrett just went out to start his safety walk-around. I told him we'd be right there."

"Code 100? Where's the scene?" Liz asked, zipping up her flight suit and following Nikki.

"I think Garrett said it's a head-on collision on 93 northbound. He wants us to let him know if we're on board to fly, given the conditions."

"Three-to-go, one-to-say-no," Liz said. "That's our motto on days like this. All three of us need to be in agreement or we don't fly. Make sure you go with your gut, Nikki. You are the newest crew member, but every vote counts."

Nikki and Liz entered the hangar and immediately headed over to their lockers. As Nikki was getting her helmet secured, Liz opened the double locked box to retrieve the narcotics she might need at the scene. Once they were ready, they approached the helicopter, where Garrett had just finished his external safety inspection and was climbing into the cockpit. Both Nikki and Liz completed their walk-around, too, making sure to double check all the latches were locked, all doors were free of obstructions and secure, and all fluid indicators were at the proper levels.

Garrett was busy prepping the controls and double checking the conditions from the cockpit when Nikki and Liz climbed into the back of the helicopter and settled into their seats. He had a thorough list he went over before every take-off and asked them both to do the same with their readiness checks. The winds were whipping, and torrential rain pelted down against the body of the helicopter, making it difficult to hear even through their headsets.

"Pilot ready for take-off. Is the crew buckled in and ready?" Garrett asked.

"Buckled and ready for take-off," Liz answered first. She'd visually confirmed that both she and Nikki had their five-point-harnesses secured and were ready to go.

"Buckled and ready for take-off," Nikki said. She'd also made sure the equipment bags had been double-checked and were fastened with belts to the on-board stretcher.

"This is going to be one bumpy ride out to 93," Garrett said through his headset. "I know this weather might be a bit intimidating, but trust me, I've flown in worse. Just hang on!"

Nikki had been thrilled with her new job in Boston since day one. She had been an EMT and a paramedic for years, but no other job had ever given her an adrenaline rush like this gig. Based on the phone interview she had done from Chicago just a few months earlier, she had a feeling the Boston scene would be exciting. The way the owner described the role sounded exactly like what she was looking to do. She knew from her training what was going to be expected, but she had no idea things could get quite so intense.

"As you know," he had explained, "being a critical-care transport paramedic puts you in many different situations. Many of the calls you'll be working on are transports, but you'll also see high-risk, life-threatening situations that need immediate attention and well-skilled hands on deck. As part of the crew, it's up to you to stabilize the victim for air transport to the trauma centers at the hospitals. Your efforts, from the moment you are on-scene to the moment you transfer them to the waiting trauma team, can make a real difference in their survival and recovery. That's our mission here at Medi-Vac Rescue. We want to save as many lives as possible. We're putting together a team that can get the job done and done well."

Nikki loved living on the edge between life and death; being the one who changed fate in her patient's favor sounded like a dream job. She knew she would be a good fit.

"So, tell me what makes you the best candidate for this position?" she recalled him asking during their conversation.

"Honestly, for me, it's always been all about the rush," she said. "I knew when I graduated from high school that this type of job was my calling. You wouldn't know it now, but I was extremely ill as a child, and I believe I've already cheated death a couple of times. When I was just thirteen, I was diagnosed with an aggressive form of leukemia. For two straight years, I was forced to fight a tremendously hard battle, one that I came close to losing more than once."

"Oh, wow, I had no idea," the owner replied. "How did you get through such a tough time?"

"I'll admit, if it hadn't been for a bone marrow transplant I received at fifteen, I'm confident that I wouldn't even be here today," Nikki answered. "Coming that close to death, and beating it, has left me with a sense of invincibility and an internal drive that's hard to describe. I thrive being on the front lines, saving people's lives, and making a real difference in the world. I'm not afraid of whatever the world throws at me, and I want to keep giving back. I know I could do that as part of your team and with Medi-Vac."

"That certainly is impressive," the owner said. She could hear him taking notes. "Tell me a little bit more about your previous experience and why you want to move to Boston at this point in your career."

Nikki took a deep breath in and spoke from her heart.

"Once I became an EMT, I realized that I had the opportunity to save lives every single day. And every day of my career so far has been different. At first, I worked in the projects around Chicago, treating gunshot wounds and drug overdoses. Eventually, I moved to the business district, mostly saving victims of car accidents and heart attacks. After a couple of years there, I went on to become a paramedic. I loved my job and loved working in my community. After an incident there that involved helping a local politician's wife, I was asked to become a community liaison. I went into the public schools to teach CPR and first aid, worked with local officials to sponsor community events, and generally felt I was well liked and respected in my field. I realized I could do even more."

"It sounds like, through your leadership and fearlessness, you've really made a name for yourself out there. Why leave Chicago now?"

"Seeing my passion and drive, my manager encouraged me to take courses to further my career and open up even more advancement opportunities. After carefully considering all the options, I enrolled in a critical-care emergency medical transport program. I knew I wanted to continue doing what I did best, but in the air, where every second counted with the patients we were helping. After I graduated at the top of my class, my instructor showed me the listing for this position. It sounds exactly like what I want to be doing. I'd be honored to be part of something so important, and I can't imagine wanting a job more than I want this one right now." Nikki stopped talking and waited for a response, hoping that she'd made a good enough impression.

"Well then, all I can say is welcome aboard!" The owner's enthusiasm was obvious. "I cannot imagine anyone more qualified or passionate to be part of the team. The job is yours if you want it."

That had been just a few months earlier, and Nikki couldn't have anticipated being in a position as terrifying as the one she found herself in now. She felt her stomach do a flip as the helicopter was rocked by a wind gust.

"Have you ever seen it this bad?" Nikki signaled to Liz, who'd been with Medi-Vac since the first day.

"Honestly, no!" Liz said, clutching her seat for dear life. "Most of the time, the weather in Boston is a piece of cake for these guys to maneuver through. I can't say that about today! I hope Garrett knows what he's doing, because I'm about to lose my lunch!"

The flight out to Interstate 93 was by far the worst Nikki had experienced. She and Liz were buckled in tight and white-knuckled it most of the way. After what felt like an eternity, Garrett finally gave them a status.

"I have eyes on the accident ahead. I'm now in direct communication with the officer on site. We'll do our flyover in about one minute. Looks clear from here, but stay on the lookout for any poles or wires, or other aircraft possibly in the area."

Once Garrett was confident his landing zone was clear, he let Nikki and Liz know.

"Prepare for landing. Once we touch down, I'd like to keep the helicopter running due to this weather. That way we can take off as soon as both you and the patient are secure. Is this acceptable to both of you?" he asked.

"Yes!" they agreed, knowing that any time he could shave off would be vital. He maintained control and expertly landed the aircraft on the highway, as close as possible to the crash scene.

Nikki quickly unbuckled, took off her helmet, and exited the side door directly behind Liz. They went to the back of the helicopter, opened the rear clamshell doors, and released the latch that secured the stretcher. Both the paramedic and medical bags were still fastened to the stretcher as they quickly wheeled it toward the accident.

Positioned several yards from the crash, they witnessed the victim lying with her head cradled in an older woman's lap. The wind was howling, and freezing rain whipped against their faces as they reached the two women.

"Are you alright, ma'am?" Liz called to the older woman, who was completely soaked and shivering.

"Yes, dear, I'll be fine. This woman is the one who needs help. I heard a crack when I pulled her from the car, so I didn't want to move her again, in case she has a neck injury. She's not responding to anything I say. Please help her!"

Nikki did her best to take the victim's pulse, which wasn't looking promising. She was barely conscious and appeared to have badly injured both her skull and her right leg. The risk of hypothermia was also of paramount concern.

"We need to get her stabilized!" Nikki called to Liz, trying to be heard above the commotion and wind. They carefully moved the woman onto the waiting stretcher, where they wrapped a neck brace and other stabilization apparatus carefully around her limp body. Nikki covered the victim with blankets while Liz gathered their gear.

"Thank you for your help, ma'am. You did the right thing by not moving her more than you had to. You need to go back to your car and get warm now. Let that officer know if you need to be seen when the ambulances arrive." Liz pointed toward the trooper.

Together, Nikki and Liz wheeled the patient over to the waiting helicopter. Within moments, they'd expertly anchored the stretcher inside the fully equipped helicopter. They shut the rear doors and climbed back into their seats. Liz took the first seat, closest to the patient's head, and Nikki sat in the bench seat alongside the stretcher.

"All clear for take-off?" Garrett asked.

"All clear for take-off," both women answered. Once they were airborne and on their way to Boston Memorial, not a second was wasted. They threw the blankets off the patient, turned the heat up, and cut her clothes off to expose her chest and abdomen.

Nikki immediately hopped into a trauma assessment while Liz placed the patient on the monitor, began pre-oxygenation, and set up the needed wires. She placed five heart electrodes onto her chest, affixed the blood pressure cuff, and connected the pulse oximeter.

Nikki spoke into her headset, keeping Liz abreast of what she was finding. "I have identified an injury to the left side of her head. No other facial injuries, no obvious broken ribs, and a probable injury to her lower right leg. Lower leg injury is closed fracture, and I've identified a pulse."

At this point, Liz was drawing up the correct dosage of ketamine and rocuronium needed for a rapid sequence intubation. Since the patient was demonstrating shallow and labored breathing, they needed to get that issue addressed immediately.

"Meds ready for RSI," she confirmed. "IV has been set up. Pushing ketamine now for sedation."

Nikki was positioned and had the equipment ready for intubation.

"Pushing paralytic now," Liz confirmed, immediately after she had finished with the first medication.

Nikki waited the required forty-five seconds for the patient to relax from the narcotic. She then positioned the airway, passed the tube, and checked to make sure it was correctly situated in the trachea. Once ventilated, the patient's chest began to properly rise and fall. She confirmed the end-tidal CO_2 on the monitor.

"Looks good," Nikki said as she secured the breathing tube. Liz was already setting up the IV fluids that would be needed to keep their patient sedated and pain-free for the transport.

"Garrett, I'm all set for a patch-through," Liz directed, now that they had stabilized the patient.

"Patching through now," Garrett confirmed once he'd gotten the ER doctor on the correct communication frequency.

Liz gave the doctor an updated status on the woman lying listless before them. "Patient is a female appearing to be in her mid-thirties, approximately fifty-seven kilos. Pulled from a car wreck at highway speed. Patient was minimally responsive on our arrival. RSI intubated in the helicopter. Obvious left-sided head injury. Pupils asymmetrical. Lower right leg injury, possible fracture of right tibia and fibula. Vitals are: heart rate sixty; blood pressure 176/100; end-tidal CO_2 is forty; pulse oxygen 99 percent. Initiating mannitol for pending herniation."

Nikki continued to triage the patient while Liz communicated with the hospital. Her main concern was the obvious head injury, but the leg also needed some attention. Luckily, the injury presented as a closed fracture, so no bone was coming through the woman's skin. After assessing alignment as best she could, Nikki placed a long board along the affected leg. She immobilized above and below the fracture, then secured the foot. While she worked, Liz kept tabs on the woman's breathing and blood pressure.

"Two minutes out. Prepare for landing," Garrett called back.

The winds were whipping violently, and the ride had been choppy and erratic. As the helicopter was being set down on the helipad on top of the hospital roof, a gust caught Garrett by surprise. The force thrust the helicopter down, and the landing was brutally harsh.

"Shit!" Nikki yelled as the harness dug into her shoulders and her head slammed against the back wall.

"Damn it!" Liz shouted at the same time. The jarring landing had caught them both by surprise. Liz immediately scanned the monitor to make sure none of the wires or tubes had come free from their patient.

"Is everyone okay?" Garrett yelled into the headset. The cockpit was lit up as multiple-colored sensors illuminated, indicating possible damage to the aircraft. "I didn't see that coming!"

The crew was rattled, but Liz and Nikki shook it off quickly. They unbuckled from their seats, exited quickly through the side door, and ran to the back of the helicopter. Opening the clamshell doors, they pulled the stretcher down and out onto the hospital rooftop. Each grabbed a side of the stretcher, and together they raced into the trauma bay, where the team from the hospital was waiting.

Liz again relayed the updated vital signs and the details of what actions she and Nikki had taken. They both knew the woman's head injuries were the most serious, and the fact that she was barely conscious upon their arrival at the scene was the most worrisome.

The trauma team took over, disconnecting Medi-Vac's equipment and attaching their own. They promptly rushed the woman toward the surgical wing. As soon as they turned the corner, Nikki took a deep sigh of relief, knowing she'd done everything she could.

"Holy crap! That was ridiculously intense!" She looked over to Liz, still abuzz from the adrenaline surge. "I didn't expect that at all."

"Yeah, that was one for the books alright. I've never seen conditions like that before. You did great out there today, Nikki. We kept right in sync, even with all that bouncing around. You can ride with me any time!" Liz winked.

After several moments, Nikki's heart rate finally slowed back down to its normal rate, and she and Liz made their way down to the main floor.

"I'm going to check in with them," Liz said, pointing toward a group of nurses on shift. "I'll see if they need any more information from us."

"Sounds good, thank you. I desperately need to hunt down some coffee," Nikki replied. A chill ran up her back. "I'm going to find the cafeteria. Text if you want me to bring anything back for you. Otherwise, I'll catch up with you a little later." She could feel her hair was dripping wet, and she started to shiver from the bitter cold. Shaking the rain from her coat, she made her way down the long corridor.

Just then, Garrett came around the corner with a deeply concerned look. "What's the matter?" Nikki asked when she saw him.

He answered in a flustered tone, "Looks like the aircraft took some damage with that landing. I definitely saw a few sensors indicating one major issue, and there may be more. There's no way I can fly it back in these conditions, especially with the icing I just started seeing. I called the owner a few minutes ago, and he's going to come help assess the damage before we're allowed to move it anywhere. He already put a call in to the maintenance director too, but it sounds like he's just getting voicemail right now. Looks like we're going to be stuck here for a bit."

Nikki's heart skipped a beat. "Oh, really? Well, I was just going down to grab a coffee in the cafeteria. Wanna join me?" She offered up a flirty smile.

"Oh my God, yes. That sounds perfect. I could definitely use some caffeine right about now. Do you think they sell it by the gallon?" Garrett smiled and put his hand on the small of her back as they walked down the hallway. Nikki felt a warm rush of blood.

"That was some crazy-intense flying out there today, Ace. Admit it…even you must have been getting just a teensy bit nervous with all that wind, right?" Nikki teased. "Even though I hear you're the best, I have to confess I thought we were all going to bite it at least a couple times out there! I felt like a Ping-Pong ball in one of those lottery machines, you know, the kind that get bounced around before being sucked into the tube? Thank God you knew what you were doing. I definitely wouldn't have wanted to fly with any other pilot today." Garrett just shrugged and smiled. Nikki could see his face flush from the praise.

"You're too kind, Nikki Jamison. I appreciate that, but I have to give a little credit to that amazing piece of machinery we were all just in. It could have been much worse. Not to mention, you and Liz were pretty incredible out there too, you know! I think you made record time getting the patient stabilized considering what you were facing. I just hope the owner doesn't fire me over that landing. I've seen pilots let go for a lot less than that."

15

"So, what interests you about joining the Coast Guard, young man?" The well-dressed officer walked over to Garrett, who was reading through the pamphlets laid out along the display table. The Coast Guard booth at the college job fair was by far one of the more interesting ones he'd seen that day.

"Oh, I'm not really sure. It looks pretty fun. I've always wanted to fly, I guess. *Top Gun* was my favorite movie growing up, must have seen it a thousand times!" Garrett laughed out loud. "Something about that adrenaline rush has always appealed to me. Plus, the Ray-Bans were pretty cool, you have to admit."

"Well, most of our officers are on water-based craft, of course, but we certainly can always use good helicopter pilots. I'm not positive, but I'm pretty sure they're also the ones who get to wear the coolest sunglasses," the officer said with a chuckle. "Being a pilot for us isn't exactly the same as being a fighter pilot, but those are the guys who see some of the most intense action in the Coast Guard, for sure. Especially the search and rescue teams. They put themselves in some seriously risky situations. Do you think you're cut out for that type of work?"

"Absolutely! That sounds really cool, actually. I can't imagine sitting at a boring desk job all day, like most of these guys are going to have to do!" Garrett answered. He looked around the room filled with classmates talking to corporate recruiters. "I need to be moving, you know, in on the action. Even here at school, most days after class I'm out on my snowboard or bike or skateboard. If it's risky and gets my heart pumping, count me in! What do I have to do to become a pilot for the Guard?"

"Well, first you must have at least a bachelor's degree, which I'm assuming you will have in just a few months," the recruiter said. "Of course, you'll have to complete the seventeen-week Officer Candidate School, too. By the looks of you, I'm guessing you'll have no problem passing the physical fitness exam, or the Class 1 Flight Physical. We also check your vision. It must be correctable to 20/20, and uncorrected vision must be at least 20/50. Finally, you must have normal color vision, depth perception, and field of vision. Do you think you'll have trouble with any of that?"

"No, sir, that's all a no-brainer. My vision is perfect. And then I can fly?" Garrett was surprised at how easy it sounded.

"Not so fast, Maverick," the recruiter answered, laughing. "That's just the beginning. If you want to fly the helicopters, you then get shipped down to flight training at the Naval Flight Training program in Florida, at Pensacola and Whiting Field. That training lasts approximately twenty months, and it's hardcore. Once you finish your training there, you may, just may, qualify to fly a helicopter at the Coast Guard's Aviation Training Center in Mobile, Alabama. You have to prove yourself worthy first!"

"Wow! That all sounds awesome! Then I get to do the search-and-rescue missions?" Garrett pictured himself swooping in to save people desperately clinging to their capsized boats out at sea.

"Yes, that along with a lot of other stuff, too. Most people don't realize this, but Coast Guard aviators are officers first and pilots second. When you first start out, count on the majority of your time being spent on what we term 'collateral duty' activities. There's a lot of administrative work that you'll be doing. That's not to say you won't be flying as well...you very well could be. Helicopter pilots assist with several types of Coast Guard missions. They have to be prepared for all sorts of scenarios."

"Oh yeah? Like what else?"

"Well, for example, you could find yourself patrolling waterways and coastlines for illegal activity. You'd be surprised at how many drugs are still coming in. You also have to be able to fly safely in all kinds of weather, some of the worst you can imagine. You'd have to know your aircraft inside and out—it's up to the pilot to make sure that everything, including the instruments, are working properly, and that all equipment and safety gear is on board and in working condition at all times. And you need to be good in emergency situations. Things can change on a dime out there, and you need to stay cool and solve problems as they come up. There's a lot riding on their shoulders. Still think you're up for this challenge, young man?"

Garrett looked the recruiter square in the eye. "Sir, I've never been so sure of anything in my life! This is exactly the type of thing I've been looking for! Where do I sign up, and when can I start?" Garrett eagerly filled out the initial paperwork and set a date to meet with the recruiter the following week.

"We'll finalize everything when you come down to the recruitment center. I'll let you know what to bring with you the day before. Training can begin right after you graduate if you'd like. Keep those grades up through graduation, and I'll see you next week, son." Garrett shook the officer's hand and raced back to his dorm to call his parents. He couldn't wait to get started.

16

"Okay, now that it's behind us, I guess I can admit it…that was a little more hairy than I was anticipating today," Garrett confessed. He handed Nikki her coffee while they found a spot at a table near the large window in the hospital's cafeteria. The freezing rain continued to drive down, pelting hard against the glass pane. Nikki took the drenched coat off her arm and draped it over a nearby chair to dry.

"Ah ha! I thought so!" she teased. "I genuinely can't get over how you can fly in this mess. Was it ever this bad when you flew for the Coast Guard?" Garrett cautiously took a sip from the steaming hot coffee, trying to avoid burning his lip.

"Oh yeah, sometimes," he answered. "You wouldn't believe some of the stories I have. The rescues out at sea during tropical storms were just like you see in the movies. There were a few times we had to save people in twenty- to thirty-foot swells with winds over thirty-five knots. That's just over forty miles per hour. Honestly, I still don't know how we did it. It gets pretty intense out there. I guess you just have to be able to block everything else out and focus solely on the task right in front of you. I suppose I was relatively good at that."

"What was your job on those missions? Did you do anything else besides fly?" Nikki leaned in, soaking up every word. She hadn't gotten to spend much alone time with Garrett, and being this close was sending tingles up her spine. She got distracted with how green his eyes were and how they were especially striking in contrast with his dark hair and chiseled jaw line.

He is so good-looking, she thought. *The fact that those biceps are bulging from under his shirt is just frosting on the cake. A cake I'd like to take a big bite from.* She found herself giggling out loud and quickly bit her lip so he wouldn't notice. She couldn't help but keep staring, watching every adorable gesture he made.

"Oh, I was pretty much responsible for getting out to the event site," Garrett continued, seemingly oblivious to her infatuation. "My job was to keep the helicopter totally steady while the rescue swimmer went down to save the victims. It's actually a lot harder than you might think. We routinely had to attend special training sessions to be able to do those types of missions. The Coast Guard sent me to the Advanced Rescue Swimmer School after I got through my first round of flight training. I guess they saw potential in me. I'm sure all the incessant begging helped, too!" Garrett chuckled at his own joke.

"Wow, that sounds like a lot of training. I didn't realize how much schooling pilots needed," Nikki said. "I guess it makes sense, though. You had to be prepared for just about any situation, after all."

"Honestly, I loved every second of it and hounded my teachers to send me for training as much as possible," Garrett responded. "I knew it was exactly what I wanted and needed to be doing. It's the most alive I've ever felt."

"I totally get what you're saying about knowing that's what you wanted to do. I felt the exact same way when I was growing up. I knew I needed to be doing something high-octane like this, too." Nikki was surprised they hadn't been interrupted yet by a call from Daniel, the owner, or Liz, looking to join them. This was the most Garrett had talked about anything personal, and she was feeling a real connection. She started to imagine what it would be like to kiss him, and she caught herself drifting off into a trance just staring at his lips.

"Hello? Earth to Nikki. Did I lose you, space shot?" Garrett waved his hand in front of Nikki's face.

"Oh, sorry! I think I'm still coming down off the adrenaline rush. I didn't mean to zone out. I really am interested. What were you saying about the advanced training you did? What kinds of things did they have you do?" Her face flushed from the embarrassment of being caught.

"Advanced training is where Coast Guard helicopter pilots and rescue swimmer crews are trained to perform rescues in heavy weather and dangerous surf conditions. They actually bring active rescue swimmers from air stations around the country to train with us. Our instructors come up with crazy simulations and have us work together to practice rescues in the surf, on high seas in the open ocean, and along cliffs and caves all along the coast. We practice how to hover as close as possible to whatever surface we are working on, while simultaneously lowering a tethered rescue swimmer to recover someone who might be stranded or injured. Talk about elite forces, those guys are some real bad-asses!" Nikki enjoyed watching Garrett's face light up with enthusiasm.

"Well, that certainly explains how you stayed so calm out there today. I hate to admit it, but I was freaking out just a smidge, if you couldn't already tell. I knew we were in good hands, but c'mon! That was insane. I'm just glad we were able to keep our patient stabilized with it being so choppy. She wasn't looking so good. I know that head injury is pretty serious. I imagine they are doing surgery on her right now, don't you think?"

Nikki paused and took a sip from her coffee. "She's one lucky lady that you were the one flying today. If it had taken any longer to get out to her, things probably would be different. I just hope she's going to make it." Nikki shuddered, then changed the topic. "So anyway, if you loved what you were doing for the Coast Guard so much, what made you leave them? It sounds like you were one of their best pilots."

Garrett looked out the window and watched the storm for a few moments before responding. Heaviness seemed to set in, and he took a deep breath before looking back at Nikki.

"Well, the truth is, I lost someone close to me out there. It should've never happened, and I know it wasn't my fault, but I felt responsible. I just couldn't get my head back into the job after the accident. I would just freeze up as soon as I got back into the cockpit. I was a mess."

Stunned, Nikki didn't know how to react. "Oh, my God, I had no idea. I'm so sorry. That must have been awful for you."

"I know I shouldn't still be beating myself up, but I still feel so guilty. He was my best friend, really more like a brother, and I couldn't protect him out there. I couldn't save him. There was nothing I could do; it was just a freak thing."

"Do you mind if I ask what happened?" Nikki asked. "You don't have to tell me if you don't want too, but I'm a good listener."

"No, it's alright. I don't mind telling you. I actually appreciate you even asking." Garrett gulped down the rest of his coffee.

"It happened back when I was stationed up in Alaska. Early in 2004, we received a distress call from a twenty-eight-foot fishing vessel taking on water about twenty miles southwest of Dutch Harbor. My team was quickly launched to search for the boat, but the weather conditions were terrible. Visibility was way down due to a severe snowstorm, the seas were running at about twenty to twenty-five feet, and the wind was blowing at thirty knots with gusts up to sixty-five knots. We knew there were three crew members on board and all were wearing survival suits. When we finally got out to the site, the tall rigging was swaying violently from side to side and the back of the boat was already underwater.

"I tried several times to get the rescue basket close enough to the three people on the boat. The seas were just so rough that I couldn't get it within reach with everything else we were dealing with. My buddy Jay, our rescue swimmer, convinced them that their only chance was to jump into the water and swim to the rescue basket, where

I could put it down safely. It was a huge risk, but frankly the only chance they had.

"The first two off the boat were able to get to the basket and hoisted up safely into the aircraft. You can't imagine how relieved we all were as they came up. The third man, however, must've had a leak in his survival suit. When he jumped in, it immediately filled with water. After several attempts to get into the basket, it became apparent that he couldn't lift himself in with all that extra weight. He was exhausted and freezing, just clinging onto the outside of the basket for dear life. I knew hypothermia was likely setting in as well.

"I told Jay that he didn't have to go down if he felt that the conditions were too dangerous, but he insisted. He knew he was the only chance this guy had. Within seconds, Jay was in the water swimming to assist him. It must have been like swimming in a washing machine, the water was so turbulent. He was the best, though, and managed to get the guy into the rescue basket, even as bad as it was down there. Once we got the third guy up to safety, all we had to do was bring Jay back up.

"That's when the swells picked up. We were being slammed by extremely gusty winds, and Jay got dragged through an enormous sea swell. There must have been some debris from the boat we hadn't seen in the water, because something struck and killed him instantly."

Garrett looked into Nikki's eyes. "He was just hanging there from the rope, not moving, not screaming, just hanging there. I still can't get that image out of my head to this day. Every time I think about it, I can't believe it actually happened. I was in shock for days afterwards. I couldn't let it go. I replayed that day over and over in my head and kept thinking what if? You know, what if the guy didn't have a leak in his suit? What if I had convinced Jay not to go down? What if I'd seen whatever hit him sooner and could move him out of the way? What if? What if?" Garrett was so choked up he could hardly speak.

Nikki reached over and took Garrett's hand into hers. "It sounds like you guys did everything right. Like you said, it was just one of those freak things that no one could prepare for or prevent. I'm so sad for you that this happened. It sounds like your friend was the real deal, and you know that his life meant something to everyone he rescued. He was a hero, Garrett. That's an amazing thing to leave behind. I'm just so sorry that you had to go through that." Nikki gave him a minute to compose himself.

"Yeah, it really sucked. He was such a great guy. The best. And you want to know the worst part? He was planning to get married later that year. We had literally just been talking about hiking the Grand Canyon and rafting down the Colorado River for his bachelor party weekend. It all just seemed so pointless after that. I couldn't focus, and I couldn't do my job the way I needed to. So that's basically why I got out. Once my time was up, I decided that I wasn't going to reenlist. I knew I needed to take some time away and get my head screwed back on straight. That's when I went back to my hometown of Boulder for a bit. I needed my family and friends around me, and my plan was to take the summer to figure out what I wanted to do next."

Trying to lighten the mood she asked, "Were you glad you went back home? It must have been nice to be around your friends again. Sometimes a change of scenery can work wonders."

Garrett nodded. "Yeah, at first I was. I knew I needed to take myself out of life-and-death situations for a while and get away from all that stress. I just wanted to chill out and be low-key for a bit. My plan was to sleep in late every day and bartend at night at a restaurant I had worked at back in high school. Good plan, right? But no. That's not my luck, I guess. Get this…just a month after I got back home, I almost died!" Garrett laughed and added, "Can you friggin' believe that? Talk about irony. After risking my life every damn day without even a scratch in the Guard, it's in Boulder that I almost kick it!"

"What? What do you mean? How is that possible?" Nikki saw his mood had lightened so she knew he wasn't upset by whatever happened, but she couldn't possibly imagine what was coming next. "What the heck happened?"

Garrett leaned in with his eyes wide and started moving his hands around as if painting the picture for her.

"So, like I was saying, I'm home about a month and begin noticing that being so lazy every day for the last several weeks is starting to give me a nasty beer gut. Real attractive, right? I'd totally stopped running and lifting, which I'd pretty much been doing every single day in the Guard, and I was feeling overall like a big, gross, unmotivated blob. Think Pillsbury Dough Boy, if you will. I decide that I need to do something about it and pronto. On a complete whim, I decide to enter a triathlon scheduled for that same morning. No training. No prep. Just going to show up and do it. I still had my old bike in the garage, so I brushed off the spider webs, put some air into the tires, grabbed my bathing suit and running shoes, and off I go."

"Are you crazy?" Nikki chuckled. "Wouldn't it have been a better idea to maybe just go for a run first? Ya know, start off a little less ambitious? So what happened, tough guy? Did you almost drown trying to do the swim or something?"

"No! Believe it or not, I actually kicked ass on the swim! I think I was in the top ten at that point, if you can imagine that. I was crushing it. I did pretty well on the bike leg, too. I kept up in the front of the pack through sheer will and stubbornness, cuz let me tell you, my legs were screaming! But, like a total idiot, I hadn't eaten much that morning, and I only brought one water bottle with me. I was dying of hunger and thirst most of the ride, but I just kept filling up my bottle whenever I hit a water station. I ended up skipping the final one, though, because stopping that frequently was taking up too much time, and I figured I'd be able to get something to eat and drink before the start of the run. Sometimes they have those energy bars and stuff that the athletes can just grab."

"So you almost died of dehydration?" Nikki guessed. "Did you keel over, too weak to go on?" She put her hand to her throat, tipped her head back, and whispered, "I'm so thirsty" with a scratchy voice as if she, too, was dying of thirst.

"Oh ha, ha! Very funny! No wise guy, actually I was able to get some water at the start of the run. But I think it was too late. I was already feeling parched and still had the full six-plus mile run in front of me. Of course, being in the baking sun wasn't helping either. It was really hot that day, and my calf muscles started cramping up pretty badly a couple miles in."

"Alright then, that must be it! You almost died from severe leg cramps, right?" She stood and started hobbling around, grabbing her calf muscle and pleading, "Help me! Help me! My legs, it's my legs!" She knew she looked ridiculous, but she loved the fact that Garrett was laughing hysterically and giving her his undivided attention.

"I'm getting there, spaz!" he retorted as he stood and gently grasped her arm, leading her back to the chair. He smiled, giving her a little squeeze as she sat back down. "It might be easier for me to just show you," he added, moving a few chairs out of the way so he had some open space to replay the events for her.

"So, as I was saying," he started, then giving her a sarcastic smirk added, "before being so rudely interrupted, I might point out, is that my legs were cramping up so badly, I had to find a spot to sit down. I was pissed because I was still doing surprisingly well up until this point, way better than I was expecting, and I knew this was going to kill my time. Anyway, as I came up around a corner, I saw a tree in the distance with some fallen branches and even better, some shade!"

Garrett pulled a chair over and pretended it was a tree branch. "I make my way over and sit on one of these big rotted branches that must have fallen years before, but I don't care, because it is a lot cooler under there. This way I have a chance to give my legs a break. I'm sitting there literally about ten seconds when bam! I feel a sharp prick, like what I thought was a thorn, pinch me right in the ass cheek! Then bam! It happens again!" He jumped up out of the chair holding his behind with both hands. "I jump up at rocket speed and quickly realize that I've just unknowingly sat directly on top of a huge bee hive that had, of course, made its nest in the branch. Yup! Just my luck!"

Nikki laughed hysterically. "Oh, you've got to be kidding! So I think I've got it then! You must be allergic to bees!"

"Well, that's just the thing!" Garrett answered. "I didn't think I was, but apparently, after talking to my parents, I found out I'd never been stung as a child, so no one ever knew! Well, guess what, everyone? I am! Evidently, I'm deathly allergic to bee stings. So I get stung at least these two times and immediately know something is drastically wrong. All of a sudden, I start breaking out with these red blotchy hives, and I'm itching like crazy all over my body. My throat starts tightening up, and I'm having a lot of trouble breathing. Of course, I start to panic. I'm not even on the course anymore and know I have to get back so I have a chance of someone seeing me. The last thing I remember is starting to feel dizzy and seeing that tunnel vision, like when everything is just about to go dark. I'm pretty sure I was just about to pass out."

"Oh, my God! I can't believe this! Then what happened? Someone must have seen you, right? You were in anaphylactic shock, Garrett. There's no way you should have survived out there!" Nikki's paramedic knowledge was kicking in, and she was mentally going over many scenarios to figure out how he could've survived. "You literally would have only seconds to survive without help! You know this, right?"

Garrett nodded in agreement, eager to continue acting out his tale. "Exactly! That's the crazy part about this story. So there I am, apparently lying on the ground just a few yards off the course, probably thinking this is it for me, when all of a sudden I'm jolted back into reality by an EpiPen needle being blasted into my quad! I'm in such a fog at this point, I'm not even sure where I am or what's happening. This young woman is kneeling beside me asking if I can hear her, letting me know that she just gave me a shot of epinephrine and that someone has gone for help. The next thing I remember, the first-aid volunteers are right by my side, helping me up and getting me into a jeep and over to the medical tent. Everything was so surreal, as if I were in a dream state." He stood and made his way back over to Nikki and took a deep breath in.

"I kept looking around and asking if anyone had seen the woman, but no one had any idea who I was talking about. I never did see that woman again, not that I even remembered what she looked like. My eyes were so swollen it wouldn't have mattered anyway, I suppose. I wanted to try to find her after the race, but I was stuck getting IV fluids for a couple hours, and by the time they were willing to let me go, most people had already left. Crazy, huh?"

Nikki was shocked by how lucky Garrett was. By all accounts, he should've died. "Do you know how lucky you were that whoever that was even had an EpiPen on her? And what about the fact that she was close enough behind you in the race to get to you in time? And then knew when she saw you that you were having an allergic reaction and needed that specific shot?" Nikki's voice escalated at each realization. "Garrett, that really was a miracle. You're lucky to be alive. Like, insanely lucky."

"I know, I know. It truly was a miracle. I still think about that woman all the time. I wish I could've thanked her in person. She was literally my guardian angel that day, and I have no idea who she was or even where she might be. I wish I knew. I really wish I knew." Garrett's attention drifted back toward the window. Outside, the winds were howling, and freezing rain continued to ping off the glass.

17

It was almost show time. Jillian felt nervous energy gripping her stomach as she positioned her bike at the transition site for the Boulder Triathlon. This was her first Olympic-distance qualifying race and she was excited it was in her new hometown. She wanted to make sure she had everything set up perfectly and ready to go. She visualized the events in her head, mapping out each entry and exit point, and methodically going back over her strategy. She knew the course inside and out, as she'd already been training on it diligently for months.

Besides being a challenging race, she still couldn't believe how beautiful the scenery was along the route. It was nothing like she could've imagined living back in Boston. She took a deep breath and felt grateful to be living in such an incredible place, doing what she loved.

"Make sure your dry clothes and whatever else you may need for the ride are kept on a towel or in a marked bag near your bikes, people! Your race number should be clearly labeled on everything, including both arms and legs!" One of the race coordinators was shouting reminders through a megaphone to all athletes within earshot.

Jillian took a moment to double check her gear. The tire pressure on her bike was perfect. She confirmed she had a spare tube and a

CO2 pump in her repair bag, just in case. Her cycling shoes were already clipped into the pedals and fastened with elastic bands to keep them in place. Her helmet was unfastened; sunglasses were inside and ready to go.

"Check, check, and check!" she said out loud. Luckily, she was early enough to grab a spot at the end of one of the racks, so she'd be able to find her bike quickly once she came out of the water. Every precious second was going to count in this competition and she knew it.

She double-checked that her biking shorts, tank top, electrolyte drinks, and gel replenishment packs were on hand for the ride. She confirmed that she had her dry socks rolled up and tucked into her shoes, along with a dry towel and sun block. Based on the weather report, she knew the sun and heat were going to be factors during the bike ride and run segments later on. Finally, she made sure that she'd packed her EpiPen and that it was already snug inside her waist pack. With her bee allergy, she didn't go anywhere without it.

Since she'd already dropped her running gear off at the second transition site, she was mentally going over that list, too. Running shoes, another pair of dry socks, extra replenishment drinks, and a dry towel was all she would need. She'd been practicing her transitions and was confident she'd be able to do them quickly during the race. Everything had been mapped out, labeled, and positioned to be easy to find. She felt ready. The only thing missing was her race partner.

Jillian wished Gabby was there with her, especially when she found herself standing all alone by her bike. For months, they'd spent countless hours training in preparation for the race. They'd even created a countdown chart on the calendar that hung in their kitchen. Each night leading up to the race, they'd excitedly check off that day's box with a big red X. Being each other's good luck charms since their early races back in college had been the norm. Jillian felt a little exposed not having her friend by her side.

With just three days to go, Gabby had accidently tripped on their front stairs and badly twisted her ankle. It swelled up like a purple and blue balloon, and just like that, she was out of the race. The timing couldn't have been worse. Both of them had worked so hard, and Jillian felt awful that Gabby wouldn't have a chance to compete, especially since she was on track to beat her personal best.

Before leaving the apartment earlier that morning, Jillian tried to cheer her up. "Don't worry, Gabs," she said. "I'll do my best to represent both of us out there today. Next race, I'll bubble wrap you for the entire month beforehand." Gabby managed a laugh, but Jillian knew she was devastated.

"Just promise to call me as soon as you finish. Hopefully you'll have some good news about qualifying!" Gabby replied, trying her best not to show her disappointment. "I know you can do it, Jill. This is your race today. I may be stuck here on the couch with this stupid boot on my foot, but I'll be rooting for you all the way!"

Jillian silently vowed not to let Gabby down.

"Okay, athletes, please make your way over to the vans," the commanding voice crackled through the megaphone. "The drivers will be taking you up to the starting gates at the reservoir in the next few minutes. Race time is twenty minutes from now!"

Jillian's stomach tightened again with anticipation. She knew the start time would be there in a blink. She boarded one of the vans and looked around, trying to determine who her competition may be. There were quite a few other women whom she calculated would be in her age division. After carefully sizing them up, she felt even more confident about her chances in the race. She'd faced many of them in other local races and knew she could beat them.

Today is my day, she encouraged herself. She knew she was in the best shape of her life, and her goal was to place in the top three. That would earn her a coveted qualifier spot at the regional competition the following month. This was the dream she'd been working toward.

As they filtered out of the vans, Jillian snaked her way up to the front of the pack. When the race director gave the five-minute warning, she put her swim cap and goggles on and looked straight ahead. All she focused on was the reservoir directly in front of her. She visualized the course she planned to swim and did her best to block out the muddled conversations and nervous chatter around her. There were hundreds of participants gathered in the small space, all waiting for the same sound.

Bang!

The starting gun fired, and Jillian sprinted into the water, bumping elbows with a few of the athletes next to her. All were vying for a front position. Luckily, her quickness off the gun allowed her to be one of the first in the water. She started swimming as soon as the water got deep enough and quickly found a strategic spot with a comfortable pace, drafting behind one of the leaders.

This was perfect positioning. She calmed down and got her breathing under control. She was exactly where she needed to be. By being out in front of the masses, she was able to maximize her swim stroke, rather than being thrashed around and losing precious seconds. She felt almost giddy with how well the race had started off.

Okay, Jill, she reminded herself, *just swim like you trained for. Conserve the energy you'll need for the bike ride and run later. Stay in your head, and stay completely focused.*

She felt her hands cut through the cool water with each stroke. Her legs remained strong with each flutter kick and she was feeling optimistic.

The swim component consisted of a fifteen-hundred meter loop. Having been able to train there the last couple of months was proving to be hugely advantageous. Not only was she confident of the course, but she also knew she was right on track with the timing.

I bet I'm making excellent time right now, she thought, proud that she hadn't had to pull her head up to check direction more than a couple times. *This feels pretty fast, so just remember to maintain a slow and steady breathing rate.* All of her conditioning was paying off. When she passed the halfway point, she was still feeling invigorated. Confident she'd held her position toward the front of the pack, she concentrated solely on her stroke and maintaining her pace.

Once close enough to the shore and only knee deep, Jillian pulled herself up and out of the water. She ran onto the beach area and quickly glanced at the time clock as she headed toward her bike. It matched her watch, which she couldn't believe. "No way!" she shouted aloud. She'd just finished the swim leg in 20:34 and it looked like she was the third woman out of the water. This was her fastest swim time at that distance to date. She felt a wave of excitement, realizing she was actually on pace to accomplish her goal. She knew she needed to stay focused.

Stripping off her goggles and swim cap, Jillian hustled over to her bike and tossed them onto the ground. The gear she'd previously laid out on her towel was sitting just as she left it and in the order she needed it. She grabbed her bike shorts and tank top and hurried into the unoccupied changing tent right next to her station. There she quickly peeled off her wet bathing suit, slipped into the pair of dry shorts, and pulled on the fresh top. Once back at her bike, she sat down, finished drying off her damp feet, and took the carefully rolled-up socks out of the cycling shoes.

"Thank you, Gabby. You're one brilliant babe!" she sung out to no one in particular as she sped through this step. Gabby had taught her this time-saving trick long ago. Having socks prepped like this allowed her to quickly roll them onto her feet, especially when they were still a little sticky from the moisture.

She put her sunglasses on, then the helmet. This way, the glasses were secure under the straps and wouldn't get knocked off when she pulled the helmet off at the next transition site, another handy tip she'd picked up from her training group. She double-checked that the helmet strap was buckled securely before getting on her bike so she wouldn't get disqualified. Stupid mistakes had prevented even the best athletes from winning, and she wasn't about to let that happen to her. Finally, she clipped on her hydration waist-belt, which was loaded with two electrolyte drinks, the energy gels, and her EpiPen.

Grabbing her bike off the rack, she passed the mounting line before getting on. There, she slipped her feet into her cycling shoes and put the bike into a lower gear so it would be easier to pedal when starting out. *Fuel,* she reminded herself, and she quickly ingested one of the gel packs. The raspberry-flavored goop easily slid down the back of her throat, replacing the carbohydrates she'd just burned during the swim. A quick check of her watch showed that this transition took just over three minutes. Since she'd allowed for three and a half, she was elated. She sipped off one of the electrolyte drinks and looked up at the breathtaking Flatiron mountain range in front of her.

Time to start pedaling, Jill, she said to herself, pushing down hard with her right foot to set the bike in motion.

Jillian had kept her position as the third-place woman as the bike leg began. Several men had either started ahead of her or passed her as she navigated the first ten miles. Since the etiquette when biking is to ride single file, except when passing, she easily counted each rider as they went by. To this point, only men had passed her, but she remembered seeing a few women right on her tail coming out of the last transition. She stayed mindful that some of her competitors might try to overtake her within the next several miles.

Just stick to the plan, she thought as she settled into a comfortable rhythm. *You have just over twenty-three total miles of rolling hills to conquer. You have trained this course, and you are ready for this. Watch the road, watch your pace, hydrate often, and watch your back.*

Jillian found that saying these specific tips in a steady cadence kept her calm and focused. These were the same words she'd heard from her coaches, from Gabby, and from her other training partners over the past few months. Now it was her turn to follow through.

After a few more miles were behind her, she reached down to grab another sip off her water bottle. She also checked her watch and saw that her time was still good. She kept herself motivated by telling herself that she was riding at her fastest time, and if there were other women who could do better than her, then so be it. She knew she was tough, and she'd done all she could to prepare. If anyone tried to challenge her now, she was definitely ready to put up one heck of a fight.

The mantra in her head was working well so far. She maintained her confidence until just after mile marker eighteen when she hit a hill with a surprising headwind. Her legs were already aching and tired, and with the challenging climb and the wind in her face, her pace inevitably slowed. A few male riders who'd been close behind started to pull ahead on her left. She allowed them to pass easily, knowing that they, too, were jockeying for a better position. With the steady incline proving difficult for some, the strategic riders who'd been conserving their energy were now taking the opportunity to make their move to pass.

I wish my legs weren't feeling quite so friggin' heavy, Jillian thought as yet another male rider pulled ahead.

A few moments later, she heard a woman's voice coming from behind. The rider yelled, "Passing on your left," as she overtook Jill. Pangs of disappointment flashed through as Jillian watched her competitor easily glide up the hill.

"Damn it!" Jillian yelled. She lifted herself out of the saddle, pushing down harder on the pedals in an attempt to power up the seemingly never-ending hill. She knew she couldn't afford to let the woman get too far ahead. "C'mon, Jill!" she chanted over and over to help push through the pain. She knew that as long as she could keep the woman in her sights, she'd remain determined to take back her position at some point along the course.

Whatever you do, she convinced herself, *don't you dare quit now!*

Jillian eagerly peeled opened another gel pack and sucked it down to get a much-needed energy boost. It also helped calm her down, and she was able to refocus on her mission. *Keep your pace, just keep your pace and you'll be fine. Don't try to catch up now or you will hit a wall on the run. Stick to the training plan. You so got this,* she reminded herself. She took a deep breath and slowed back down to her planned and practiced pace until she finally made it over the crest of the hill.

"Woo hoo!" she howled at the top of her lungs, celebrating that the hardest part of the ride was now behind her. She gulped down the rest of the water from one of her bottles and allowed her legs to recover a bit. She knew from practice that this course was mostly a downhill ride over the next couple of miles.

As she approached the final cycling check point and water station, she knew she had less than two miles to go. She glanced at her spare water bottle to make sure she had enough fluids left. There were only a few ounces remaining. The heat was making her sweat more than she'd prepared for, but she calculated she could wait and fill both bottles again at the transition site for the run.

This might be the best chance to reclaim my position in third place for my division, and I cannot risk losing even a few seconds off my time making an unnecessary stop, Jillian rationalized. *I hope I don't regret it,* she thought as she whizzed by the water stop. She gave a quick wave to the cheering volunteers manning the station.

When the final transition area came into sight, she downshifted, upped her cadence, and started spinning to loosen her legs in preparation for the run. When she was just a few yards away, she slowed down and released her buckles so she could slip out of her bike shoes a little faster. She quickly scanned to find the location of the dismount line and wasted no time getting there. The time clock read 1:13:56. Jillian was astonished that she had just beaten her goal by two full minutes, especially with the trouble she had on the hill. She double checked her own watch again to make sure she was in sync, and got over to the spot where her running gear was laid out. As quickly as she could, she lifted her bike into the waiting rack and grabbed her running shoes.

Although still a bit wobbly after coming off the bike, she was energized knowing that she was crushing her calculated times.

With this pace, she thought, *I'll still be able to finish in the top three if I can just get my position back soon. I'll definitely have to maintain my planned running pace of seven-minute miles. If I can do that for all six miles, I should be able to clinch a top spot.*

Jillian scanned the transition area and saw the woman who had passed her earlier on the hill. She was just starting on her run. After pulling on her running shoes, Jillian hastily filled her water bottles and checked her waist pack one last time. She was confident that she would be the faster runner and headed toward the course, ready to prove it to herself.

Her legs felt painfully heavy as she took her first few strides. Most of the blood in her body had settled into her quads due to the heavy demands she'd just placed on them while biking. She sensed them slightly trembling beneath her and felt a tad off balance. Taking a sip from her water bottle, a bead of sweat dripped into and stung her eye. "Ugh!" she grunted and angrily wiped the sweat off her forehead with her fingertips, flicking it onto the ground beside her. "Damn it!" she grunted again, feeling the burning sensation linger. The heat from the sun was way more intense than she'd prepared for, and it was making her nervous.

After a few more strides, she realized it was taking longer than expected to bounce back, and she was getting discouraged by how sluggish she still felt. "Let's go, down there!" she yelled, looking down at her legs. "I need you to work your magic, like right now, please!" she pleaded. Just then, she was passed by an older man who gave her a strange look as he went by. Jillian laughed nervously, quickly realizing what that must have looked like from behind.

"I was talking to my legs!" she shouted. She could feel her face get even more flushed than it already was from the embarrassment. The surge of adrenaline from her humiliation gave her an unexpected boost. Ironically, she was able to find her groove again and gradually picked up the pace. When she realized she was less than seventy yards behind her rival, she completely forgot the heat and the pain and focused on what lied ahead.

When Jillian passed the two-mile marker, she looked down at her watch. The first two miles had taken just about fourteen and a half minutes. She knew she needed to make up the lost time due to her slow start. The woman she was trying to pass had just turned a corner, and Jillian decided that once she had her in her sights again, she'd make a move to pass. She'd been steadily closing the gap and was now only about forty yards behind. She calculated that if she could get far enough ahead within the next mile, there would be no way she wouldn't place in the top three.

Rounding the corner, Jillian was ready to pick up the pace. Just as she started to speed up, something moving in her peripheral vision caught her eye. She looked to her right, where she saw what appeared to be a man crawling along the ground several yards off the course. She was forced to make a split-second decision: stay the course and hope that he was alright, assume that someone else would help, or stop running and sacrifice what was likely going to be a qualifying time for the race.

Her instinct told her something was quite dire. She knew in her gut that she needed to check things out to see exactly how bad things were. She sprinted over to where the man was lying face-down and shook him firmly on the shoulder.

"Are you okay? Sir, can you hear me?" she shouted. She continued to poke at him, but got no response. She cautiously walked to his left side, put both hands on his right arm, and turned him over so he was face up. She immediately started yelling and waving her arms frantically, trying to get the attention of other runners who were just turning the corner and coming into view.

"Someone go get help! Call 911! This man is having an allergic reaction and needs medical attention right now! Hurry! Someone please hurry!"

Jillian looked back down at the young man. His face was red and blotchy, and he was wheezing, visibly struggling for air. His eyes and lips were swollen shut with hives, and he was obviously in anaphylactic shock.

Wasting no time, Jillian zipped open her waist pack and grabbed the EpiPen. She yanked off the safety cap to expose the needle and forcefully stabbed the device directly into the man's outer thigh. The shock caused him to flinch and he let out a labored moan. Using a circular motion, Jillian rubbed the injection site for several seconds, helping to disperse the administered epinephrine. She kept her fingers on his pulse and was relieved when she sensed his heart rate starting to creep back up. As he began taking deeper breaths, she knew the medicine was working.

Other runners started to gather around the scene. "The medical staff is on their way! They should be here any second!" one of the runners shouted toward Jillian. He hurried over to join the group. "You should get back to the race, you were way out front. Really, you should just go!" He pointed back toward the course. "I'll stay here until the medics come get him. You'd better get going so you still have a chance!"

Jillian wasn't sure what she should do. She'd already been delayed several minutes. She hesitated for a moment, but then saw a jeep pulling around the corner and heading straight toward the group. The medical symbols on the sides and front of the vehicle assured her that he would be in good hands.

"Yeah, okay! Here, let them know I gave him this!" she said, shoving the empty EpiPen cartridge into his hand. "Thank you!" she shouted as she sprinted back onto the course.

The time clock for the run read forty-seven minutes as Jillian crossed the finish line. Five women in her age division had come in ahead of her. She knew she hadn't earned a qualifying spot in the regional triathlon.

Exhausted from the effort, she was even more heartbroken with the outcome. As her eyes welled with tears, she slowly made her way back to the transition sites and gathered her gear. Her head was pounding from a combination of the intense heat, utter disappointment, probable dehydration, and stress.

"Hey, it's me," she said to Gabby as she finally pulled out of the parking lot. "No, and I can't talk about it now, I'm just so disappointed." Jillian's voice cracked through the phone as she started to sob. "It's so hot out here, Gabby. I just need to take a cold shower. Then I'm going to be in my bed with the air conditioner on and the lights off for the rest of the day. I have a throbbing headache and my skull literally feels like it's going to explode. The only way I'm getting rid of this pain is to sleep it off. I should be home in about fifteen minutes. You're not going to fucking believe what happened to me again. I'll tell you more about it when I get home."

18

D r. Ethan Carter stood over the surgical scrub sink and carefully brushed under each fingernail, along each side of every finger, between his fingers, then the back and front of each hand. The warm water slowly washed away the foamy antimicrobial suds. By habit, he counted out the two full minutes required for this part of the sterilization process. He kept his hands higher than his elbows and moved up his arm to the next section to be sterilized, methodically repeating the process. He'd prepped for surgery hundreds of times as a resident in his young career, but now that he was a full-fledged neurosurgeon, everything felt even more critical. He needed everything to go just right.

"I'm glad you both are joining me on the procedure today," Dr. Louis Prentice, Ethan's mentor and the head of neurosurgery, broke the silence. Ethan, along with Ben Hastings, one of the third-year residents, were both scrubbing in for that morning's surgery. Ethan would be assisting with the surgery, while Ben planned to observe.

A couple hours earlier they'd all met to go over the scheduled procedure one last time. Dr. Prentice summarized the plan in full detail. "The patient, a professional basketball player, is going to be undergoing surgery to remove a benign tumor that has caused blindness in his left eye. Ethan, you'll take over once I've removed the tumor. Your aim is to reduce the swelling on the optic nerve in order to speed up his recovery time. Ben, you'll be strictly observing today. As you both know, this surgery will determine the fate of the man's career, and it needs to be flawless." Both men nodded in agreement.

Ethan felt privileged to have been called on. He was confident that he'd not only be able to help salvage the man's eyesight, but also reduce the standard recovery time significantly. Following the success of his latest article published in the *Journal of Neurosurgery*, requests for his surgical assistance had been even more frequent. Everyone was hearing about the young hot-shot doctor who'd perfected a technique that was changing the face of certain types of surgery. Ethan knew his skills were ideal for this procedure.

"So glad to have you aboard, young man," Dr. Prentice had reminded him earlier that morning. He patted him on the shoulder as they all headed toward the surgical suites. Ethan had been recruited to come out east just a few months prior, at the beginning of the year. A brand new neurosurgical wing had just been completed at Boston Memorial, and Dr. Prentice, the former chairman of the Department of Neurosciences at the California School of Medicine, was hired to lead the team.

"Glad to be here, sir. Thank you again for bringing me out," Ethan answered. He knew he had distinguished himself back in California as being not only the youngest, but also one of the best and brightest students to come through the neurosurgery program there in quite some time. Dr. Prentice told him he'd been watching his progress closely and had kept Ethan in mind when it was time to hire his own staff.

While still in medical school, Ethan pioneered a technique that was less invasive and even more precise than what had currently been being done. The technique was saving lives because it reduced much of the swelling that often accompanied specific types of brain surgeries. Recovery times were shorter, and negative side-effects had been lessened considerably. The success of his methodology positioned him as a budding pioneer in the field, and Dr. Prentice told Ethan he wanted talent like this working with him in Boston. Ethan was honored to be asked and grateful for the opportunity.

Ethan finished washing his hands and forearms and leaned over to turn the water lever off with his elbow. "Paging Dr. Carter! Dr. Carter, please call extension 107, stat!" a voice blasted out over the intercom. He hesitated, knowing that picking up the phone would negate the sterilization procedure he'd just completed.

"Go ahead. You are the primary point surgeon on staff today. You should get that," Dr. Prentice instructed. Ethan dried his hands and quickly dialed the extension. He nodded as he listened and directed his attention toward Dr. Prentice. He carefully relayed the details of the emergency unfolding as the information was being given to him.

"There's a medi-flight in transit right now. The patient is stabilized, but in critical condition. Female, mid-thirties, with a probable head impact injury and possible compound fracture to the lower right leg. Vitals weak but holding, intubated, possible herniation of the brain." Ethan hung up and jumped into action.

"We need to prep the OR now!" he called out to the personnel in the area. "I'm calling imaging to be ready for an emergency CT scan. Let's move, people!" Ethan knew he would need to determine quickly if the woman sustained any fractures to her skull, if there was bleeding in the brain, if any blood clots had formed, or anything else that might impact what he did next.

"Ben, I want you to go with Dr. Carter," Dr. Prentice instructed. "You can learn something from him on this. I'll be able to handle the eye surgery on my own." Dr. Prentice ushered Ben toward the rest of the trauma team, who were gathering outside the operating suites awaiting further instructions. "Follow his lead on this and let me know if he needs me for anything."

Ethan, along with the rest of the trauma squad, prepared for the helicopter's arrival. They knew that every second counted. The winds and driving rain outside were most likely going to be problematic, and additional staff prepped for transfer from the incoming medical helicopter. The entire team hustled up to the rooftop entrance and waited for their cue. Within seconds they saw the approaching Medi-Vac helicopter. They grabbed their equipment, positioned themselves appropriately, and prepared for it to land.

Bam! The descending helicopter landed hard on the roof. A strong gust of wind had slammed it down, pounding it onto the cement landing pad. Several seconds passed before the critical care nurse and transport paramedic emerged from the side door, fighting against the wind and rain to make their way back to the clamshell doors. Once opened, they pulled out the occupied stretcher and extended the contractible legs.

The trauma team rushed onto the wet, icy landing pad to meet the incoming crew. All hands grabbed the rails of the stretcher, and together they wheeled the victim into the covered entrance. As they made their way down the ramps inside the building, the transport nurse called out the vitals.

The trauma team expertly took over control, disconnecting Medi-Vac's equipment and connecting their own. Both the in-flight EMT and nurse followed closely in case any other information was needed. Once they'd reached the surgical wing, the patient was rushed directly to imaging for a CT scan of her injured skull.

The large CT scanner sat idle and ready when the gurney rushed through the doors. The team carefully and methodically lifted the woman onto the narrow, motorized table that had been positioned to slide into the tunnel. Straps and pillows were gently placed to position her head and ensure that she stayed completely still. With great precision, the table was moved into the scanner so the process could begin.

Buzzing, clicking, and whirring noises quickly filled the room as the x-ray tube rotated. Each rotation yielded several thin cross-sectioned images of her head, slowly painting a clearer picture of Jillian's injury.

The radiologist pointed to the scans and explained, "As you can see here, a convex shape is clearly emerging from these images. Because its expansion stops here at the skull's sutures, where the dura mater is tightly attached to the skull, it's obvious that we're seeing the results of a hemorrhage."

Pointing to another spot on the scan, she continued, "Again, from another angle, we can tell it has pressed inward toward the brain here. The image is conclusive in my opinion. My diagnosis is that this woman has suffered a traumatic acute hematoma on the left fronto-temporal area. Based on my experience, I would conclude that immediate surgery will be needed or death is probable."

The scans confirmed what Ethan anticipated all along. He elaborated the findings to his team as they headed back toward the operating rooms. "A brain hemorrhage has occurred and is quite possibly still bleeding. Based on what we know about the nature of the accident, an epidural hematoma has formed on the left side of her head, most likely due to the impact it sustained when it slammed against the driver's side window of the car. Emergency surgery is necessary to remove the blood clot, stop the bleeding, and reduce the increasing intracranial pressure and swelling. Every minute that passes is potentially doing more damage to her brain."

Ethan again found himself scrubbing up in preparation for surgery. Waiting any longer could result in her death, and Ethan wasn't going to let that happen. He used the opportunity to mentor Ben, who was also scrubbing up and planned to be in the operating room during the procedure. "Okay, Ben, tell me what procedure this diagnosis requires, how you would proceed, and why. Be specific."

"Yes, sir. This diagnosis will require a craniotomy. We need to perform the removal of an epidural hematoma, which is a hemorrhage, from around the dura mater, the firm fibrous tissue covering the brain. Depending on the size and location, this blood clot could result in death by pushing the brain, causing it to herniate through the base of the skull."

"Yes, that's excellent," Ethan said. "Now, tell me the steps that I'll be following in chronological order with this surgery. Include the possible risks of each." Ethan started the third round of scrubbing his hands and arms.

Ben thought back to his studies, then elaborated, "The patient will be taken into the operating room and put to sleep under general anesthesia. Her head will be partially shaved to expose the area of operation. She'll then be placed in three fixation points using Mayfield head pins, which will keep her head perfectly still during the procedure. Using an antibiotic solution, the area where surgery is to be performed will be prepped and draped." Ben took a breath and looked over to Ethan, who'd just finished putting his surgical gloves on.

"Go on, what happens next?" Ethan prompted him to continue.

"Next, you'll make an incision and reflect the scalp over the area of the hematoma. You'll then use an air powered drill to make a hole in the skull. Finally, you'll add an attachment to cut open and remove a flap of skull. At that point, the hematoma should be clearly visible. You'll then remove it from the surface of the dura mater. Any open arteries or other visible bleeding points will be cauterized. Once that's complete, you'll then close and reposition the flap of skull as closely as possible, using titanium plates to hold the bone together." Ben paused and waited for Ethan's response.

"There's one more step we need to do before we completely close. What is it?" Ethan asked. Both men were now fully draped in their surgical gear and ready to head into the operating room. The patient had been brought in, and the anesthesiologist had begun sedation.

Ben thought for a moment before adding, "Yes, of course. A pressure monitor will be needed to be placed into the brain to allow the postoperative monitoring of pressure within the brain."

Ethan nodded and added, "What about risks? I wanted you to detail the risks associated with each phase."

"Well, there are always the general risks such as bleeding, infection, stroke, paralysis, and coma," Ben started. "With the anesthesia, there could be blood clots in the legs, a heart attack, or possibly even a reaction to the anesthetic. There's also the possibility that the surgery may not be able to remove the entire hematoma or stop all of the bleeding. It's possible that the scalp or bone won't heal post-operatively, there may be injury to the scalp from the Mayfield pins, and potentially we may see erosion of the plates used to close the skull through the skin after healing. There may be a need to do another surgery if there's residual pooling of blood or if the swelling can't be controlled as well. Oh, and if there's an injury to the brain itself, the results could include weakness, seizures, stroke, paralysis, coma, or even death." He finished and waited to see if he had remembered everything correctly.

Ethan nodded approvingly. "Well, we aren't going to let any of those things happen today, now are we?" he said and motioned Ben to follow him into the operating room.

Walking in, he was confident he'd perform the surgery flawlessly, and with his specialized technique he knew that the risks of permanent damage or side effects due to undue swelling would be minimal. He positioned himself in the spot he would perform the surgery and greeted the surgical team surrounding his patient, just as he did before every surgery.

Ethan looked each person in the eye for several seconds as he spoke. "Each of you in this room has dedicated your life to saving the lives of others. Thank you for your contribution and expertise here today. I'm proud to stand beside you and do the work that we're here to do. Now, let all of us put forth our best efforts." With that, he instructed his playlist of classical music to be turned on and focused his attention to the job in front of him: saving this woman's life.

19

"**Y**our father and I are incredibly proud of you, honey!" Ethan heard his mother approaching from behind and braced himself for the inevitable hug. She wrapped her arms around her only son and squeezed. It wasn't quite the all-out bear squeeze he was used to, so he assumed she was at least being mindful not to crush his gown. It was high school graduation day after all, and not only had he finished two full years ahead of schedule, but he was also receiving the award for academic excellence. He waited for her to release him, then finished positioning the honors cords around his neck and adjusted his cap in the hallway mirror.

"Thanks, Mom. I appreciate that. How does this look?" he asked, worried that he had pinned it with the mortar board on crookedly. He tucked a few loose strands of blond hair under the cap and took a step back so he could get a better angle of the full getup.

"Oh Ethan, you look so handsome! I still can't believe you're actually graduating today." She crossed her hands over her chest in pride. "Did you ever think this would be happening so soon?"

"Well, that's kinda been the plan since last year, so yeah. I'd better be getting my diploma after all that!" He laughed, shaking his head as he walked over and grabbed a pen from the kitchen counter.

He scratched something out onto a note card he was holding, then scribbled over it and added something else.

"Putting the final touches on your valedictorian speech, are you?" she inquired. "You'll probably be delivering that in just over an hour. Are you sure you don't want to practice your speech before we get there?" Ethan pretended he didn't hear her as he finished making his notes.

When they were on their way out to the driveway, she asked again. "One last chance, Mr. Valedictorian. You know I'm dying to hear what you're going to say. Reciting it ahead of time might be a good way to ease any nervousness. You know the old adage: practice makes perfect. How about it?"

"Nice try, Mom, but you're going to have to wait just like everyone else. Don't worry, I won't tell any embarrassing stories from my childhood, and I promise I didn't forget to thank you and Dad!" Ethan winked at his mother, knowing how excited she was. He held her car door open as she got in, still beaming with pride. "And yes, I'm wearing clean underwear if that's what you were going to ask me next," he said with a mischievous smile.

After they found a spot in the crowded high school parking lot, Ethan gave his parents a quick hug, then ran ahead to catch up with a few friends. As they filed in, those in the graduating class made their way up to the chairs in the front of the auditorium. The graduates had been practicing for the commencement ceremony all week and easily found their spots, clearly labeled and arranged in alphabetical order.

Ethan had spent the last few nights thinking about and writing down what he planned to say during his speech. He was honored to be giving it, but he started to feel a little apprehensive as more and more people filled the room. He patted his pocket to make sure his note cards were within reach.

When Principal Walker finally started the commencement ceremony, Ethan found himself wiping sweat off his palms onto his graduation gown. He tried to pay attention to some of the other speakers, but found it difficult to focus on anything they were saying. He was anxious to get his speech over and done with.

Finally the principal announced, "Now I would like to introduce this year's valedictorian. He's a young man who has exemplified what it means to be both a student and a scholar. He has an unquenchable thirst for knowledge, an unstoppable drive for learning, and has completed all of his classes here at the AP or Honors level by the ripe old age of just sixteen. This makes him the youngest graduate we've had pass through these halls. We know he's going to do great things in the world. It's my absolute pleasure to introduce Ethan Carter!" Principal Walker looked toward Ethan as the crowd began clapping loudly. Ethan's heart raced as he made his way up to the podium and cleared his throat.

"Thank you, Principal Walker," he started, noting a slight crackle in his voice. He felt his face get a little flushed. "Greetings to everyone in this year's graduating class. Welcome to the parents, teachers, family, and friends who are all here today. I'm honored to be standing here before you." He began feeling a bit more confident. He took a deep breath and continued.

"To be honest, when I found out that I was going to be delivering the valedictorian speech here today, I wasn't sure what I should talk about. I didn't want to just come up here and talk about the same old thing you hear with lots of these types of speeches. Things like, 'Hard work will pay off' or, 'Life is short, so you need to follow your dreams' and, 'It's only possible to set yourself apart from everyone else through going the extra mile with unyielding determination.'

"It's not that I don't believe these sentiments are accurate…it's just that I think we have to be open to, and on the lookout for, a couple of other variables, too. What are these other variables, you might ask? Well, these may be things you don't necessarily even believe in, but they're forces that I know to be true based on my own personal experience. Specifically, I'm talking about taking advantage of two key things that can be rare, but also pivotal, in one's life. These two things are luck and opportunity." Ethan took another deep breath and scanned the crowd. He felt all eyes on him and caught his mother smiling out of the corner of his eye.

"For all intents and purposes, I shouldn't even be here in front of you today. The truth is that I should have died when I was just six years old. Most of you don't know this about me. But the fact is, I firmly believe that I came within just seconds from drowning in my cousin's pool one summer night, long ago. That's where my story should have ended. But I got lucky. You see, I do believe in luck.

"It was luck that the girl babysitting me that night happened to get up and check my room at that exact moment. It was luck that she thought to look outside for me, rather than assume I was just playing a silly hiding game like we'd been doing earlier that night. It was luck that she was a strong swimmer and reached me in time to get me pulled up and out of the water. It was luck that she knew, even at the young age of twelve, how to administer CPR and was able to clear my lungs and get me to breathe again." Ethan glanced toward his parents. He saw his mother wiping tears from her eyes.

"Now, this brings me to the second thing we need to be on the lookout for in life, which is opportunity. Because I've had this specific piece of luck in my life, I've also been given a tremendous opportunity to make the most of it. I've tried not to take this responsibility for granted. My parents, whom I'm so grateful to, have also encouraged me to not only recognize, but more importantly, to take advantage of many opportunities as they've crossed my path.

"As human beings, we often pass over opportunities or miss their significance completely because we assume that we'll always get another shot. Or we think that something even better will come along. I personally think this way of thinking is a huge mistake. Instead, I propose that you seize these opportunities the moment they present themselves, because the fact is, you may never get that second chance.

"I also think that the timing of how things happen in life is critical. Opportunities arise as a way for us to learn a valuable lesson, grow as a person, or make a real impact on our own life and the lives of those around us. Don't wait to take action! Don't wait to take advantage of an opportunity! Don't wait for something that you think will be better to come along, because in doing so, your whole life may very well pass you by."

Ethan felt his enthusiasm rising and could see the guests in the first few rows nodding in agreement. He waited a few moments before continuing to allow the crowd time to absorb what he was saying.

"Whenever I had a curiosity growing up, my parents would encourage me to explore whatever it was. As a young child, I took lessons twice a week in order to learn how to play the piano. In middle school, I went to weekend workshops at the technical college to learn about physics, astronomy, and robotics. Over our summer vacations in high school, I volunteered to help build houses for communities in need and spent time at the local food pantry unloading boxes and stocking shelves. Along my path, I've looked at each of these opportunities as a way to increase my knowledge, to learn more about all kinds of people, and be open to what each of us can individually contribute to the greater good. Ultimately, these experiences helped me figure out where my place in this world would be."

Ethan paused and flipped to the final note card in the stack. It was slightly crumpled and still a bit damp from sweat. He looked back up and tried to make eye contact with several people in the crowd.

"So, where has all this led me, you may wonder? Well, to tell you the truth, it led me right back to the edge of that swimming pool that summer night ten years ago. Without a little luck, none of these experiences, nor me even being here today, would have been possible. I think of all the people in this world who may never get the kind of luck I had that night. For most, there's unfortunately nothing I personally will be able to do about that. But what I'm hoping is that by taking advantage of the tremendous opportunity I've been given to go to the California School of Medicine on a full scholarship, I'll be able to make a real difference in the future. Maybe, just maybe, I can be that little piece of luck for many, many people who will someday cross my path."

Ethan paused, took a breath, then continued. "I encourage all of you graduating today to pay attention to the luck that will come into your lives. You may not know when or how it will come, nor even what it might look like, but have faith that it will. The key is to be ready to take advantage of that luck and be open to whatever opportunity it brings along with it. Remember, the two always go hand-in-hand.

"Through your actions, each and every one of you has the power to send a ripple throughout the entire world. One that could bring positive change, new opportunities, and maybe even a little luck to someone else in need. Know that we're all connected, and that with hard work, determination, and a little luck, you really can realize your dreams and reach your true potential. Maybe you'll even surprise yourself in the process.

"In closing, I want to say thank you to my parents, to the teachers who have encouraged and challenged me along the way, to my classmates and friends, and finally, to that girl who saved my life and was my little piece of luck that pivotal night so long ago. Wherever you are, whoever you may be, may luck always be on your side!"

20

For the first time in as long as she could remember, Barbara Richards was completely on her own. She sat in lonely silence at the kitchen table, watching the freezing rain pelt against the window. Little clumps of ice had started to gather and slowly slide down the pane, forming a row of slush on the outer sill. A steady draft leaked in from the weathered window casing, sending a shiver down her back. She trembled and pulled her cardigan sweater snugly around her shoulders. Nothing could beat back the chill.

Oh, my poor Joe, what have you done? What have you gone and done? It's so empty now, she thought as the forceful winds whipped against the outside of the house.

Barbara stared blankly at the several stacks of dishes on the table. Jillian had neatly piled them there just a few hours before. They'd been carefully washed and dried, and were now waiting to be returned to their rightful place in the cabinets. Glancing toward the stove, she let out a deep sigh. The blackened, smoke-stained ceiling and cabinets reminded her of the mess that had been made.

Just a few nights prior, Joe, her husband of thirty-six years, decided to wake up around midnight to cook an egg. Forgetting that he'd turned the burner on, and after adding way too much oil to the pan, he wandered out of the kitchen and into the living room. He turned on the television, rested his head on the couch pillow, and immediately fell asleep.

The piercing sound of wailing smoke detectors forced Barbara, dazed and disoriented, from their bedroom. Coming into the kitchen, she was confronted by a wall of heavy smoke and flames shooting up from a frying pan on the stove. Quick thinking, and her experience working in a restaurant kitchen years earlier, prevented what could have been a catastrophic disaster.

Barbara grabbed a lid and immediately covered the fire. Using a towel to cover her hand, she turned off the heat and gently moved the pan away from the red-hot burner to the other side of the stove. Since flames were still poking out through the cracks in the lid, she grabbed a box of baking powder from the cabinet next to the stove and sprinkled it over the pan, quickly dousing any remaining flames. When she found Joe sound asleep on the couch, she covered him with blankets and opened the windows and doors to allow the thick smoke to clear.

She knew the time had come.

Ring-ring. Ring-ring. The phone had been beckoning for several moments before the sound snapped Barbara back into the present. She got up and slowly made her way across the kitchen to the phone hanging on the opposite wall.

"Hello?" she answered, worried that something had happened to Joe in the nursing home.

"Hello, is this Mrs. Richards at 118 Fitzwilliam Street?" Barbara didn't recognize the voice, but could sense the authority and urgency in the caller's tone.

"Yes, who is this please?" she answered cautiously.

"Mrs. Richards, this is Sergeant Nelson from the Massachusetts State Police. I need to verify some information with you. Do you have a daughter named Jillian Richards who may have rented a silver-colored Ford Fusion recently?"

Barbara hesitated a moment to think.

"Yes, I do have a daughter named Jillian, and I know she rented a car while she was here in Boston," she answered. "I'm not sure what kind of car it was, to be honest. I do think it was silver colored, though. Or maybe grey. I cannot say for sure, they all look so similar these days. She's not here right now, I'm sorry. She left hours ago to go back to Boulder, Colorado. Has something happened to her rental car? Did she leave something behind?"

There was a pause before the officer started speaking again.

"I'm sorry to have to tell you this, Mrs. Richards, but we believe your daughter has been in a serious car accident. She has been taken by medical helicopter to Boston Memorial. The car we believe she was driving collided with a tractor-trailer on the highway, then caught fire. The driver was removed from the vehicle before the fire started, thankfully, but we think her identification must have still been inside. We used the partial license plate to track down her information through the car rental agency. That's why it has taken so long to contact you."

Barbara fell to her knees.

Sergeant Nelson, apparently awaiting a response, prompted, "Ma'am? Are you still there? Are you okay?"

Barbara felt as if she had been kicked in the stomach, unable to speak.

"Mrs. Richards, would you like me to send another officer to come pick you up and take you to Boston Memorial?"

It took all of her strength to say, "Yes, please. I will be waiting," before hanging up the phone, slumping down onto the kitchen floor, and sobbing uncontrollably.

21

Daniel Bryant called Garrett Holden's cell phone as he pulled into the underground parking garage at Boston Memorial in his Mercedes S600. It had been roughly two and a half hours since he found out about the accident with the helicopter. With the conditions as bad as they were, it had taken him this long to navigate his way safely into the city. Luckily, the freezing rain had stopped, and he only had to contend with strong winds for the last couple miles.

"Hey, Garrett, it's me. I'm here in the parking garage, finally. Sorry you've all had to wait so long. The roads are still slick, and I hit a few detours rerouting us around accidents. Crews are just putting salt down on the roads now. Anyway, I'm on my way up. Where should I meet you?" Daniel was anxious to see how much damage the Medi-Vac helicopter sustained with the hard landing. With his investment of just over six million dollars, he needed to find out how bad things were and what this might end up costing to repair. He stepped into the elevator and pushed the button to take him up to the hospital lobby.

"Hey, no problem, Mr. Bryant. We've been killing time in the cafeteria. I'll meet you right at the bank of elevators in the lobby, then we can head up to the roof together. I should be there in two minutes," Garrett answered.

As soon as he hung up with Daniel, Garrett looked back to Nikki. "Hey, want to join me up on the roof with boss-man? He just got here and wants to check out the damage to the helicopter. I guess he still can't get a hold of his maintenance director, but the guy knows a lot about these machines in his own right. You up for a little field trip?" Garrett flashed his handsome smile and hoped he could entice Nikki to come along.

"Sure, sounds like a plan," she said, grabbing her coat. "My calendar just happens to be free the rest of the day, lucky for you!"

Daniel greeted Garrett and Nikki as they came into the lobby. "Hi, guys, thanks again for sticking around for so long. It's probably better that you weren't out on those roads anyway. It took forever to get here! So, Garrett, tell me what you think we are looking at with the bird up on the roof. How much damage are we talking?"

Garrett knew that even though Daniel was well versed on all aspects of the helicopter, he trusted his expertise and wanted his opinion before they headed up.

"Honestly, with the winds and rain as bad as they were, I didn't get a chance to inspect it as much as I would have liked to when we first landed. Now that the rain has stopped, I'm glad we'll have some time to check it out together. I should be able to give you a much better idea of what we are looking at," Garrett answered. He led them all over to a separate bank of elevators that would take them to the roof.

As they rode up, Daniel made eye contact with Nikki and smiled. "How did the patient do today?" he asked, seeming genuinely concerned. "It must have been quite a mission with the conditions the way they were!"

Nikki nodded in agreement. "It was unbelievable. By far the worst conditions I've ever experienced or flown in. You should've seen this guy, though," she said, patting Garrett on his shoulder. "He was amazing out there. Handled everything like a pro. If it weren't for his mad flying skills, I think her chances of making it would be pretty slim. As a matter of fact, I think she's still in surgery now. Unfortunately, she sustained a pretty serious head injury."

Daniel looked at Garrett, who flushed, then shifted his weight from one leg to the other and redirected the attention back to Daniel with a compliment.

"She was lucky that Medi-Vac was even an option. Honestly, if she pulls through, having that incredible piece of machinery is what saved her life. What you're doing with this company is quite remarkable, sir. I'm just sorry that landing caught me by surprise. That's never happened to me before."

Daniel felt humbled by the praise. "Well, I'm just glad that we all could be there for her when she needed us most. And I'm not upset about any damage, Garrett. I'm the one who put you in this situation, and I know that your priority was saving her life, which is what it sounds like you've helped to do. That's why we're all doing this, right?"

Daniel noticed Nikki subtly nudge Garrett and wink. He knew they both must be feeling relieved to hear him say this. When the elevator doors opened, they made their way to the rooftop entrance.

"Okay, Captain, let's see what we've got with our H145," Daniel said as he led the way over to the Airbus helicopter. Garrett followed closely, obviously ready to start his detailed inspection of the aircraft, as well as explain what all the lit up sensors meant.

Garrett opened the cockpit door and invited Daniel to sit beside him in the adjacent seat.

"The main indicators are showing that we experienced a mast moment exceedance. I also heard the accompanying gong indicator with the landing, so I'm confident that's what happened."

"Oh, I see." Daniel nodded. "I've heard of that happening before. Can you explain for me in layman's terms what that means?"

"Yeah, of course. With a rigid rotor system like the one Airbus has, a hard landing is capable of transmitting high bending forces to the main rotor shaft. That's the main bar that comes up through the top of the helicopter and attaches to the rotor blades. In this case, it sensed too much deflection with the force of the landing, so the alarm and sensors went off."

"Okay, that makes sense," Daniel acknowledged. "What does that mean as far as repairs that will be needed?"

"Well, first we're going to have to determine what percentage was reached with this incident. There are certain levels that can be tolerated, which would still allow us to fly. Once we know that number, protocol will indicate where, when, and if it needs to be addressed right now."

"What about all these other lit sensors? Are they showing additional damage?" Daniel asked, pointing to the many illuminated buttons on the control panel.

"No, those just need to be reset. I don't think any of the electrical systems were affected by the impact because everything was still working. All those sensors are still showing operational, even after that landing. So right now I think we should hop back out and evaluate any external damage," Garrett advised. "There could be things that the sensors didn't pick up." Both he and Daniel got out so he could begin his walk around the helicopter.

"I'm going to visually inspect the main landing gear, the main rotor, and, of course, the airframe structure. I will also check to see if there are any blades rubbing on the Fenestron shrouded tail rotor, which can happen with hard landings. If I see anything, I will point it out to you," Garrett confirmed. Daniel gave him an approving nod.

"In the meantime, Nikki, if you could please take pictures as I go through, it might be helpful to have a record of this," Garrett continued. Nikki took out her phone, selected the camera icon, and gladly followed, snapping several shots.

Garrett explained what he was doing as he methodically checked the fuselage for any cracks, distortions, or fluid leaks. He meticulously inspected the rotors to see if they'd been damaged or bent. Inch by inch, he combed over the entire structure looking for any sheared rivets, buckling, or splits along the frame. He checked and double checked to make sure he'd inspected every component carefully and thoroughly.

When he finished, he looked to Daniel and smiled. "Well, boss, it looks like I have some good news for you. First of all, be thankful Airbus built in the energy-absorbing safety feature to this model. Because of that, the fuselage, seats, and skid landing gear all look fine. The hydraulic system seems to be perfectly intact, fluid levels all look good, and all the electrical sensors are still showing clear after the reset. It appears that the only real issue was with the mast moment."

Garrett walked to the front of the helicopter and looked again. "As far as I can tell, there are no other structural issues whatsoever. I'm confident I'll be able to fly this back to the hangar, even with the incident we experienced. I suggest we wait a while longer, just to make sure the storm completely passes. We'll need to get the maintenance director to do his inspection before it can be dispatched again, of course. He could potentially find something I missed, but I think we're in pretty good shape, considering."

Nikki's phone rang. It was Liz, calling with some news about their patient.

"That was Liz," she told the men after she hung up. "She's been with the trauma nurses since we got here. It sounds like our patient is going to be coming out of surgery soon. She asked if I would go sit with her in the waiting area until we can find out the prognosis. If it's alright with you guys, I'm going to head down now to keep her company. Are you all set up here for now?"

"Yes, of course, Nikki, you should go down," Daniel said. "Thank you for your excellent effort today. I'm lucky to have such a caring and brave team on my staff." He motioned to Garrett as well. "You're welcome to accompany her if you'd like. I'm going to take a few more pictures for the insurance company, then I'll join you. Like you said, it's best to wait for these winds to die down completely before you attempt to move the helicopter anyway. Go ahead, I'll see you both soon."

Garrett and Nikki made their way down to the third floor and followed the signs toward the neurosurgical wing. Liz was already there and waved to them as they came into the waiting area. "I'm glad you guys are here. I'm going to run down to the caf to grab a quick bite with the other nurses. None of us have eaten all day. I'll be back up in a few. Do you mind waiting here until I get back?"

Nikki shook her head. "No, not at all. You go eat," she answered. "We'll stay right here until we can get a status. I'll text you if I hear anything." They found a place to sit in the empty room and turned their attention to the television hanging against the sterile blue wall in front of them. The meteorologist on the news channel was giving another update on the weather.

"I'm glad to see this storm is finally moving out," Nikki mumbled. She let out a yawn, then rested her head on Garrett's sturdy shoulder and closed her tired eyes.

"Yeah, they're saying it's pretty much died down at this point," Garrett answered. "Do you want to fly back with me when it's time to bring the helicopter back?"

He got no reply. Nikki had already drifted off to sleep.

22

"**M**ae Roberts?" the emergency room nurse called out. She peeked out from behind the door of the triage area and scanned the area. The waiting room was overcrowded and noisy, filled with restless patients waiting to be seen. Mae acknowledged her by raising her hand and did her best to lift herself up and out of the uncomfortable chair she'd been sitting in for the past several hours. Her hips and lower back had tightened up due to the long wait, and as she stood, she cringed and buckled over in agony.

"Ohhh," she groaned. Another painful spasm hit, sending sharp, shooting pains into her legs. She grabbed the chair's arm behind her to prevent falling.

"Just wait right there," the nurse shouted when she realized Mae was having trouble. She quickly brought a wheelchair over.

"Is that a little better?" she asked, helping Mae sit back down slowly. "There you go, that should help. Lift your feet right onto these for me." She motioned and guided Mae's feet onto the footrest brackets. "That should be a little more comfortable," she said with a kind smile. Mae leaned back into the wheelchair.

"Yes, much better, thank you," Mae answered when she was finally able to take a deep breath. The nurse wheeled the chair into the office where there was some privacy. "I appreciate your help. That was quite embarrassing."

"Well, you are safe now. As I like to say, once you're in my office, welcome to the inner sanctum," the nurse said and winked at Mae. "My name is Jackie. I'm the triage nurse on duty today. Sorry the wait has been so long out there. Several of our staff couldn't make it in with the weather we were getting earlier and, of course, we've been slammed."

Mae saw Jackie look at her ripped stockings, crinkled clothing, and disheveled hair, and could only imagine what she must be thinking.

"So, what brings you here today, Mae?" Jackie asked.

Mae didn't know where to begin. She cautiously tried to shift her weight in the chair to get a little more comfortable, but every motion was painful. She placed her right hand behind her and rested it on her lower back.

"Well, I think I may have injured my back pulling an unconscious woman out of a car earlier today. It feels like I've pulled a muscle right through here, and I'm getting waves of pain down into both of my legs. I had one just now out in the waiting room."

The nurse wrote this information down. Pointing to a chart with faces on it ranging from a happy smiling face to a miserable crying face, she asked Mae to rate her pain.

"Right now sitting here, I'm about here." Mae pointed to an unhappy face in the middle of the chart. "But then when a spasm hits, I'm here." She pointed all the way over to the miserable crying face. "I've never experienced pain like this before. What do you think it could be?"

Jackie wrote something else and looked up. "Well, first of all, let's go back to the part where you pulled a woman from a car. Where and when did this happen?" Jackie looked up with a curious but kind expression.

Mae took a moment to compose her thoughts, then elaborated, "Well, I was on Interstate 93 several hours ago heading to pick up my granddaughter, Lucy, at Logan Airport. The weather was awful, of course, and a freak accident happened right in front of me. A car must have slid out and ended up slamming into a tractor-trailer. I was the first on the scene, if you can believe that! When I got over to the car, I tried to get the woman driver out as quickly as I could, but she was unconscious and had a leg pinned under the dashboard. From the blood I saw, I know she badly injured her head. I assume she crushed her leg as well. She was really stuck in there. I actually had to cut the seatbelt, wrap it around her, and pull her out, if you can imagine. We both fell backward and landed pretty hard on the ground. All of the weight came down on me. I could feel something happen near my tailbone right away. Luckily, I was able to get up and drag us both out of harm's way. It's a good thing, too, because as soon as I did, the car caught on fire! It was horrible!"

Obviously stunned, Jackie shook her head as she wrote everything that Mae was saying on her chart. "The woman wasn't moving, and I had to stay with her out in that awful storm until help could reach us. I had no choice but to sit on the hard, frozen highway for quite some time. Once I stood to get back to my car, these awful spasms started. I could hardly walk, they were so painful! The police officers on the scene were so busy, I didn't want to trouble them. So I decided to come straight here. Do you think you can help me, Jackie?" Mae asked, looking genuinely uncomfortable.

"Wow, Mae, that is an unbelievable story. I can't imagine how scary that must have been for you," Jackie said, placing the chart down on the desk. "It sounds like you probably injured yourself either pulling the woman out of the car or landing hard on the pavement. I'm going to put you in an exam room and have one of our doctors see you as soon as possible. Hopefully it's just a bad sprain or a bruise, and some muscle relaxers and ice will do the trick. Worst case, you may need to get an x-ray if they think you injured a disc. They should be able to help you figure this out." Jackie smiled reassuringly as she jotted down her final notes, then added, "By the way, what ended up happening with getting your granddaughter from the airport?"

"Oh, yes, thank you for asking," Mae answered. "Luckily, her flight was delayed due to the weather, and she never ended up leaving Boulder. That was fortunate for me! I was so worried she was all alone waiting for me at Logan Airport. That would have been just awful. I think we're going to try for a visit over her next school vacation or during the summer instead. Sometime when we know for sure the weather will be more cooperative!"

Jackie laughed as she wheeled Mae down the hall toward an exam room. "That sounds like a much better idea to me. Good luck to you, Mae. I hope everything works out with that back. And don't forget to tell your granddaughter that her grandmother was a superhero today!"

23

As Jackie headed back toward the waiting room in the emergency department, she saw an older woman come through the doors. The woman appeared to be panicking, frantically scouring the area. "Jillian? Jillian, are you in here?" she was shouting, scanning each row of chairs, still overflowing with those waiting to be seen. Jackie could see that the woman's erratic behavior was obviously making people uncomfortable.

"Excuse me, ma'am, how can I help you?" Jackie asked, approaching her quickly.

"It's my daughter, Jillian. I'm looking for her. The police officer who just dropped me off said she most likely came in through the emergency department. This is the emergency department, right? I just found out she was in a car crash a few hours ago. Have you seen her? I'm so worried. My poor Jillian."

Jackie gently put her hand on the woman's arm, guided her into the office, and sat her down. "What's your name, ma'am? I'll see what I can find out. Please just take a deep breath and try to calm down."

Barbara did what she was told. She took a deep breath and tried to compose herself. "I'm sorry. I'm really sorry. I didn't mean to upset anyone. My name is Barbara Richards. My daughter Jillian was in a terrible crash and brought to this hospital earlier today. That's all I was told."

Jackie took a moment to let this sink in.

"Was your daughter traveling on I-93 that you know of? I think I may have just heard about that accident myself." Jackie typed Jillian's name into her computer. "It will only take a moment for the status report to pop up on my screen. Give me a sec to scan through the details."

"Yes, of course!" Barbara answered emphatically. "She was on her way to the airport earlier this morning. What's the screen showing you? Do you know where she is now? I need to see her! When can I see her?"

"Well, from what I can see here, it looks like your daughter is currently in surgery upstairs. I'll put in a request for someone to escort you up there right away. Can I get you a glass of water, or do you need anything else while you wait?" Jackie asked.

"Surgery? What for? Does it say on your screen what's happened? Please tell me what's happened to my daughter!" Barbara pleaded. "Oh, my God. This can't be happening."

Knowing what Mae had just told her about the seriousness of the accident, Jackie thought it best not to let Barbara know any more of the details she'd heard. *Oh, this poor woman,* she thought. *She has no idea how bad this might be.*

"You look white as a sheet. I think it might be a good idea to have you lie down for a few minutes," Jackie suggested. "Here, let me help you." Jackie offered a hand and led Barbara over to a cot in the corner of the triage room.

"I understand how upsetting this must be," Jackie said. "I don't have any of the specifics for you right now, I'm sorry. I promise I'll have you brought up to where she is as soon as possible. When you get up there, ask to speak with a doctor directly. They'll be able to let you know exactly what's going on."

Jackie had Barbara rest in the triage area until the escort could come for her. With it being so busy, it took close to twenty-five minutes for someone to come down. As Jackie watched Barbara heading up to the neurosurgical wing, she wondered if she should let Mae know that the mother of the woman she'd helped earlier was there in the hospital. She processed a few more patients, so by the time her shift was over, another hour had already gone by. Jackie handed off all the active paperwork to the nurse who came in to relieve her, grabbed her things, and headed toward the exam rooms. She was hoping Mae hadn't left yet.

"Hello again, Jackie!" Mae greeted her when she saw her poke her head into the exam room. She'd just finished being treated. "What are you doing back down here? Did I forget something in your office?"

Jackie smiled. "No, Mae, I just wanted to check in on you. What did the doctor say about your back?" Mae had just finished putting her coat on and was holding a small piece of paper.

"You were right! The doctor said I most likely sprained my lower back pulling the woman out of the car. He wrote me a prescription for some muscle relaxers. The ibuprofen they already gave me is helping a lot, and they say I should be fine in just a few days. I'll probably be getting a lovely bruise on my tailbone to show off, too. Thank goodness it wasn't anything worse than that!"

"Yes, thank goodness!" Jackie responded, then hesitated, still debating if she should share the information she had. She rationalized that she would want to know if it were her, so she decided to just blurt it out.

"Mae, I thought you should know something." She paused again. "I thought you should know that the woman who you pulled from the car today is here, up in surgery, and her mother just arrived at the hospital a short time ago. From what you said, you may have been one of the last people to see her daughter. I just thought that if it were me, I might have some questions about my daughter and about the accident, especially if things don't go well. I hate to say it that way, but do you know what I mean?" Jackie was thinking she probably broke all kinds of privacy laws, but it felt like something she needed to do.

"Oh, heavens." Mae sounded surprised. "Well, I guess it didn't even occur to me that the woman from the accident would be brought here as well. Yes, yes, of course, I know what you mean. I would want to talk to someone who was actually there at the accident, too. Someone who actually saw and helped my daughter. I definitely know what you're saying." Mae paused for a second, apparently deep in thought, then asked, "What do you think I should do? Should I see if I can find her? Where would I even look?"

"Neurosurgery is on the third floor. If you take a left off the elevators and walk a short distance down the corridor, you'll see the waiting area. I can't give you any more information about the patient, but I think it's safe to say that if you decided to venture up there, things would naturally fall into place." Jackie offered up an encouraging smile.

"Okay then, I guess I'll be on my way. My kids have been calling me for the last few hours wondering if I was ever coming back home! I'm glad the storm has finally cleared out. Be safe getting home, Mae, and good luck with your back." Jackie turned and headed down the hallway toward the exit.

Mae finished gathering her things from the exam room and slowly walked down the hallway, which led her to the large bank of elevators in the main lobby. She was cautious not to make any quick movements that might trigger another spasm. As she approached the elevators, a well-dressed middle-aged man with slightly windswept hair looked over, acknowledging Mae. He held the open elevator door and waited for her to get in.

"Thank you for waiting so patiently for me. That was very kind." Mae smiled, feeling a bit embarrassed by how she must look. "I guess chivalry isn't dead after all!"

"You're quite welcome, and that's nice to hear. It's truly my pleasure. Which floor would you like today?" the gentleman asked.

"Third floor please. Thank you." Mae was anxious to get upstairs so she could sit down and rest her back. She was worried it would spasm again at any moment. She watched the man push the button, lighting up the number three. The elevator doors closed, and Mae felt the upward momentum.

"That's where I'm headed, too," the man responded.

"You look so familiar to me," Mae said, looking more closely at his features now. "Have we met before? I feel like I know you from somewhere."

He chuckled, his face lighting up by her reaction.

"My name is Daniel Bryant. I don't think we've met, but it's nice to meet you now." He reached over and shook Mae's hand. Mae was positive she'd seen him before, but couldn't quite place where.

"Well, either you have an identical twin somewhere, or I've definitely seen you before. I never forget a face," Mae added with a smile.

"You may recognize me from a few local commercials I've been on recently. I run a few businesses in the Boston area," Daniel offered. "Could that be it?"

Mae nodded, positive now that's where she'd seen him. "Yes, yes! I knew I'd seen you before. It must have been on TV. Channel five, right? Well, congratulations to you. That must be very exciting."

When the elevator doors opened, they both turned left and started down the hall toward the waiting area.

"Are you visiting someone in neurosurgery today?" Daniel asked. He politely walked alongside at her slow-moving pace.

"I'm not really sure," Mae answered. "It's a bit of a complicated story, but I guess I'm just coming up to see if I can offer any support to the family of a car crash victim from an accident that occurred earlier today. I don't know them personally, but I happened to be there at the crash scene. I suppose I thought I might be able to help in some way. That must sound a bit odd to you, I'm sure."

"No, actually that sounds rather kind," Daniel answered. "This may be a complete coincidence, but was the victim brought here by Medi-Vac that you know of?"

Mae nodded. "Yes, she was, as a matter of fact. It was quite the ordeal seeing that helicopter in action this morning. Everyone was moving so quickly, I could hardly keep up. How do you know about that? Were you there, too?"

"No, I wasn't there, but I work with Medi-Vac, the company that owns that helicopter. I heard about what happened and wanted to come offer my help, too. I'm just glad they could be of service today. With the weather we had earlier, it must have been pretty scary for everyone involved."

"Well, ain't that the truth! It was so hectic, and the woman wasn't in very good condition when they brought her here, unfortunately. I'm praying the doctors doing the surgery are able to save her life. She was still so young. Such a tragedy."

As they entered the waiting area, Mae found her way over to a row of empty chairs. "If you'll excuse me, I need to sit for a bit. I can feel my back starting to tighten again."

"Yes, of course," Daniel replied. "I completely understand."

Mae chose a seat against the back wall, grateful for the chance to rest.

Daniel walked over to greet Garrett and Nikki, whom he saw was sound asleep with her head against Garrett's shoulder. "Any news?" Daniel whispered when Garrett looked up.

"No. Still nothing yet. I think that might be the victim's mother talking with her doctor, though." Garrett motioned his head toward a small conference room with glass panels adjoining the waiting area. "She's been in there with him for just a few minutes."

A few moments of silence passed while they watched the woman and the doctor speaking behind the privacy of the glass. The woman was nodding at each word the doctor spoke, and they could see she had a deeply concerned look.

"Did you finish getting what you needed on the roof?" Garrett turned and quietly asked Daniel. "Do you think we took enough pictures for the insurance company?"

"Yeah, I think so. The storm has finally moved out, too, so once we're done here, I think you'll be okay to fly it back if you're up for that. Thanks again for all of your help today. You handled everything like a real pro. I knew you would," Daniel said as he patted Garrett on the back. "I know the damage could've been much worse, and I appreciate having such a seasoned pilot flying for me."

Daniel glanced around the room and noticed a Keurig machine on a table against the back wall where Mae was resting. He could almost taste how good it would be as he got up, walked over, and made two cups of steaming hot coffee. He took a few steps over to where Mae was sitting and graciously offered her one as he sat beside her.

"Thank you, I sure could use it," Mae said, taking the hot cup into her hands. She lifted the lid and gently blew the steam away. "Boy, that smells good," she said. "I didn't realize how much I needed this until just now," she added, taking a small sip. As they sat and made small talk, Daniel felt grateful for the moment of peace.

"Is that the woman's family you were just speaking with?" Mae asked him after a few moments.

"Oh, no. Those are more folks from Medi-Vac. Looks like there are a few of us here today who are all worried about the same person. Hopefully we'll hear something soon."

Several minutes later, the doctor stood up and opened the door of the small conference room. The noise of the clicking handle broke the dead silence of the room, and Nikki was startled awake. Without hesitation, she jumped up from her chair and approached the doctor, quickly reading his name tag.

"Hi, Dr. Carter is it? We're the medical team that brought the patient with the head injury here earlier today. Is there any news about her condition that you can share?" she asked.

"Oh? Hello." The doctor seemed startled for a moment, apparently surprised by the group before him. "I'm afraid I can't share any details about the patient to nonfamily members at this time, I'm sorry. I assume you are the paramedic?" he asked Nikki.

"Yes," Nikki responded. "And this is the pilot." She motioned to Garrett as he stood and walked over to join her. "And that is the owner of Medi-Vac." She pointed across the room to Daniel. "And, well, I'm not exactly sure who you are?" Nikki looked toward Mae, who was attempting to stand next to Daniel.

"This is Mae, the woman who pulled the victim from the car at the accident site earlier today," Daniel answered for Mae. He helped her to her feet, and they moved to join the others.

"Well, I'm impressed that all of you have come here to wait on her behalf. I don't think I've ever seen anything quite like this before," Ethan said.

"I realize that you can't give us any of her personal information," Nikki said, "but we were hoping for some fragment of encouraging news."

Ethan nodded. "I understand your concern. Although I can't give you any specific information, I can say that, without a doubt, each of you has made a real impact here today. Please know that your actions certainly changed the odds in her favor."

Nikki reached over and touched his arm. "I'm sure we can all say the same about you, Dr. Carter. We're all hoping for the best."

Complete silence descended over the little group. Nikki reflected on her role in the unknown woman's destiny, realizing that each person who stood beside her had also played an important part.

"Okay, guys," she said, finally breaking the solemn silence. "We should get back to work. I'm sure Dr. Carter has other patients he needs to get to. I'm going to go find Liz and we'll meet you all back at the hangar in an hour."

24

Barbara stared straight ahead as the elevator doors opened onto the third floor. A large sign with an arrow hung on the wall in front of her. "Neurosurgical Wing," written in big block letters, pointed to the left. She was having trouble making sense of any of this.

"This can't be happening," she muttered as she followed her escort down the empty corridor. "Jillian was just sitting on my couch a couple of hours ago. She should've been halfway back to Boulder by now. Jillian is supposed to be heading back to David as we speak. She has her race in a few days…she's worked so hard for it. There's no way she can miss it. This can't be right. I literally just gave her a hug this morning. She said she would come back in a couple weeks." Barbara was desperately searching for some reassurance that a grave mistake had been made.

"Please wait in here, ma'am," her escort said kindly as he led her into a private, glassed-in consultation room in the empty waiting area. "I'll let them know you're here and have someone come and speak with you as soon as possible. Good luck with your daughter. I wish you both the best."

With that, he let the receptionist know she was there and offered a small wave as he left. Barbara sat in stunned silence, staring blankly at the wall for quite some time before the doctor came in.

"You must be Mrs. Richards?" The doctor extended his hand as he walked into the small, private room and closed the heavy wooden door behind him. "I'm sure this has all come as a complete shock to you. I'm so sorry to have to be the bearer of such news."

"Yes, I'm still not sure what's happened to Jillian," she said. "I just can't believe any of this. I don't understand what's going on and what I'm doing here. Where is she now, and when can I see her?" Barbara was shaking and having difficulty getting the words out.

"I totally understand how upsetting this must be. I'm going to do my best to walk you through the surgery that we just completed on Jillian. I'm also going to explain exactly what is happening with her now and what we can expect going forward," he said.

"The first thing I want to let you know is that the surgery went as well as we could have hoped for. I'm confident that your daughter is going to pull through. That being said, it's important for you to know that she's still in critical condition, and the next several hours are going to be paramount in her recovery." He took a slip of paper from his folder and placed it on the table. Barbara could see the outline of a skull on the page. He unclipped a pen from his front pocket and began to sketch something out.

"We suspect your daughter suffered a blow to the frontotemporal region of her skull when her head hit the driver-side window in the car she was driving. We classify an injury of this nature as a traumatic brain injury. Luckily, there was no fracture; however, during the impact, her brain crashed back and forth inside her skull, causing some damage. A CT scan done upon her arrival here at the hospital earlier today showed evidence of bleeding and the formation of a hematoma." The doctor spoke slowly and clearly, carefully drawing out the location of the injuries he was describing.

Barbara watched and listened intently, trying to absorb everything he said. "What exactly does that mean?" she asked.

"I will try my best to explain in layman's terms," he continued. "After the initial impact occurs, the brain often undergoes a delayed trauma. This mainly consists of swelling, where it pushes itself against the skull, thereby reducing the flow of oxygen-rich blood. This is called secondary injury, which is quite often even more dangerous than the initial impact injury. In Jillian's case, we found that she had developed a hematoma, or a blood clot, that forms when a major blood vessel ruptures."

"So her brain is bleeding?" Barbara asked.

"Well, it was," the doctor answered. "You see, our body's natural reaction when we bleed is to clot, which is basically how we stop the bleed. The blood clot that Jillian had formed was rather large, and we feared that it was also compressing her brain."

Barbara felt numb, but she nodded. "How did you fix this?" she asked with tears welling in her eyes. "She's going to be okay, right? Please tell me she's going to be alright!"

The doctor nodded and continued to draw as he spoke.

"A clot that forms between the skull and the dura lining of the brain is called an epidural hematoma. This is what Jillian had. We had to do a procedure called a craniotomy to repair the bleeding vessels and to remove the large blood clot. Ultimately, we had to relieve the high intracranial pressure she was experiencing."

Barbara looked at the drawing with all the lines and shaded in areas. She saw where the doctor indicated he had to cut and drill. She visualized her daughter lying there all alone, getting plates and screws affixed to her skull. She suddenly felt like she was going to faint.

"I think I need a minute to process all of this. Can I take a minute please?" Barbara asked as she broke into a cold sweat. She wished her husband was by her side to help her digest the complicated information. She wished she had a shoulder to cry on or someone to share the burden with.

"I don't think I can do this by myself," she said out loud. "This is an awful lot to take in all at once."

"Yes, of course. Take your time. I realize this is a lot to process," the doctor answered softly. "We can take a break if you need to. I'm on your schedule now."

Barbara took several moments to compose herself. She commanded herself to shake any doubt out of her head. She was alone now, and she had to stay strong. She knew she had to be there for Jillian.

Once she was ready, she asked, as optimistically as she could, "So, are you saying that the surgery you just did has fixed all of this?"

He waited a beat, then answered cautiously, "The surgery we did was successful in removing the hematoma and stopping the bleed for now. Hopefully we were able to address the entire area affected. I also placed an intracranial pressure monitor within her skull to measure pressure inside her head. This will allow us to intervene quickly if the pressure becomes too high. This is what we need to be watching closely for the next several hours."

"Were there any other injuries?" Barbara asked, not knowing how much more she could handle.

"Yes, unfortunately there were. We also suspect that Jillian sustained a spiral fracture to her right tibia. She was pinned inside the car, and the force needed to pull her out possibly twisted the bone to the point of it breaking. Luckily the fracture appears stable, whereas the bone has maintained its alignment. We'll most likely not have to do surgery on the leg, but she'll definitely need a cast and possibly some physical therapy going forward."

"When will you know for sure how bad her leg is?" Barbara asked.

"For now, we have stabilized her leg with a long splint. We will plan to do another set of x-rays, but a cast will not go on for three to five days. That will allow any swelling to go down. Our main concern was the head injury, of course."

Barbara knew this was just the beginning, and that the ramifications would be huge. "My daughter is an elite athlete. Did you know that? She was getting ready to compete in an important triathlon. Do you think she'll ever be able to run or compete again?"

"I honestly wish I could tell you she'll be back to her old self in no time," the doctor answered. "But the truth is, we just don't know yet. It's still too early to predict what's going to happen with her recovery."

"So, what do we do now?" Barbara asked, wiping away tears.

"After surgery, Jillian was taken to the recovery room, where her vital signs are being monitored now. We're waiting for her to come out of the anesthesia. She's on a ventilator, which we'll keep in place until she's fully recovered from the anesthesia. Once she's awake, she'll be transferred to the neuroscience intensive care unit for close observation and monitoring. You should be prepared for her to be at this hospital for at least several days and possibly up to a week."

Barbara could feel the anguish in her expression. As the doctor stood, he asked, "Would you like to see her now? I can have you brought down to recovery if you think you're ready. I think it would be important for her to see you when she wakes up."

Barbara stood slowly, then spontaneously hugged Jillian's doctor tightly around his torso. As she did, tears started to stream down her cheeks. She started trembling as the realization of everything that had just happened hit her all at once.

"Thank you," she cried, sobbing into the shoulder of his hospital scrubs. "I'm so sorry to be falling apart like this, but thank you for saving my baby girl. I couldn't live without her. I'm so grateful for what you have done for her. Thank you so very much."

"It's going to be okay," he reassured her, breaking one of his arms free and wrapping it around her shoulder. "Your daughter has a long road in front of her, but I am confident she's going to be okay. I'll get one of the nurses to bring you down to see her in a few minutes. She's going to need you now more than ever."

25

SIX HOURS, ELEVEN MINUTES
AFTER IMPACT
BOSTON MEMORIAL HOSPITAL, BOSTON

Jillian lay in recovery, connected to a breathing ventilator with tubes and wires coming out from every angle. The machine's lights flashed and signaled her vitals with a steady cadence of beeps and clicks. Jillian's head, completely wrapped in bandages, had a catheter snaking out from a small hole in her skull. Her right leg was slightly flexed and wrapped in a splint. Her eyes were swollen and she was still, aside from an involuntarily twitch from time to time.

"Oh, Jillian! My poor baby!" Barbara gasped as she stepped into the recovery room, feeling her knees weaken. She didn't recognize the woman lying in the bed before her.

My Jillian is so young, so vibrant and so full of life, she thought. *This can't be her. Please don't let this be her.* She froze, unable to move past the doorway.

"Would you like to come in and sit by her side?" the critical care nurse asked. "It's okay. You can come in."

"Oh, hello. I'm so sorry, I didn't see you there. Yes, I think I would. Thank you." Barbara gathered her composure and hesitantly walked over. She sat in the chair closest to Jillian, scooting it a few inches until it touched the side of the metal bed frame. She reached up and placed Jillian's familiar hand in her own.

Looking at Jillian, Barbara said in a meek voice, "This is my daughter. I just found out about the accident she was in a short while ago. I think I'm still a bit shaken. I know this is her, but I just can't believe it. It's quite a shock to see her like this. My poor baby." Barbara paused for a moment, lifted Jillian's hand, and kissed the top of it. "When is she supposed to wake up?"

"It may be another half hour or so," the nurse said, looking up from the chart she was writing something on. "Some take more time than others to completely come out of the anesthesia, but I would say it won't be too much longer. She's been coming in and out for a bit now. You're welcome to stay here as long as you'd like." The nurse offered Barbara a slight, comforting smile. "When was the last time you saw your daughter?"

Tears welled in Barbara's eyes again as she thought back to that morning.

"It was only a few hours ago. She just left my house this morning to head to the airport. She was going back to her home in Boulder, Colorado. She lives there with her fiancé, David. I just had to call him to tell him the news. Poor David. He's in complete shock. Well, I guess it's safe to say we all are. I still can't believe this. My poor sweet child." Barbara was sobbing again.

The nurse walked over and put her hand on Barbara's shoulder. She reached over to a box of Kleenex on the nearby window ledge and handed her a bunch. "I know this must look just horrific to you right now, but I can assure you that your daughter is doing really well considering what she's been through. She made it through the surgery like a rock star, and her vitals all look spot on. I've been doing this for a long time, and my gut tells me that she's a fighter. I know that having you here is going to make all the difference when she wakes up."

This was just what Barbara needed to hear. She nodded as she wiped away tears. "She really is a rock star!" She managed a slight chuckle at the nurse's intuitive visual. "She's just such a special person, and I can't imagine losing her. She's too young and has so much to look forward to. She was supposed to be competing in a triathlon in a few days, then she was going to finish planning her wedding. It's just so unfair. She just has to pull through."

The nurse poured a cup of water into a spare Styrofoam cup and handed it to Barbara.

"I can tell that you love her very much. I bet she's an amazing person. I can already sense she's lucky to have you for her mother."

Barbara was grateful. "Oh, it's me who's the lucky one! If it weren't for Jillian, my dream of being a mother would never have come true. I got pregnant later in life. I was already thirty-eight, if you can believe it. Honestly, I didn't even know if I could have children, especially at that age. Back then it was almost unheard of to get pregnant that late in life. I sure did want one, though." Barbara looked back to Jillian and kissed the top of her hand again.

"I was so fortunate to meet her father when I did. And I was so thankful that he wanted a child, too. We were both lucky it happened so quickly, and we had this beautiful, healthy baby girl." Tears streamed down Barbara's face. She stood and leaned close to her daughter's head. She kissed the small patch of skin exposed on her cheek and whispered softly into her ear.

"Right, Jill? You're my beautiful baby girl, and I need you to fight like crazy to come back to me. Can you hear me, sweetheart? I need you to wake up and tell me that everything is going to be okay. You're still the strongest and bravest person I know, and I love you so very much. It's time to wake up now, my sweet girl."

Barbara sat back down in the chair and rested her head on the bed alongside Jillian's hand. She lay there for a long time, quietly wiping her tears, reflecting on all the precious memories she'd had with her daughter. She thought about how incredible it felt to hold Jillian as a baby, to smell the top of her little head, and to make her giggle uncontrollably. She remembered how proud she and Joe always were to watch Jillian compete in her sports, always pushing herself to be the best athlete she could be. She couldn't have been more excited to see her daughter find a home she loved in Boulder with a good man she was about to marry.

"Come back, Jill. It's time to come back now," Barbara whispered over and over as she rested with her eyes closed, still holding Jillian's hand. She drifted off to sleep.

"Barbara?" The nurse gently nudged her shoulder. "Barbara, it's time to get up now. Jillian has started to wake up. We're going to take her off the ventilator, so she can breathe on her own. She should be opening her eyes any second now. Maybe if you talk to her it will help."

Barbara stood and gently rubbed her daughter's hand while they removed the tube from her windpipe. "Hello, my beautiful. It's Mom. I'm right here by your side. It's time to wake up now, Jillian. Open your eyes; I'm right here with you." She and a few of the other intensive care nurses who'd come in to help stood by the bedside and waited. Several moments passed as Barbara continued to speak soothingly to Jillian, trying to entice her to react with the sound of a familiar voice.

"I'm…so…thirsty."

Jillian's lips moved so subtly and her voice was so soft that Barbara and the nurses weren't even sure they actually heard her speak.

"Jill, this is Mom. I'm right here, darling. What did you say? Can you open your eyes for me? Try to open your eyes if you can."

They saw a slight flutter, then another—then Jillian opened her eyes as much as she could through the swelling and puffiness. She looked at her mother for a few seconds, then as the recognition registered, smiled ever so slightly. Barbara felt a wave of relief wash over her.

"Mom? Where am I?" Jillian asked in a scratchy voice.

"We're in the hospital. You've been in a terrible accident, honey. They had to do surgery to remove a blood clot from your brain and stop it from bleeding. Try not to move right now. You have bandages on your head, and these IVs are keeping the medicines you need pumping into your body." Barbara pointed to the splint on Jillian's leg and added, "You also have a broken bone in your leg, so they put that in a splint. Just try to stay still until we can talk to your doctor."

Jillian stared blankly at her mother for several moments.

"Can I please talk to Dr. Carter now? I need to speak with him right away," Jillian whispered, still sounding a bit groggy from the medications. Barbara looked up at the nurse who was taking Jillian's blood pressure and pulse.

"I think she wants to talk with her doctor now. Is that a possibility?" Barbara asked, sitting on the edge of the bed to be closer to her daughter.

The nurse finished writing down her vitals on the chart and answered, "Yes, of course. I've already paged him to come down. It should only be a few more minutes."

Barbara slowly started to feed crushed ice chips into Jillian's mouth. This kept her occupied for a while, but after waiting for some time, Jillian got agitated. She struggled to put her words together, but managed to slowly let out, "Mom, why hasn't the doctor come to see me yet? What's taking him so long?"

"I'm not sure, honey," she answered. "I'm sure he'll be down shortly. Can I do anything to make you more comfortable right now?"

"No, but can you go let my friends know that I'm going to be okay? Please get them from the waiting room and have them come in. I'd like to see them now. I know they're all worried."

Barbara stared at her daughter in confusion.

"What was that, Jill? Who are you asking for, sweetheart? I'm not sure what you are asking me to do? Is someone here that you know?"

Jillian saw the nurse look at Barbara and shrug, shaking her head as if she too was confused by the request.

Jillian got impatient. Her voice took on an annoyed tone. "Mom, they're waiting for me right down the hall. Please go get them and bring them here. I need to thank them in person. They saved my life today. Please, Mom!"

Barbara stood and whispered to the nurse, "I'm not sure what's happening. She's insistent that I go get these people from the waiting area down the hall, but I have no idea who she's talking about."

She paused, then looked over at her daughter, who'd obviously heard everything she said. Jillian had a noticeable urgency in her eyes.

"Jill, I'll go down to the waiting area right now to see who's there. You just rest and stay calm right now. I promise I'll be right back." Barbara kissed her daughter on the forehead, left the room, and walked down the hallway back toward the receptionist.

As Barbara opened the door to the waiting room, she scanned the entire area. Rows of sterile, empty chairs and a few coffee tables littered with ripped magazines lined the walls. There was no one there except for an older Asian woman sitting in the corner chair reading an old *Good Housekeeping* magazine.

"Excuse me, have you been sitting in here for a while?" Barbara walked over and politely asked the woman.

"Yes, I've been here for over an hour already! My doctor got tied up in surgery and is running behind, I guess. Why do you ask? Have you been waiting a long time, too? They never get you in when they say they will. I think it's high time we start charging them for the time they make us wait. That would be something. Isn't our time worth just as much as theirs? This isn't the first time I've had to wait, either. Last time I was here, they made me wait an hour and a half, then they made me reschedule. Imagine that! You're welcome to wait here with me if you'd like. What time was your appointment supposed to be?"

Barbara wasn't quite sure how to respond to the flurry of questions and commentary.

"Oh, no, I don't have an appointment today. I'm looking for a few people my daughter thought might be in here waiting for her right now. I think she's confused, though. It's probably just the anesthesia wearing off. Anyway, thank you for your time. I hope you don't have to wait much longer." Barbara smiled and walked back through the door to the receptionist sitting just inside.

"By any chance have you seen anyone waiting in the lobby area earlier today? My daughter thought some of her friends, or perhaps some people who helped her earlier today, might have come to see her."

The receptionist just shook her head. "I don't think so. No one who wasn't a patient has been here since I just started my shift earlier this morning. I'm sorry. I wish I could help." Barbara nodded and walked back down to Jillian's room.

The nurses were busy taking Jillian's temperature and changing an IV bag when Barbara came back into the room.

"Did you see them, Mom?" Jillian asked as soon as she saw her mother. "Are they still waiting for me? Did you tell them to come down to see me now?"

"Honey, I'm so sorry to disappoint you, but no one was out there," she said softly as she sat back down beside her and caressed her cheek. "I'm not sure who you were expecting to be there. How did you say you knew these people again? Did you remember something about the accident?"

Just then the doctor walked in. "Well, look who's awake. It's nice to see you, Jillian." An older man with graying hair, glasses, and grey scrubs walked over to Jillian.

"My name is Dr. Rosen. I'm the surgeon who performed your procedure earlier today. Has anyone explained to you what happened yet?" the doctor asked as he took out a small flashlight and shined it into Jillian's eyes. "I apologize for the bright light here. I just need to check for pupil reaction."

Jillian was upset and confused. She turned her head away from the doctor and shot her mother a look of panic.

Seeing her reaction, the doctor continued, "I understand this might be upsetting. Just take your time. Can you tell me your full name? Do you know where you are right now?"

Annoyed, Jillian answered reluctantly. "My name is Jillian Richards. My mother told me that I'm in a hospital because of a bad car accident. I know I had surgery on my head. I'd like to speak with Dr. Carter now. Can someone please tell Dr. Carter I only want to speak with him?"

Dr. Rosen looked at the nurses still in the room. "Do we know who she's talking about?" he asked them, confused. He directed his attention back to Jillian. "Could that be one of your doctors from back home? We don't have anyone on staff here by that name that I know of, and I've been here for over twenty years."

Dr. Rosen looked to Barbara, who was now standing by Jillian's side, holding her hand and trying to comfort her. "I'm not sure who she's asking for. Maybe you can find out if she has another doctor by that name? Maybe it's her doctor from back home?"

"No!" Jillian croaked. "Dr. Carter is my surgeon! He's the one who fixed my head. He's in the waiting room right now with the others. You need to go get them! They saved me today, and they're all here waiting. Stop lying to me! Why are you all lying to me?" She started to weep.

"Jillian, you need to calm down. No one is lying to you sweetheart. We're all trying to help." Barbara looked to Dr. Rosen apologetically. "This really is not like her at all. I've never seen her get that upset so quickly."

Dr. Rosen turned back to the head nurse. "Please give her a sedative to calm her down. Let's allow her to rest a bit more before we continue with the neuro checks. Have you been able to have her move her arms and leg or do a strength assessment yet?"

The nurse shook her head as she added the medicine to Jillian's IV port. "Not yet, but she just woke up a short while ago. We'll do that after she has a chance to rest. In the meantime, we'll have the compression sleeve put on her left leg and get that started." The nurse looked to Barbara to explain. "They help prevent blood clots from forming by compressing the leg veins to keep blood moving."

Barbara watched her daughter drift off, then addressed the doctor directly. "Why was she asking for all of these strangers? She said they saved her today. I have no idea what she's talking about. Could this be a sign that she's going to have permanent brain damage? I'm worried about her behavior. Is this normal?"

Dr. Rosen paused before answering, carefully choosing his words. "It's hard to say what's normal or not normal with the human brain after it's sustained an injury like Jillian's. I can say that it's common for a person to be disoriented and confused after waking up from a procedure like she just underwent, not to mention the trauma she's experienced. It's also common for someone under anesthesia to experience hallucinations, which are a known side effect. They can be rather upsetting in some cases. If that's what these are, they should wear off fairly quickly. The fact that she knows her name and where she is leads me to believe that these delusions will be temporary."

"But what if it's not the medication talking?" Barbara pushed. "What if Jillian really believes these people exist? She seemed pretty adamant. I'm worried she's going to be angry with me if she thinks I'm keeping something from her."

"I understand your concern and wish I could give you a definitive answer. We're just not sure how much activity a brain experiences or records during a comatose phase like the one she was in. It's impossible to determine what thoughts, if any, she may have been having through all of this."

"Do you think the people she thought were here were just part of a dream?" Barbara asked.

"I suppose it's possible she was suspended in a dreamlike state for a while after the impact. Perhaps these people she thinks she's remembering are just part of her subconscious or imagination, or maybe they are a jumbled compilation of old memories. I've seen cases where a certain sound or smell at the time of the accident can work its way into a person's subconscious and create a memory of something that never really happened."

Barbara wasn't convinced and frowned.

"The human brain is a wonderful and mysterious thing in many ways," Dr. Rosen continued. "Quite a bit of its potential is still untapped, that's for sure. The important thing is that we were able to intervene when we did. I know you're worried, but we need to be patient. Let's wait to see what happens in a few hours, then a few days, then in a few weeks. Like we talked about, it's going to be a long road to recovery. My experience and instinct tell me she's going make a full recovery. It might just take some time."

"Well, I certainly hope your instinct is correct," Barbara answered. "I've never seen Jillian act that way before. What if we were just too late?"

"I'm confident that I was able to remove the entire clot and stop the bleed, and everything looked as good as could be expected when I closed her back up. The behavior you just saw and these imagined memories could very well be the result of the swelling, the brain's attempt to reconcile for lost time, or like I mentioned, a temporary side-effect from some of the medications we used for the anesthesia," Dr. Rosen offered. "In the meantime, let's focus on getting her breathing normalized and moving her arms and left leg as much as possible. I'll have the orthopedic doctor come take a look at her injured leg as soon as possible, and once she's in a cast we can get her up and moving. If it would make you feel better, I can also order a psych eval when she's up for it. We have a lot of work to do, and Jillian is going to need all the support she can get. Do you have the help you're going to need over the next several weeks to months?"

The doctor was kind and compassionate, and Barbara knew he was being upfront with her. "Yes, her fiancé is on his way now, and we'll both be here as long as she needs us to be. I know you're right, it's just going to be hard to be so patient when I'm this worried. Thank you again for everything you did for her today. I just want my Jillian back."

"We'll do everything possible to get your daughter back to her old self, I can promise you that. It's just going to take time." Dr. Rosen rested one hand on Jillian's arm and the other on Barbara's shoulder.

"The one thing you both have working in your favor is that your daughter is a survivor. She proved that to me today on the operating table. She just needs to keep that same tenacity and spirit to get through her recovery now."

"Yes, she certainly is tough," agreed Barbara. "From the looks of things, she's going to need to work harder than ever before. It's a good thing she knows what it takes to push herself. I'm sure none of us have any idea how challenging this is going to be."

"Try not to be too discouraged," Dr. Rosen answered. "We'll be with you every step of the way, and Jillian will have every possible resource available. If she is half as strong as you say she is, I know she will excel through her recovery."

"Okay, I'll have to trust you," Barbara said. "My daughter has brought good luck to so many people in her life already...hopefully the universe will send some of that back to her now."

26

The vaulted, red rock slates of the Flatiron mountain range stood valiantly in the distance. Overhead, white clouds slowly drifted by against the deep blue sky. It was race day, and the athletes were busily preparing their transition stations for the Boulder Invitational Triathlon. The excitement in the air was palpable.

"Jillian!" a familiar voice shouted from behind. "Hey, Jillian! I'm so glad I found you before the race started. I didn't know which transition site you'd be at." It was Gabby. She wheeled her bike over to where Jillian was standing and gave her an enormous hug.

"What a day, huh? Did you ever think you'd be back here so soon? I didn't even know if I'd be able to find you with all the people here. Can you believe how many athletes are competing?"

"I know, it's crazy!" Jillian said, hugging back, happy to see her friend. "I've already been here for a couple hours, believe it or not. I forgot how much work is involved in getting ready for these things!" she laughed.

Gabby placed her bike in an open rack next to where they were standing and began to position her gear on a towel. Jillian watched her friend carefully prepare each item she'd need when she came out of the water, just like she'd done herself so many times before.

"Hey, babe!" David called out as he approached Jillian and Gabby. He was holding something up in the air. "They just handed these to me. I think they want us to wear them today." He hugged Gabby hello, then kissed Jillian on her cheek. "Here, this one is yours," he said, handing Jillian a tightly rolled up tie-dyed t-shirt. She quickly unfolded it and showed the back to Gabby. In big bold letters the word "VOLUNTEER" was written across the top.

"I love it!" Jillian exclaimed, smiling at David. "The only trouble is, how am I ever going to get this tiny shirt to fit over this behemoth?" She grinned from ear to ear as she rubbed her very pregnant belly. "I think we might have to wait until this time next year for me to actually fit into this thing!"

"Well, hopefully you'll be wearing your own number again by that point, silly," David teased and kissed her forehead. "Isn't that what you've been working so hard toward all these months?"

"Yeah!" Gabby chimed in. "Plus, you still owe me doing this race together. First it was my ankle, then your accident, now the baby! We have to make it work one of these times!"

"Attention, athletes, please make your way to the waiting vans. They will bring you to the starting gates. Please double check your race numbers are visible. Race time is in twenty minutes," the race director's voice crackled over the megaphone. Gabby finished what she was doing and stood to give Jillian one last hug.

"Well, I'm certainly ready to have my training partner back full-time as soon as possible, so let's get moving on this whole delivery thing if you don't mind!" she teased.

"I'm working on it, believe me. I want this bowling ball out too, like yesterday!" Jillian said with a smirk. "We'll get to do this race together one of these years, I promise!"

"Now, wish me luck, you two!" Gabby commanded in a playful voice. She grabbed her swim cap and goggles and jogged over to join the others making their way onto the idling vans.

"We wish you lots of luck, Gabby!" David shouted after her.

"Just make sure you stay on the course and watch out for those nasty headwinds on the final hill!" Jillian yelled. "And stay away from any bees!" she added, waving as she watched the vans fill up with enthusiastic athletes.

"Are you doing okay?" David turned to her and asked, tucking a loose strand of hair behind her ear. Jillian leaned over and kissed him softly on his lips.

"Yes, I am, and thank you for asking. How could I not be okay? I have the most handsome husband, a beautiful baby girl coming to join our family in just a few weeks, all of this beauty surrounding me, and have regained just about all of my strength. What could be any better?"

"Well, yeah, that's all true. Especially the part about the handsome husband," he said, adding a wink. "But seriously, I know this race has some not-so-great memories tied to it for you. I just want to make sure you aren't doubting your decision to be here."

"No, I'm glad we're here. I wanted to help out today. I'll admit that earlier I was thinking about the day of the car accident, though, and all those memories came crashing back. I wonder if the guy I stabbed with my EpiPen ever comes back to do this race. That was what? Thirteen or fourteen years ago, I think? Who knows, I could have already bumped into him five times today. I wouldn't recognize him even if I was talking directly to him. Unless maybe his eyes were swollen shut and he was covered in hives again!" Jillian laughed.

"Yeah, but if that was the case, I don't think he would be doing too much talking! What did you say he was in your vision? A pilot of some sort?"

"He was the life-flight medical helicopter pilot. You have to admit, I had a pretty vivid imagination for someone so close to death. I sure was convinced those people were really saving me after the crash. Why you all didn't just throw me in the loony bin back then, I'll never know!"

"Loony bin? No way. You're too smart for that. I have my own theory on what happened that day, and it doesn't include you being a crazy person."

"Oh, really? Do tell! I don't think I knew you had an actual theory about it. What is it then, oh wise one?"

"Well, knowing you as well as I do, it wouldn't surprise me one bit to conclude that you willed yourself to survive. Let's face it…no one I know has more determination than you do when it comes to reaching a goal. I think you masterminded that entire scenario so you'd survive what most of us mere mortals would've never been able to. It took some pretty clever engineering to include all those players from your past."

"Hmm, interesting theory," Jillian responded, impressed that he'd put such thought into it. "But then, how do you explain the fact that they felt so real, and yet I have no idea who those people are, or what they do, or where they live, or anything about them, really?"

"Think about it," he continued. "You really did save five people in your lifetime, right? That alone is a miracle. I know you didn't know them personally, or have a way to keep in touch with any of them, but somehow they stayed with you. It's like they lived somewhere deep in your psyche. And they were there for you when you needed them most. There has to be something to it. You gave each of those people the most precious gift: a second chance. I think they became like your cosmic guardian angels or something."

"Cosmic guardian angels? You don't think that sounds a bit hokey?" Jillian asked. "Maybe it's time I should consider putting you in the loony bin!"

David just smiled.

"Nope. All my marbles are intact, thank you very much. I think what happened to you is pretty cool, actually. Not the accident, of course, but the way the things that needed to come together that day did. Hey, you're the one who's always making the argument that whatever energy we put out into the universe comes back, one way or another, right? That day was your proof. I think that because you are you, a kind and loving person, it was your destiny to survive. You deserved to make it through all of that, Jill. I just hope you don't have any regrets when you look back on all of this. I know it hasn't been easy."

Jillian took a few moments to let his words sink in. "No regrets," she finally answered. "I would've preferred not to have had to go through that year of rehab, of course, but in a way, even that taught me a few things. I think it taught us all a few things."

"Oh yeah? Like what?" David asked.

"Well for starters, it taught me that there's more to life than just winning medals. I guess the real lesson for me was that it made me finally realize the significance of what it meant to save those people. For some reason, I was the lucky one who got to give them each their second chance. Now it's my turn for a second chance, right? I never understood how powerful that was at the time. It's a gift really…and I'm not gonna take mine for granted."

"Well, this past year-and-a-half sure taught me how strong you are, babe," David said. "I couldn't be more proud of you, blue-eyes."

"Ya know, the truth is, even though I know it happened differently, I like believing I was saved the way I imagined. It makes me feel connected, like everything that happened to me had a larger purpose. It gives me hope that everything is going to be okay."

"Well then it will be," David said, wrapping his arm around her shoulder.

"So what I never got that gold medal or can't be out competing today. What I have right here and right now is so much more than I could've ever dreamed," Jillian said, leaning up and kissing David.

Taking one last look around, Jillian wrapped her arms around his waist and rested her head against his chest. A warm breeze brushed across her face and she felt an overwhelming wave of gratitude.

"Any way you look at it, I'm one lucky girl."

THE END

87049264R10122

Made in the USA
Columbia, SC
09 January 2018